DANGER AHEAD

Lady Samantha Mayne had never blinked in the face of the most risky enterprises. She had eagerly volunteered to soar through the air in her brother's strange invention called a glider, and hadn't minded coming down with a crash. She had chosen the most powerful of stallions to mount, and without hesitation taken the highest of fences.

But now she had dared dress in a gown that displayed to the full how feminine a form she really had. And now Lord Charles Laverstock's eyes were on her, his arms were around her . . .

. . . and as his lips came down on hers, Samantha had to wonder if this time she had taken one chance too many. . . .

———————————————————

EMILY HENDRICKSON lives at Lake Tahoe, Nevada, with her retired airline-pilot husband. Of all the many places she had traveled to around the world, England is her favorite and a natural choice as a setting for her novels. Although writing claims most of her time, she enjoys gardening, water-colors, and sewing for her granddaughters as well as the occasional trip with her husband.

Queen
of the May

Emily Hendrickson

A SIGNET BOOK

NEW AMERICAN LIBRARY

A DIVISION OF PENGUIN BOOKS USA INC.

NAL BOOKS ARE AVAILABLE AT QUANTITY DISCOUNTS WHEN USED TO PROMOTE
PRODUCTS OR SERVICES. FOR INFORMATION PLEASE WRITE TO PREMIUM MARKETING
DIVISION, NEW AMERICAN LIBRARY, 1633 BROADWAY, NEW YORK, NEW YORK 10019.

SIGNET TRADEMARK REG. U.S.PAT. OFF. AND FOREIGN COUNTRIES
REGISTERED TRADEMARK—MARCA REGISTRADA
HECHO EN DRESDEN, TN, U.S.A.

SIGNET, SIGNET CLASSIC, MENTOR, ONYX, PLUME, MERIDIAN
and NAL BOOKS are published by New American Library, a division of
Penguin Books USA Inc., 1633 Broadway, New York, New York 10019

First Printing, December, 1989

1 2 3 4 5 6 7 8 9

PRINTED IN THE UNITED STATES OF AMERICA

To John, my loyal partner and strong supporter,
as well as in-house aviation expert

Sir George Cayley, English scientist and inventor, first designed a glider of sorts in 1799. In 1809 he published an article in *Nicholson's Journal* on aerial navigation. In this he laid down, for the first time, the basic rules of heavier-than-air flight. He also described a flying machine that reminds one of our present hang gliders, which some think he piloted in 1809. Had a lightweight engine been developed at that time, it is believed powered flight would have begun a hundred years sooner. In 1853 he constructed a glider that carried his unwilling coachman nine hundred feet in the first manned flight. The coachman resigned, pointing out he had been hired to drive, not fly.

Cayley wrote in the *Mechanics Magazine* that a glider could not only be steered, but taken aloft, dropped from a balloon, and flown to a distance about five or six times the distance horizontally that the balloon is above the earth. He didn't test this particular theory.

I wish to give special thanks for materials and assistance to the Smithsonian National Air and Space Museum Branch Library in Washington, D.C., and the Victoria and Albert Science Museum Library in London.

You must wake and call me early, call me early, mother dear;
Tomorrow 'ill be the happiest time of all the glad New Year;
Of all the glad New Year, mother, the maddest, merriest day;
For I'm to be Queen o' the May, mother, I'm to be Queen o'
the May.

Alfred, Lord Tennyson, "The May Queen"

1

"Are you *certain* I will not get hurt?" Sam glanced up at her big brother, George, with a dubious expression on her face. "I have not forgotten the time you had me out on this very hill in a storm with a kite and a brass key, so as to test Mr. Franklin's notion of electricity. Papa said I could have been killed." Even her indulgent parent had been upset at this outrageous incident.

"I am more careful now," the inventive George Mayne assured the slight figure standing so defiantly before him. "If you follow my instructions, there is no way in which you can get injured. According to my calculations the glider will not carry anyone heavier than you. So you see, I need you, little sister. It will fly, never fear. If Sir George Cayley can do it, so can I." He hoped his confidence was catching.

Sam, otherwise known as Lady Samantha Mayne, nervously brushed her hands down her nankeen breeches, fatalistically shrugged her shoulders beneath her soft cambric shirt, and climbed into the slight craft resting on the curve of the hill. To her, it resembled nothing more than a wee boat with a rudder aft and a peculiar horizontal sail above. With impatient fingers she tucked a stray curl beneath the ridiculous jockey cap perched atop her head before looking once again at her brother. Intrepid she might be, but this was beyond the experiments she had helped George with in the past. Yet he seemed so certain that they would not fail. She had adored her older brother from the time she could toddle after him, watching with fascination as he had devised variations on a Chinese flying top. Now she could not think of disappointing him by a refusal to assist.

"Just remember that Sir George only wrote the theory, he hasn't tested it himself other than in models such as you have

11

done," she reminded. "Although you have flown all those models—and lovely they looked, too—it does not follow that I shall succeed with my part of this test." She turned from the frowning face of her dear—and only—brother to study the elevator-cum-rudder hinged to the back of the craft and wondered if it would really work, or if she would crash into the gentle valley stretching out beyond where she waited. She had no wish to end her brief life, although George seemed determined to do his best to accomplish this deed one way or another.

In the distance Sam could see a flock of Scarborough gulls wheeling and soaring. Would she join them? Her heart raced at the very thought. To be the first woman to join the birds! She glanced to the far side of the valley where Aunt Lavinia, dressed in her usual white, fluttered a handkerchief with maidenly enthusiasm. She had read the tea leaves in Sam's cup this morning and pronounced this "the" day to go.

That was all George had needed. Drawn at first to Sir George Cayley's theories because of the shared first name, Sam's brother had become obsessed with the notion of manned flight. He had the silly idea that these guided gliders might be used in the war against the French. George thought that once he got his flying machine to fly, it could be lifted high in the air beneath a balloon, then released to soar over enemy lines to observe troop movements. Obviously an absurd notion. But one had to humor these genius types.

It seemed to Sam that all her life she had indulged her brother. She had dressed in breeches to please him and help him with his fantastical schemes. As time had passed, Sam became interested to the point where she would not give up her assistance. "To think I passed by the wonder of a Season in London for all this," she murmured, unheard by George. She was certain this was far more exciting, although at this moment she wondered if a dance floor might not be safer.

Sam looked up at the diagonal bracing, running a finger along the wire to check its tautness. The thin tension wheels the family coachman had clucked his tongue over began to roll along the ground while George and four grooms ran down the hill pulling the ropes that would drop away once Sam was aloft. Sam braced herself, keeping a steady eye on the rudder as she gently bounced over the ground. A breeze blew up the southeastern slope giving lift to the slight craft.

She was flying! No longer could she feel the bump of the wheels as they rolled over the grassy slope. Instead, the soft warm wind caressed her face, rushed past her ears, and the canvas over her head gave a very faint flutter. She had joined the birds! Sam swallowed with care, darting a swift glance at the trees marching up the slope across the far side. She caught a quick glimpse of white—Lavinia, no doubt—and further along, a slash of blue—perhaps one of the grooms.

The long valley ran between two slopes rising toward woods on either side. Her brother had explained that the valley was ideal for testing his glider in that it was so similar to Cayley's own terrain.

Sam's earlier fears fell away as she exultantly glanced to where she could see George below, capering about and waving his Belcher handkerchief. She was actually soaring like the gulls! She gave an experimental nudge to the rudder and observed how the craft altered direction a bit. Then she tried the elevator control. It seemed slow to respond.

She saw the ground of the opposite side coming closer and closer. She was going to land. Recalling George's instructions, she tried to raise the nose of the craft. This was the part of the flight that was truly dangerous, no matter how reassuring George might be. Sam had watched countless of those little model gliders George had tested crash into bits and pieces when they dived into the ground. She tried to ignore the flutterings in her stomach and maintain the calm needed to minimize the damage. Control the rudder-elevator, she reminded herself. The elevator failed to respond as it ought.

The nose of the little bird dropped, there was a loud bang as she hit the ground, then the tail fell off. Total silence followed. Not even the gulls could be heard.

Sam sat still for a moment, then she took a deep breath before checking each limb to make sure she was all there—in one piece. She began climbing over the edge of the boat-shaped craft, eager to meet her brother for a celebration. Her nankeen breeches caught on a splinter and she exploded with a fluency picked up from George.

The sound of crashing through the brush brought her head up. It had to be George. "Don't just stand there like a looby, get me out of here!" She twisted around and found it wasn't George after all. A blue-clad stranger—a tall, dark-haired, and much too handsome stranger—stared up at her as though she were an apparition. He could hardly be blamed, she supposed. After all, how often did one see a white bird of this size come sailing across a valley almost to one's feet? Those gray eyes gazed at her with such disbelief. Well, she was real enough. She would feel it come the morrow.

Charles Winford, Marquess of Laverstock, had stopped to watch. He had been heading purposefully toward Mayne Court when he had caught sight of this fantastic vision, this enormous white bird soaring high in the air across the valley. Fascinated, he sent his valet and carriage on to the estate and turned his horse off the road to discover more. Drawing closer, he had seen it was a peculiar craft with a slim figure, a young boy, steering a rudder-like extension as he sailed across the dale. When it became obvious the young lad would crash to the ground, Charles jumped from his horse, pushing through the underbrush to reach the remains, whatever they might be.

Charles frowned at the language, hurrying forward to lift the lad from the boat-shaped affair where a splinter had well and truly snagged him. Only it wasn't a him. Charles caught his breath in amazement as a jockey cap fell from *her* head.

Her strange golden eyes framed by sooty lashes were far too large in that little heart-shaped face, and that mouth, now split in an engaging grin, was too wide for perfect beauty. Why the chit even had a dusting of freckles on her pert little nose. Worst of all was her hair. Spilling over her shoulders in sensuous abandon, the wealth of golden-red silk now released from the silly cap was most certainly out of fashion this year—or any year, for that matter. Shades of red were always suspect for some odd reason.

Yet his hand itched to touch her petal-soft skin, and he

couldn't help but admire that enchanting figure so dashingly revealed in those disgraceful breeches she ought not to be wearing. The urge to thread his hands through that glorious hair was incredibly strong. Against the deep green of the woods she looked like a tiger flower in the wildest of gardens.

She was utterly scandalous! Yet he was extremely intrigued with this unusual beauty. Weary with his efforts at the War Office, he had come for a change of scene . . . for that and another reason no one need know about.

And now he felt as though someone had dealt him a blow to his solar plexus. A hard blow.

"Well, are you not going to help me? Can you not see I am caught?" Samantha's voice was alive with annoyance touched with humor. Why was it she had this particular effect on gentlemen?

Charles was jolted from his preoccupation with this shocking young woman. He moved swiftly to her side and lifted her slight body from where she was snagged, disengaging her successfully from the splinter without further damaging those clinging breeches he tried—unsuccessfully—not to look at. She was delightfully curved in such delicious places. Charles drew himself up. No matter what her dress, a young lady was not to be ogled as though she might be a maidservant. For as sure as he breathed, her speech proclaimed her as a member of the gentry. He set her gently on her feet, then watched as she jumped up and down with obvious happiness.

Samantha danced about in glee, then enthusiastically threw her arms about the stranger. "We did it! We did it! I flew with the birds!" Her hug was not returned. Sam dropped her arms, suddenly aware of her impropriety as she glanced up at the bemused face of the man who had retrieved her from the glider.

At that moment George, followed by two of the grooms, came crashing through the brush to join Samantha and the stranger. At last Samantha was able to hug and kiss her brother with great delight at their accomplishment. George grinned with a masculine embarrassment at this, meeting the glance of the amused stranger with male understanding.

In his usual forthright manner, George nodded in greeting after disengaging himself from Sam. "Hullo." He bestowed a puppy-friendly look on the newcomer, extending his hand.

"I'm Laverstock." Charles stood looking expectantly at poor George, who had never been known for his polish in social niceties.

"Uh . . . George Mayne, and this is my little sister, Samantha." George had remembered to include Samantha, for which she was most grateful this time.

"Lady Samantha. Sir." Laverstock's bow was exquisite in polite courtesy. He addressed George. "Do forgive me for trespassing. I must confess that I was terribly curious about this thing your sister was piloting. However, I was on my way to your home, so perhaps it is as well."

Samantha's heart did another lurch, but quite different from the lurches of excitement she had felt in the glider. "You were coming to our home?" she echoed, then edged behind George as she recalled her most unorthodox and unladylike attire.

Charles caught the movement and almost smiled. "I have a letter from your father in London. He suggested I come up here to get away from the War Office for a bit. Thought the sea air might do me good."

The poor man must have been ill. Samantha's caring heart went out to him. She sidled around the sturdy body of her brother to offer her sympathy just as Aunt Lavinia drifted up to join them.

Lady Lavinia Mayne had never married, devoting her life to raising the children of her brother, the Earl of Cranswick, after his wife died giving birth to a boy, who also died shortly thereafter. Her white hair escaped from her hat in wisps around a much-lined face. Faded blue eyes assessed the situation with shrewd accuracy. Garbed in an outdated dress of white muslin and an enormous hat of questionable vintage, she peered up at the newcomer. George murmured his name to her.

She nodded in polite greeting. "I am Lady Lavinia Mayne, my lord. We are pleased to welcome you to Mayne Court. Though not precisely, because we aren't at the Court at the moment, are we? But we shall be shortly, for it is just over there beyond that grove of trees." Lavinia waved a vague hand in the direction from which she had come while thinking rather hard. "Samantha, why don't you hurry along and change for tea, my dear? Those clothes must be vastly uncomfortable for you.''

Aunt Lavinia knew full well how Sam loathed wearing dresses and that she considered breeches to be by far the more agreeable. Sam could only conclude that her aunt had decided Lord Laverstock made her feel uncomfortable in breeches—which he did, with his sidelong glances at her. The expression in those gray eyes of his was indecipherable.

Sam sketched a curtsy, awkward to do while wearing breeches, then marched off to the Court. Aunt Lavinia would rely on Sam to alert the staff that a guest was arriving. Tea would be prepared and a room would be whisked into readiness.

While she hurried along the narrow path Sam considered the guest her father had sent up to them from London. In addition to those inscrutable gray eyes, he had dark brown hair and a slash of a mouth, which when not disapproving might be nicer in shape. He possessed a firm jaw, something of which her father was bound to approve. He always declared—on those infrequent visits from town—that Samantha would need a firm hand.

Sam stopped in her tracks as she considered the thought that now struck her. Had her dearest papa sent this London lord especially for her? She gave a skip of joy as the notion slowly whirled about in her brain, then settled down to take root. That was it. Her precious papa must have cleverly persuaded this gentleman to take a rest from the rigors of his work at the War Office while all the time intending to send him to his dear daughter Sam as a present!

But Lord Laverstock seemed a bit of a stuffed shirt. Such dignity and ruffled feathers at the sight of Samantha in her breeches—it was nigh unto laughable. Only, Sam sighed, it was nothing to amuse one. She really must do something about herself.

A rustling not far away brought Lady Emma Fanshawe into view. She was impeccably dressed and seated upon her horse in a manner Sam could only admire. Sam much preferred to ride astride. How Emma could manage the side saddle was marvelous to behold.

''Hullo, Cousin Emma. Did you know we have a guest?'' Then Sam had an awful thought. Suppose Lord Laverstock didn't know he had been sent up here for Sam and took a notion to admire Emma instead. With her soft brown eyes, appealing brown curls, and a feminine manner much liked by Aunt Lavinia, Emma could be competition.

Not observing the narrowing of Sam's large golden eyes, Emma nodded graciously. "I had occasion to greet them. Lord Laverstock and George are assisting the men with righting the flying machine. Tell me, did you really soar in that contraption? How I wish I might have seen it."

Samantha shrugged, then walking alongside Emma, continued on her way to the house, suddenly desirous of a bath and fresh clothes. Next to Emma she felt positively horrid. "George thought it might be bad luck to have a lot of people watching. Aunt Lavinia came, of course." Sam struggled with her manners, then bowed to the inevitable. "You will be joining us for tea, will you not? Since Aunt Lavinia does not hold with nuncheon, it is bound to be a generous one."

Emma gave a gentle smile, and nodded with her usual grace. Really, no one had a right to be so . . . so dainty and feminine. Sam failed to recall that they were of similar height and build— only, one girl had grown up to be all genteel woman, the other, a saucy hoyden.

"I would be very pleased to join the group. Is not your Cousin Alfred due to arrive as well?" They had arrived at the tall red-brick house, a fine example of baroque architecture, while she spoke.

Sam paused at the entrance to the house to look over her shoulder at her cousin Emma as the lovely girl gave the reins of her horse to a groom. Emma and Alfred were of no relation. Emma was her mother's niece while Alfred was on her father's side of the family. The two had fought as children. The youthful Alfred had declared that little Emma was the worst sort of female. Now Sam cast a worried glance up the staircase, then looked at Emma.

"I believe he may be here already, or at least will be shortly. You won't quarrel with him, will you? It would never do for our other guest to find this a hornet's nest."

Emma was spending the year with Samantha while her parents, the earl and his countess, were abroad. George had

sent her on an errand so the delicate nerves he feared would
not send her into spasms while watching Sam glide through the
air.

"I? Quarrel? Never!" The musical trill of laughter from
Emma's perfect lips for the first time grated on Sam's nerves.
"Unless he starts it first," Emma murmured.

"We had best get changed before the others arrive. Tell me,
did you ever meet Lord Laverstock while you were in London
for your Season?" Sam tossed out this casual question while
the girls rushed up the staircase.

"Oh, yes. He is much admired. He is an excellent dancer
and always displays the most elegant taste in his dress. His
behavior is above reproach. I understand his home is simply
divine," said Emma breathlessly as they turned the corner at
the top of the stairs.

Samantha's heart sank a trifle. Elegant and divine were hardly
words applicable to herself. Perhaps he might be attracted to
an opposite? Her own behavior—gliding across the valley while
wearing boy's clothing—was scarcely such as to appeal to a high
stickler. Never one to brood before a looking glass, Sam placed
little value in her unusual appearance, nor did she understand
the impact of her rare beauty upon a susceptible masculine heart.

"Emma . . . would you be so kind as to help me choose a
gown? For once I would like to go down for tea and not have
Aunt Lavinia scold me." Sam gave her cousin a pleading look.
It was necessary to know more about Lord Laverstock and she
might take advantage of the time to probe.

Emma smiled at her guileless cousin, so transparent in her
desire to improve her dress. "Of course. Permit me to slip on
something else first and I shall be with you directly."

Sam entered her room with a thoughtful frown. Hetty, the
patient maid who continually tried to urge Sam into better ways,
entered shortly after, casting a disparaging eye on the breeches
being tossed on the bed by the absent-minded young lady.

"What your sainted mother would say to this if she but saw
it, I canna' say." Hetty picked up the breeches, folding them
to stow in a drawer. She knew better then to try to eliminate
them from the wardrobe of her charge.

"Rubbish. And what might she say of my dear aunt? I can

see how she would smile at the sight of Lavinia reading her tea leaves at the table. What I wear is not so very disgraceful. I would like a bath, please.'' Sam issued the order in a careful voice, conscious she would startle the maid.

Hetty rose up sharply, giving Sam a surprised stare. "Aye. A bath. In the middle of the day, no less.'' She started toward the door. "Best see to it right away afore you change that mind of yourn.''

Left alone, Sam whirled about the room in her wrapper, a cream lutestring and lace confection brought up from London by her fond father in hopes it might stir his daughter to more ladylike behavior. She must plan. Something told her—that bemused look, perhaps—that Lord Laverstock would not care for a hoyden. Not everyone succumbed to Sam's questionable charm the way her doting parent did.

A gentle tapping at the door brought Emma, to Sam's relief. "What would you like to wear this afternoon, dear cousin?''

Sam's ebullience faded as she considered her wardrobe. She sighed with resignation. "You had best take a look. Goodness knows I have no idea as to what might be proper. Hetty would turn me out in a dun-colored gown with a neck up to here.'' She drew a line below her jaw and grimaced as she plunked herself down on the edge of her bed.

Hetty bustled in followed by a line of maids bearing pails of steaming water. While Emma searched for a suitable gown for her to wear, Sam slithered into the nicely hot water in the hip bath behind her screen. She lathered herself with freesia-scented soap, all the while furiously wondering how she might find out more about their guest. She hoped Papa had sent instructions for her along with Laverstock. What was the good of such a present without directions on how to capture him? It seemed she was strictly on her own in this.

"I believe this gown your papa sent up from London last month would be quite appropriate, Samantha,'' murmured Emma in her sweet manner.

Sam peeped around the screen where she now dried herself with a Turkish towel to discover an amber satin-cloth gown she privately thought insipid being displayed for her. It was excessively plain, ornamented in front with rows of white silk

trimming, called frostwork, and in back with small pearl
buttons. The full lace sleeves caught about the middle of the
arm looked silly to Sam's eyes. She glanced up to see Emma's
hopeful expression.

Unable to disappoint her cousin, Sam valiantly nodded with
what she hoped was enthusiasm. "Just the very thing." The
narrowness of the skirt gave her pause until she recalled she
would be walking with Emma, who always tripped along in the
most dainty and refined manner.

When Sam eventually studied her reflection in the looking
glass, she was pleasantly surprised at what she saw. She
looked . . . almost elegant. Her hair had been pinned up in a
Psyche knot and those sleeves did seem rather nice. Only the
vast expanse of bosom displayed bothered Sam. She turned
troubled eyes to Emma, her tutor.

" 'Tis all the fashion in London, my dear. Your father always
sends the very latest thing. Come now, or we shall be late for
tea." Emma beamed a smile of pride at her achievement, and
hoped Samantha would for once not rip the hem of her gown
with her tendency to stride.

"Mind you," Sam confided as they walked down the stairs
together. "I do not care for a mincing walk, but I shall try to
shorten my usual stride, dear Emma. Gads, but 'tis a nasty bit
of work to be a lady."

Emma shuddered and wondered if creating a lady might not
be too great a task if Samantha was the raw material.

The others had assembled in the drawing room. George was
staring out the window in an abstracted manner, then, at their
entrance, turned to give Sam a sweet smile. "Well done, Sam."

Forgetting all her resolutions about being a proper lady,
Samantha joyously hurried across the room, mindful of her skirt,
to throw herself into her brother's arms, accepting his hug with
contentment. She had pleased her big brother. She peeped up
at him and scolded, "You must do something about that
elevator. It did not respond as it ought, I believe."

Someone cleared his throat and Samantha recollected where
she was and who else was present. A delicate flush stained her
cheeks, much to Aunt Lavinia's amazement.

"Your brother is most favored to have a sister willing to assist him.'' Lord Laverstock bestowed a serious look on Samantha that quite subdued her.

At that moment a personage entered the room, ignoring Peters, who hovered behind him. The foppish dandy dressed in lilac and primrose made an elegant leg, then crossed to greet Aunt Lavinia, bowing low over her hand.

''Percival Twistleton, I declare,'' exclaimed Aunt Lavinia. ''We have not seen your face in an age, it seems. I trust your parents are well?''

''Well enough.'' The newcomer gazed around with a puzzled frown. ''I thought Alfred was to be here. I received a note from him just yesterday that he intended to visit.'' Percy's high voice was full of his bewilderment. ''I decided to pop up for a visit.''

A voice from the doorway spun the exquisite around. Another gentlemen entered as different from Percival as chalk from cheese. ''I am late, I fear,'' answered Alfred Mayne ruefully. ''Good to see you all once again. Laverstock, what brings you so far from London?''

''Fatigue.'' The deep voice seemed faintly amused, though Sam noted the gray eyes were keenly observant.

Sam gave her cousin Alfred a forgiving smile. ''Papa sent Lord Laverstock up here to Yorkshire to see if the sea air might do him good. There is a letter, I believe.'' She fixed her golden gaze upon Laverstock, concerned at the reserved look she found on his face. My, he was a stuffy one. If she did not know better she would think he disapproved of her gown. He had certainly looked at her bosom hard enough. Perhaps she was a trifle full there, but that could not be helped in the least. If Papa thought the gown acceptable, it was fine with her.

Sam walked daintily to where Laverstock stood by the mantel. He gave her a narrow look, then extracted the thin epistle from a pocket to place in her outstretched hand.

She glanced at the letter, but there was not one word of direction as to how she was to capture this marvelous gentleman for her very own. Evidently Papa had confidence in her. She squared her shoulders at the very thought, and looked up at Laverstock with an utterly captivating smile. Not accustomed to making an effort to charm, she had no notion of how breathtaking the result could be when she chose to expend it.

Her large golden eyes seemed alight with inner fire and the mouth that was a trifle too wide enchanted the gentleman accustomed to far more expert wiles.

Samantha swung away from Laverstock to study Percival. Really, the man grew more preposterous every year. "You have missed the event of the day, Percy. I flew across the valley in George's glider. It was vastly thrilling." Her cheeks bloomed with faint color and her eyes sparkled with remembered excitement. "Only think, the silly man believes he can attach one of those gliders beneath a balloon so it can be used to spy on the French. They might shoot the person flying it, I should not wonder! Of course, if he could get that elevator thing working properly, he might be able to keep it aloft for some time, and then it could glide back to the other side of the lines. It is far more easy to manage than a balloon." Her voice was musing as she considered the problem aloud.

"Samantha," cautioned George. He cast a glance at Cousin Alfred, wondering what he was doing here this time.

"Oh, pooh, George. 'Tis not as though something will actually come of it . . . is it? Besides, Laverstock can be trusted, for Papa sent him. And the rest are family. Almost." She dismissed Percival. Still, it was odd he had turned up at this time of year when he might normally be found in town. The same might hold with Laverstock. Or even Alfred, for pity's sake. She shrugged her shoulders, liking the feel of the delicate lace against her skin.

Gaily, she turned to Aunt Lavinia. "Tea, if you please, dear Aunt. I am famished."

Emma suppressed the moan that almost slipped out. Really, to turn Samantha into a lady was asking a great deal of a person.

2

D inner was not the most pleasant meal ever served in the old house. Emma studied Alfred with curious and sometimes hostile eyes. Alfred ignored Emma as though she weren't seated across the table from him.

Percival chatted with Alfred between paying Samantha outrageous compliments, which, as usual, she ignored. She had become so accustomed to his silly gallantries that she was totally deaf to them.

At the head of the table, Aunt Lavinia surveyed her family as well as the newcomer. She didn't consider Percival a stranger. Alfred and George's old school friend often came to visit, usually when short of funds. Had he been of a different nature, she might have thought he had an interest in Samantha. As it was, she had decided he could not bear his family, a feeling she shared, and that he felt at home with the Maynes. She had never quite decided whether that was flattering or not.

Lord Laverstock was rather quiet, watching the faces of those around the table, listening to the animated chatter between Samantha and her brother, George. Laverstock possessed a perfect politeness and a somewhat haughty courtesy. Lavinia wondered how in the world he would survive the informal atmosphere in Mayne Court for the weeks he intended to remain. Although he had said he was on a repairing lease, Lavinia was no fool. She wondered what the true reason might be. Her tea leaves of the morning had revealed something most interesting. A secret smile hovered over her mouth as she continued to watch the group between bites of roast fowl.

George ought to have been paying attention to Emma rather than amiably arguing with his sister. At last it was Laverstock who remembered his manners. "You are spending a visit with the Maynes?"

Emma glanced at Alfred, gave a twitch of annoyance, then smiled graciously at Laverstock. "My uncle was so kind as to suggest that I stay here while my parents are abroad. Indeed, this is almost like home to me."

At this, Alfred looked up to catch her eye. "On the shelf now, are you, Emma? I trust you are good company for Aunt Lavinia. As I recall, you share an interest in gardens."

Emma flushed and stiffened as she glared at Alfred. "My status in life can be of no concern to you, cousin. Although I confess to admiring Aunt Lavinia's garden." Emma turned to Laverstock with more animation than he had heretofore seen in her. "Aunt has the most charming plan to her garden. There are delightful beds of flowers, all white, of course, with clever statues here and there. She has a greenhouse filled with interesting botanical specimens too fragile to survive in our climate. Beyond all this can be found a variety of walks affording delicious vistas. It is a neatly ordered place, one you can enjoy at leisure while you visit here. If you seek restoration of the spirit, it will certainly soothe."

Laverstock inclined his head, then caught sight of the curious effect Emma's words had on Alfred. Though ostensibly in conversation with the dandy, Percival, Alfred had hung on every word spoken by the demure Emma. Odd behavior for a man who seemed to dislike the young woman. But then, things were often not what they appeared.

"I still say the elevator control needs to be changed," argued Samantha quietly. "It was decidedly sluggish. Had I been better able to control the up and down of the craft, I might not have crashed quite so badly."

Shaking his head, George denied there was anything wrong with his design. "It follows the principles set down by Cayley, and everything else the man wrote has been proven correct."

"Hah!" Seeing that Laverstock was now watching their discussion, Sam appealed to him. "Cayley wrote that in the not too distant future man would conquer the air. That full-sized editions of his little model flying machine would leave the ground carrying passengers and fully under control; people will be able to leave one place and fly to another previously determined, landing there in safety!" She turned her unusual eyes on her brother, adding, "In safety, George—not crashing into the ground and falling into bits and pieces. And many people? Nonsense. Those gliders are merely toys. They could never serve a useful purpose."

George gave her a disgruntled look in return. "I still say that the glider, improved a bit from the one you used today, could be suspended from a hot-air balloon and released to fly over the battle lines. Balloons are too big, too cumbersome for such a task. Cayley thought the glider could do such a task. Think how Wellington would benefit from the knowledge of French troop formations."

"Utter folly. You would need mere boys to fly it . . . or a young woman such as myself. Am I not right, my lord? I cannot see the generals permitting such an event to occur." Samantha sparkled with glee at the image this thought provoked.

"Samantha! Such scandalous thoughts! The very idea of a woman partaking in war is repugnant to anyone of sensibilities." Aunt Lavinia raised her eyebrows in horrified reaction to the statement uttered by her unconventional niece.

Seeking to direct the conversation in a less volatile direction, Laverstock inquired, "What is to be found in the local area for diversion?"

Samantha exchanged a cautious look with Lavinia. "There is always something to do for one of an inquiring mind. If you stay with us long enough, you will partake of the annual May Day celebrations. That is a delight you would not wish to miss, I am certain."

Aunt Lavinia frowned at this remark. She could foresee trouble up ahead. Heaven knew what notion Samantha might take into her head. The meal having reached its conclusion, Lavinia rose and motioned to the two young women to follow her. They left the men in temporary silence.

George watched as Peters, the butler, poured out port for each of the men, then dismissed him with a vague wave of his hand.

"Do you think it really could be done, George?" Alfred

intently studied the boyish face of his cousin. "The survey from the air, that is."

Laverstock added, "It would take a very sturdy craft."

"Lightness is of the prime importance," George countered. With one hand he tried to demonstrate. "A curved surface will lift if driven against the wind, the lighter the better. Like a leaf. The problem is power. There is nothing at the moment to provide the thrust needed for propulsion—hence the idea to use a balloon. Actually, it is not all that new, I understand a Swiss gentleman is attempting to do something of the sort with a bit of success. A glider gives the advantage of maneuverability that the balloon lacks, you see."

"But you think it could be done. Since you obviously could not use a woman for such a dangerous task, it would have to be someone very slight." Alfred persisted in his questions, his curiosity marked by Laverstock.

"Someone like Sam could do it," remarked George, thoughtfully.

"Surely you wouldn't permit a slip of a girl to do such a dangerous task!" Percival recoiled in horror.

"Sam ain't your usual girl. She has spunk and daring. She's a right one, she is." Sam would have floated with sheer delight had she heard her brother's encomiums. George was more inclined to scold than praise.

"Well," offered Percival, "I, for one, think it a hare-brained idea. However, if you should need assistance while I am here, I would be happy to help you. I have always prided myself on an ability with draftsmanship."

Alfred chuckled. "Clever Percy. Decided to add to your empty coffers, have you? Plan to hire out?"

"Not me. However, I could if I chose." With that, he turned to George. "Can we not rejoin the ladies? All this talk of work has quite fatigued me."

In the drawing room, Samantha had found it most difficult to refrain from pacing about. She had accomplished what she felt was a crowning achievement, and now she was being treated by her aunt like she had done something horrid.

"Do sit down, Samantha. You will wear a path in the carpet.

See how poised Emma is? Dear girl, you could be such an influence on Samantha if only she would pay attention to you." Lavinia sighed as she observed her younger niece.

Sam paused in her ramble about the room to stare at Emma as a momentous thought struck. Fiddling with the delicate lace of one of her sleeves, she considered the matter at short length before testing it. "Emma, no doubt you will agree with our aunt that I am sorely in need of polish. Since you have had the benefit of a Season in town, could you . . . would you attempt to help me? That is, I would deem it a kindness if you would."

Such a pretty speech from her hoydenish cousin touched Emma. After the cutting remark from Alfred while at the table, Emma felt a need to do something worthwhile. "I might. But you would have to agree to follow my direction."

Recalling Lord Laverstock's expression as she had hugged her brother, Sam nodded. "I fear Lord Laverstock deplores my want of conduct." Then in typical Sam fashion she blurted out, "Do you fancy him, Emma? While you were in London, did you lose your heart to him? Is that why you turned down so many offers? For you are vastly charming and quite in good looks, you know. Any man would be fortunate to wed such a lovely woman as you. And," Sam added as an afterthought, "you have an excellent dowry, as well."

"That of a certainty puts me in an enviable position," chuckled Emma, never able to become annoyed with Samantha, even at her most outrageous.

"Well, did you? For I might as well confess I am most taken with him." Samantha placed her hands on her hips, giving Emma a most beseeching look.

"No, dear cousin. My heart is elsewhere, most unfortunately, for I seem not to be able to recover it." Emma took a deep breath, a somewhat painful one it seemed to Sam. "I shall help you as best I can. Although I must confess I have my doubts." At Samantha's hurt expression, Emma shook her head. "Not about you, silly goose. About myself. How can a spinster, as Alfred called me, best advise a girl?"

"Hah! I have been trying to do it for donkey years and I have not succeeded." Lady Lavinia chortled with open glee. "I wish you well, my dear. You shall need it."

"You are both most pitiless to a girl's esteem." Sam flashed a grimace of distaste at the two, who chuckled at her pose.

"The trouble with you is that you never examine what you see in the looking glass." Lady Lavinia cocked her head, fiddling with a white enameled snuffbox, the sight of which caused Samantha to pale.

"Aunt . . . you didn't go to visit the squire today, did you?" Sam went two steps closer to examine the item in her aunt's hands.

"As a matter of fact, I did." Lavinia smiled at the snuffbox with evident pleasure. "Pretty thing, is it not?"

"Ohhhh, dear Auntie. What shall I do with you?" Sam shared an agonized look with Emma, then smiled with effort. A snuffbox to return! "Well, at least I have solved one of my problems. Emma is one of the most amiable of women and I am truly pleased that she will assist me in improving my appearance and deportment. I gather I ought to have attended that school for young ladies after all."

"Hmpf," said Aunt Lavinia, "Best be silent. I believe I hear the men approaching. Play something for us, girls."

Emma walked over to sit on the blue velvet stool before the pianoforte while Samantha picked up her lute. The gentlemen entered to the lovely sight of Emma and Samantha playing with grace and skill. The sound was soothing and gentle to the ears. Samantha seemed to acquire a charm and ladylike gentility heretofore not evinced.

Sam was lost in her dreams, as was often the case when she sat with her lute. In them, she was a queen with courtiers around her. She possessed the polish and finesse to capture the heart of the man she adored, her king, who this time had dark hair and a firm jaw line and vaguely resembled Laverstock. She sighed, then was brought to the present with polite applause as the music concluded.

"Play my favorite, Sam." George gave his sister a fond look, one she never could resist.

She bowed her head in his direction, sparkling a delightful smile at him, one that Laverstock envied. How fine it was that a brother and sister could have this peculiar closeness, a sort of bonding that went far beyond mere toleration.

The haunting strains of "Greensleeves" drifted out into the evening air. With a window open to permit the scent of spring flowers to enter and only faint candlelight to see by, it was a charming scene. The girl sat in her softly glowing amber gown, one dainty primrose slipper peeping from beneath the hem, her white-lace-covered arms cradling the old-fashioned lute. Her fingers plucked the strings with dexterity but with feeling as well, bringing a unique quality to the music.

Laverstock sat partly in the shadows, watching Samantha with keen eyes. She was breathtaking—magnificent in a strangely simple, primitive manner. She possessed an inner vibrancy, radiating an aura of liveliness even when sitting still. Something about her appealed to the deepest urges within him. Basic. That so-unfashionable golden-red hair drew his gaze. Fine silk would envy it, most women would secretly hate her for it. And he could only wish she was someone else, someone he might have for a night. No . . . not a night. He acknowledged that with all her charms, it would take longer than a night to tire of her.

Sam was drifting again. It had been exciting to soar in the sky with the birds for companions. Stimulating. How could she be expected to settle down to a mundane life, puttering with flowers and music, dabbling with embroidery or watercolors. Not that she could do any of those things, except music, which she loved as much as life itself.

Excitement. It was in her blood. She wanted to be the one who soared in a glider over the enemy lines to spy out troop movements. She did not doubt her brother could accomplish such a thing eventually if he set his mind to it. And who better to pilot the glider than herself? She had experience, something no other person had at this point.

The song ended and Sam rose with reluctance to join the others. The spell was truly broken when she caught sight of the white snuffbox sitting next to the tea pot on the tray before Aunt Lavinia. Mercy! Sam now had the task of returning the item to the squire's home without being detected. She could only hope it had not been missed as yet. What a pity Aunt possessed fingers that strayed to take things which did not belong to her. It made life incredibly complicated.

Laverstock handed a cup of tea to a suddenly distracted Lady

Samantha. "Your aunt appears to favor white, from what I have observed so far. Is there a reason?"

An enchanting smile lit Sam's face, for in spite of the problems her aunt presented, Sam dearly loved her. "How true. She read someplace that the very elegant Madame Récamier always dresses in white. Aunt Lavinia was much taken with the notion and since then has followed suit. Even her garden is done with white flowers, as Emma said."

"Your father mentioned the fascination your brother has with gliders. I had no idea he was so brilliant." Laverstock inhaled the spicy floral scent that floated about Lady Samantha, and edged closer.

"George? Well, I suppose he is brilliant, but he is no earthly good to anyone. Do you believe that he will succeed with this wild scheme of his? He lives with his head up in the clouds, along with the gulls and his gliders." Samantha shook her head, freeing a tendril of silken hair to softly glide down and curl against the nape of her neck. "Mind you, I wish he might do well. It is so depressing to fail. I am excessively fond of him, you know."

Laverstock eyed the delicate curl which curved with such loving care about the slim neck, and for the first time in his life struggled to maintain his equilibrium. He cleared his throat and sought conversation of any sort. Rescue came from a most unexpected source—Alfred.

"I say, Aunt Lavinia, how about reading our tea leaves? You have not told my fortune for some time." Alfred held out his cup with a devilish glint in his eyes.

Aunt Lavinia darted a glance at Emma, for she knew that young lady disapproved of the reading of tea leaves to tell fortunes. Emma proclaimed it a heathen custom fostered by the gypsies.

Lady Emma gave Alfred a frosty look, and said, "Alfred wants to know if he is to rise tomorrow, I expect. When one lives dangerously, one must be prepared." She flounced away from him to where George stood in amused silence. He had seen this bickering between his cousins too often in the past to take alarm at it. Emma lost her usual reserve when it came to Alfred.

"Why, Emma, I never dreamed you thought I was
dangerous." Alfred turned his face toward her, that devilish
look lighting up his ordinary brown eyes so they were most
appealing.

Emma's face flushed a delicate pink, though she refused to
act with girlish flutterings. After all, she was only one and
twenty, thought Sam. It was not as though she were an ancient.

Aunt Lavinia cleared her throat and the room fell silent.
"Very well, Alfred. You first, since you asked. Drain the last
of your tea. Swirl the tea cup around three times."

Alfred obeyed, using his left hand, then handed the cup to
his aunt. After that, she took his cup and placed it upside down
on his saucer. She turned the cup three times counter-clock-
wise in the saucer and then turned the cup over, the handle facing
her, and looked at the leaves and the patterns they formed. As
she studied it, her hands went up to touch her forehead, rubbing
at the center.

"There is trouble coming . . . yet you will do well. There
will be romance. And there will be money coming soon."

Alfred took the cup from her, glancing at Emma before
turning to Percival, grinning. "I gather I shall fare well from
this. I could do with a bit of money, though not the romance.
Trouble and romance seem to go together." Percival merely
frowned and Emma sniffed audibly.

"He has an elevated opinion of himself if he thinks there is
a miss who would chase after him," she sniped. Alfred could
put Emma out of countenance like no one else had ever managed
to do.

Samantha promptly followed the same procedure and handed
her cup to Aunt Lavinia. The older lady looked at the cup,
stiffened, and glanced up at her niece. "I see danger, Samantha.
There is a dagger in your cup tonight." Lavinia looked again
and relaxed. "However, it will not result in death." A satisfied
smile crept into her eyes, but she said no more. She had seen
romance as well, and a ring in a few months' time. It would
not do to alert Samantha, for the tea leaves could be thwarted.

Reluctantly, Emma proffered her cup, after following the
same ritual. "I do not believe this nonsense," she murmured
to George. Yet, like the others, she could not resist the lure.

Picking up the cup, Lavinia studied it before chuckling. "Good news is coming, my dear. A bird is in your cup. The closed book tells of a secret in your life. There is a mouse as well. That means you must not be timid, it could result in lost opportunities."

Alfred chortled with glee. "Emma, a timid little mouse? Not that dragon. I believe Emma would grasp opportunity with both hands given the chance."

"You are beyond what is proper, Alfred Mayne." Emma turned back on him, rigid with her disapproval of his words. Sam noted the hurt look in her sweet cousin's eyes.

Swaggering a bit, George handed Lavinia his cup. He had been cautious, yet he wanted to know if there might be a forecast regarding his glider.

"Relax, dear George." Aunt Lavinia looked at the leaves and glanced up at him. "Patience will be required, but do not be too stubborn. There will be a disappointment, yet in the future there will be success and happiness."

George was sorry that there wasn't better news of the glider. Yet he manfully hid his reaction and backed away from the sofa where his aunt sat with a thoughtful expression on her face.

"Well, I cannot allow the others to be read and not find out my own future." Percival thrust his cup at Lady Lavinia with a dainty twist of the hand. He stood one hand on his hip while awaiting her reading.

Slowly rotating the cup, Lavinia then searched the dregs with a growing frown. "You have been too extravagant, Percival. The jug in the bottom of your cup tells me you have suffered losses." She clamped her mouth shut and said no more about his fortune. She had seen a gallows in the cup. Percival had bad luck coming, but she felt it better not to tell him about it. One never knew how others might react. It could be that his creditors would follow him, pressing him for payment. Pity that the money was in Alfred's cup. Percival could have used a tidy sum to settle those bills of his.

Stepping into the sudden silence, Lord Laverstock offered his cup, properly rotated as he had seen the others do. Although he had no real wish to have his fortune told, believing it a lot of nonsense, he also was intrigued. It was obvious the old lady had scored a hit with each of her readings. He was curious to see what she might see in his tea leaves.

"A wish will be granted in the near future." Lady Lavinia grinned suddenly as she studied the contents. "See, there is a flower near the rim of the far side, telling me it will be a happy wish and come true very soon. However, there is a dagger in your cup as well, warning against haste; trouble is on the way first. The seesaw tells me that it will work out all right and the shoe indicates there will be a change in your life for the better." She had seen something else as well, but this she kept to herself, a satisfied gleam hidden as she dropped her gaze to her lap.

The group rearranged as they chattered and joked about the readings from Aunt Lavinia. George began to talk of the problems with his glider once again, asking Percival what he thought of a change in the design.

Alfred watched, shaking his head. "Percival conceals a fine mind beneath all that dandified exterior, you know," he confided to Laverstock. "Sorry to learn he is trying to outrun his creditors. I wondered what had brought him up here at this time of the year. Maybe I can lend him a hand."

"Elegant clothes can be costly. Perhaps if he stays away long enough, his next quarterly will cover the bills?" Laverstock offered, wondering again at the curious relationships being revealed in the small group.

Alfred shrugged, and with concern in his eyes, cast a glance at his old school friend in the lilac and primrose attire. Percy seemed not the same fellow, for some reason.

Across the room Samantha picked up her lute to strum a bit while she considered what her aunt had foretold would happen. Lavinia did not read tea leaves for a group very often, which made Sam concentrate on what had been said. Danger. Sam wrinkled up her nose as she considered the word, then struck a dissonant chord on her lute. Would it come through the glider? Or from something else?

3

Samantha was certain she had barely drifted to sleep when a loud crash awakened her. She sat up in bed, clutching her bedcovers about her neck as she considered the noise. What might the terrible sound be? Surely no one could make such a racket in the house and go unnoticed?

Then she listened as the sound of wind tearing at the very foundation of the house increased. The grandfather of all storms must have blown up some time after she had gone to sleep. That was the only thing that could account for the fury beyond her window. Indeed, it was guaranteed to chill her very bones with its intensity.

Slipping from her high four-poster bed, she cautiously stumbled her way to the window, peering out into the dark as though she might actually be able to see something in the blackness of the night. Nothing was visible below.

Another crash. Might it be one of the elms? She hoped not. They were such magnificent trees. Samantha withdrew from the window and returned to her bed, groping in the darkness for her tinder box. Once the little candle was lit, the room seemed warmer and less disquieting.

If the storm was frightening her, what must it be like for Emma? Sam picked up her wrapper from the foot of her bed, tugging it on to tightly enfold her. She stuffed her feet into slippers, then took her candle with her.

Opening her door, Sam tiptoed down the hall, pausing outside Emma's door before quietly opening it to peek inside.

"Oh, Samantha, thank heavens you are here. What a frightful night this is." Looking lost in her great bed with enormous feather pillows ballooning at either side of her, Emma huddled beneath her comforter. Her dainty lace cap was a bit askew on

35

those charming brown curls. The candle burning steadily in the holder on her bedside table revealed eyes wide with fear.

Sam noted with an affectionate ruefulness that even in the dead of night, with cap a-kilter, Emma looked like the polished London miss that she was. Samantha walked to the window where she began to pull the draperies together. Then she noticed a light flashing somewhere in the west wing of the house. Quickly, she yanked the draperies shut, turning to face Emma with what she hoped was a collected countenance. "Why not get a cup of chocolate? It has been my experience that a hot cup of something always makes a storm seem less a worry."

Better not to dwell on that light in the unoccupied portion of the house. Maybe someone was merely checking to see if the storm had created a leak in the roof? Sam hoped so. This was not a night to have a visit from the family ghost.

The two girls walked to the stairs, each carrying a candle in each hand to chase away the shadows that danced wildly with every step they took.

"I had never realized what a shivery old house this is, Samantha. Was George telling the truth when he was used to tell those stories about a ghost?" Emma glanced about her with obvious apprehension.

"Well, mind you, I have not seen any sort of a ghost, but he claims there is one. I have always suspected that George merely wished to keep me in my room come bedtime. It was a very different way of ensuring I did not come begging for a cup of water or a biscuit."

"Oh, you mean like the trolls-under-the-bed sort of thing Alfred used to tease us about?" Emma closely followed Samantha down the hall into the kitchen.

Coals put forth a comforting glow in the great hearth across the room. Sam placed her candles on the scrubbed wooden table before stirring up the remains of the fire, adding on a bit of wood, then pouring milk into a pan and placing it on the hob to heat.

"I believe that is the first of foolish notions men try to plant in our brains," declared Sam as she rummaged in a jar for a few biscuits.

Intrigued, Emma forgot about the storm outside and eased onto a stool by the table. "What notions?"

Sam put the biscuits on a plate and placed it on the table before Emma, then turned to locate the chocolate, sugar, and vanilla. She had acquired a very particular recipe for chocolate, one she greatly preferred.

"Like we are weaker, or that our minds cannot think as well. Or that we are afraid of our own shadows. I suspect they fear we might show them up for the poor fellows they are and so they keep repeating all that nonsense." Sam stirred the chocolate mixture into the hot milk, then poured the steaming liquid into two large mugs. The delicious fragrance of chocolate wafted across the room to tease the nose of the man who watched.

"For example, allow me to remind you of my flight this afternoon. A fragile female sort of exploit? Not on your life. Had my brother been able to find a boy who understood what must be done, he would have chosen him first. But I did it— and well, I believe."

"Were you not afraid, dear Samantha? I fear I should have been near fainting merely to watch you." Emma sipped at her chocolate, looking adorable with a chocolate mustache.

"A little," replied Sam honestly. "But it was a lovely thing to do, soaring through the air like that. I felt so free, and it was wondrous up there in the sky."

"And you could have broken that dainty neck of yours as well!" The husky male voice came from the shadows of the door, greatly startling both of the girls.

Whirling about, Sam clutched at the neck of her wrapper as Lord Laverstock emerged from the shadows into the gentle candlelight. Emma patted the nightcap atop her head as though to assure herself she was properly attired.

"My goodness, how you do startle one." Sam swallowed with care. If he had been impressive in his evening attire, he was a stunning blow in his silk robe and slippers.

"Any more of the chocolate about?"

As he made his inquiry, the cook entered the room, looking horrified at the sight of Quality in her domain.

Samantha soothed her, promising to permit her to bring in

more chocolate to the drawing room. Shepherding the others out and up to the drawing room, Sam wondered if there might be any more lights in the other wing of the house. While Laverstock stirred the fire, she crossed to the windows. She pulled the draperies closed, and noted as she did that whoever had been in the west wing was still there. She drew in a careful breath, then joined the others in the warmth and pleasantness of the revitalized fire. She didn't feel particularly like testing the ghost theory tonight.

"To continue a subject you undoubtedly would rather not, you were talking about daring women." Lord Laverstock gave her what could only be described as an inscrutable look.

Glaring at him in spite of her admiration, Sam tossed her head, effectively ridding her glorious hair of the silly scrap of a nightcap she placed there at Hetty's insistence. "And if we were?"

"You must admit your aunt was right. Women would not be suited for war." He rested an elbow against the mantel, assuming a negligent stance. Yet his eyes held a sharp awareness in them.

"We could have our uses if only men were not so narrow-minded." Sam was unyielding. After years of assisting George, she felt there was little she might not attempt.

"What is all the fuss down there? Such noise there is! I vow, I have been tossing in my bed the past hour." Aunt Lavinia entered the room with a dainty hand over her mouth to stifle a yawn. Her white silk wrapper was embroidered with flowers and a pretty cap sat atop her neatly braided hair.

"The noise of the wind woke us up, dear aunt. 'Tis a storm of some magnitude. I feel better now, as I daresay does Samantha. There is comfort in the company of others when a gale blows up." Emma rose to join Lavinia and usher her to a chair by the fireside.

The cook entered bearing a tray of chocolate and biscuits. Fortunately, she anticipated there might be a gathering on such a night, and she had brought an ample amount.

Sam looked about the room, then went to the hall to peer up the stairs. "Odd that Alfred doesn't join us. He would be the first to twit us about being frightened of the storm. I expect

Percival is cowering beneath the covers like any self-respecting mouse." She returned to the tray and helped herself to a second cup of chocolate and a large biscuit. Strolling slowly back to the fire, she continued to think while sipping at her beverage.

"With all that lightning about outside, 'tis no wonder if we be concerned. Fires are easily started that way. And do not be too hard on poor Percival." Lady Lavinia sipped at her chocolate, thinking Samantha would need a very firm hand if ever she wed.

"He is not one of life's more stalwart creatures," added Emma, "but he seems harmless."

"Fires? Oh, goodness, I never thought of that." Concentrating on the one word that penetrated, Sam thumped her cup on the table. She tightened the sash on her wrapper, dashed out into the hall, and set off to the west wing of the house.

"Lady Samantha! Wait!" Lord Laverstock followed close behind her. Catching up to her, he touched her arm to get her attention. "What makes you think there is a fire?"

"I did not say such a thing. Only, I did see a light flickering about in the west wing of the house. As it has been unoccupied for years, I am concerned."

"Why did you not say something before? Afraid?"

Sam halted in her steps, glaring up at him, unwilling to admit she was thankful for the oil lamp he had had the forethought to bring with him. "It is Emma, you see. I fear she is one of those delicate ladies whose sensibilities might be upset."

He took Sam's arm and they hurried down the hall until they came to the area she was certain she had seen light. She opened the first door and found nothing other than the holland-covered furniture of the state bedroom. Even the draperies were drawn. In the subsequent rooms, the same conditions were encountered. The wing was not a large one, and soon the two of them stood facing each other, Sam feeling exceedingly foolish.

"I am certain I saw something. I did *not* imagine it. "I'll have you know I am not that sort of female." Why Sam felt so belligerent or that she must defend herself, wasn't precisely clear to her. Why couldn't things go smoothly? It was clear Lord Laverstock had no notion that her fond papa had selected him for his daughter. Yet she quite desired him as a husband. After all, her papa was a very wise man. If he had chosen Laverstock, he must be the best, a veritable nonesuch.

"We might as well return to the others. You may not have noticed, but it is cold and damp here." He guided her back to the central part of the house, wondering why he was being so noble. With that riot of hair tumbling down her back she did not resemble a proper lady, but what a mouth-watering morsel she was, indeed.

His name suited him, somehow, thought Sam, liking the feel of his warm hand on her arm. Laverstock was such a stiffly polite man, possessing that haughty courtesy Aunt Lavinia had remarked on earlier. He seemed afraid to get near her. Sam gave her aunt a reassuring look as she entered the room. Laverstock paused to replace the oil lamp, then followed.

"What made you go haring off in such a dither, young lady?" Aunt Lavinia noted the frustrated expression in Laverstock's eyes and relaxed. Spinster she might be, but she knew a thing or two about the other sex. Nothing unseemly had occurred.

"You may rest assured there is no sign of fire." Samantha met her aunt's gaze with clear, but troubled eyes, then turned to face her cousin. "I did not wish to alarm you, Emma, but I noted a light in the state room wing earlier. When Aunt mentioned the possibility of fire, I feared that the lightning might have struck the house."

"And you couldn't leave it for the men to check, could you?" Aunt Lavinia sighed with defeat and shook her head.

Swallowing her ire, Sam said, "All is well."

"Except you do not know what caused the light," replied the practical Emma. "That ghost George teased about . . . you do not suppose . . . ?"

"Nonsense! Though I wonder where the dear boy is? Alfred ought to turn up as well. He is not as sound a sleeper, as I recall." Aunt Lavinia shifted uneasily in her chair. The tales of a family ghost were all too vivid for her liking. There must have been some substance over the years to keep the story alive.

"Did I hear someone mention my name?" Alfred entered the room, his dressing robe untidily tied about his waist and his hair looking as though he had raked it with a hay fork. Sam noted that he was dressed in shirt and pantaloons with soft slippers on his feet. If his arising had been hasty, he had dressed before joining them, though not bothering to glance in a looking glass first.

Behind him, Percival entered the room. He might be sleepy, but he was as nattily turned out as though he was planning to attend a rout, except for his elegant brocade dressing gown. "Nasty weather, what?"

"One cannot help but wonder what is keeping the old pile of bricks standing in this gale," added Alfred, after pouring out a cup of chocolate for himself.

"My, are you not a wonderful comfort!" snapped Emma.

Alfred ignored her, looking about the room with a shrewd gaze. "George is the only one not affected by this storm."

"George could sleep through anything." This statement was followed by a loud crash. Samantha and Emma jumped up to scurry across to stand by Aunt Lavinia's chair as though to draw courage from her.

Lord Laverstock and Alfred headed toward the door with Percival remaining behind.

"Must stay with the fair ones, don't y'know," Percival said with a wary eye on the doorway.

For once Sam did not wish to attempt a man's job. If the two men wished to be heroes, it was perfectly agreeable with her.

The crackle and snap of the fire in the grate and the low moaning of the wind as it tore around the eaves of the house were the only sounds to be heard. The three women and Percival remained tensely in place, waiting, watching.

Minutes ticked by, then George stumbled into the room, his face glistening with water and clothes soaking wet.

"Mercy!" exclaimed Aunt Lavinia. She clutched her wrapper about her while huddling closer to the fire.

Samantha left the chair where her aunt sat frozen with apprehension and rushed to her brother's side. "What has happened?" She caught sight of a soft wool rug on the sofa and picked it up to place over George's shoulders.

"I went down to the barn. Had to see if the glider was safe. All this wind, could be the roof might go."

"Well?"

"Roof is well enough, but for a few leaks. Someone else had been there, though. Papers were disturbed, not the way I left them."

Percival raised a hand in dismay just as Laverstock and Alfred entered the room, their hair wet and clothes spattered with rain.

Sam turned to face them. "What did you find?"

"Tree crashed down near the west part of the house, broke a window. Two of the men are there now, pulled the tree away enough so they can cover the window up."

"Gracious, such a night!"

Laverstock walked over to place a soothing hand on Aunt Lavinia's shoulder. "The wind seems to be dying down and I imagine by morning the storm will have passed. Perhaps the best thing would be to go to bed and try to sleep." He glanced about the room, looking at George, who huddled by the fire. "A good dose of brandy and dry clothes will keep George from coming down with an inflammation of the lungs."

At that, Aunt Lavinia jumped up and bustled about getting the brandy and giving a hearty tug on the bell pull. Peters entered shortly.

"See to a hot bath for George before he catches his death." As Peters bowed and left, Aunt shooed the rest of them up the stairs and to their rooms.

Samantha left Emma at her door with the admonition that if she felt concerned, she might come into Sam's room. Alone in her own bed, Sam began to think. Just before Laverstock and Alfred had returned, George had stated that someone had been in the barn. Could there be a connection to the light in the west wing? Unlikely—the barn was down the hill from the opposite end of the house. She shivered, but not from the chill of her room. Pulling the comforter up about her ears, she wondered what was going on in her home.

Samantha wandered along the garden path the next morning, trying to conceal a yawn. She toted her lute with her, searching for a secluded spot where she could escape the company and do a bit of thinking. She brushed a crumb from her gown, another of the lovely gowns from dear papa. It was a pleasing gold muslin with pretty white spots. Over it, to ward off a chill from the still dampish air, she wore a heavy shawl in an attractive paisely design.

There were branches strewn about everywhere. Two of the great elms had gone down in the storm. At the west end of the house a top sawyer cut into sections the tree that had broken the window. Another workman stowed the wood onto a cart to be hauled away to the barn. The glass from the broken window was being carefully removed. From the recesses of the barn a piece of glass was being carried up to the house. A small army of workmen scurried about the garden cleaning up the debris, something Sam normally might have observed with interest. Not so this morning.

Brushing aside some leaves, Sam sank onto a bench in a quiet portion of the garden. Scent from the white lilacs drifted around her, mixing with the fragrance of the bed of lily of the valley not far away, along with the pungency of damp ground.

What had been going on last night? She couldn't believe in a ghost, no matter if it was family tradition. No, it was something more earthly. But what?

"Feeling more the thing this morning?" The attractively husky voice startled Samantha.

"You certainly do have a way of creeping up on a person, Lord Laverstock. Is this a new trait or have you always done it?" She gave him a cross look and drew her feet beneath her gown, feeling somehow that she needed to retreat, no matter how little.

"May I?" He brushed aside a few leaves to join her on the marble bench, looking off down the garden before turning to examine Samantha. "Troubled?"

"What makes you say that?" She smiled as though she hadn't a care in the world instead of a suspicious wandering light in the middle of the night to consider. That, plus an aunt who persisted in removing articles from other people's houses. Oh, and she had best not forget George's pronouncement that someone had been poking about the barn. Her mind drifted off to dwell on the snuffbox and how she might return it to Squire

Dowdeswell's drawing room. The roads would be in a dreadful condition today after all that rain, yet she *must* see to it somehow.

"As I walked down the path you were unaware of my presence. You wore a distressing frown on that lovely countenance." His voice had a curious inflection she couldn't identify, but it was certainly intriguing.

Sam gave him a wary look. In her limited experience a man waxed poetical just when he was about to do something silly— like hold her hand or attempt a kiss. In the past she had been successful in warding off this nonsense. Now she suddenly realized that she had no interest in fending off any action on Lord Laverstock's part.

However, Lord Laverstock seemed to have no such thing in mind. He eyed the lute forgotten in Sam's lap. "Would you give me a song this morning? I must say, the lute does not quite fit in with your image as an independent and questing woman."

The lute gave a twang as Sam's fingers slipped from the proper strings. She straightened and gave him a falsely sweet smile. Rather than answer, she began to play the old madrigal "The Silver Swan." Glancing at Lord Laverstock, she sang the haunting melody, her voice clear and true.

"The silver swan, who living had no note,
    When death approached unlocked her silent throat,
    Leaning her breast against the reedy shore,
    Thus sung her first and last; and sung no more,
    Farewell all joys, O death come close mine eyes,
    More Geese than Swans now live,
    More fools than wise."

" 'Tis a sad song for a vital young woman to sing. I thought most madrigals were of the merry sort." He leaned against the back of the bench, glancing at her before staring off to the distance where he could see George directing the removal of some of the smaller trees that had fallen during the night's storm.

"True. Most are light-hearted songs, and sung by two or more." She strummed a bit of a happier melody. "Still, there is something noble and pure about the 'Swan.' 'Tis a very early song, I suspect. At least, that music book seems to be very old. Some of the other songbooks I found have madrigals, sonnets, and airs.''

"How do you happen to play a lute? An odd instrument nowadays. Most young women play a pianoforte or a harp."

She studied the fine detailing on the large pear-shaped body of her lute, toying with a turning peg. "I found it in the attic one rainy day, and with it a stack of old music. I couldn't resist trying to play it. It is quite portable and I can carry it wherever I please."

"I still say it does not suit you."

Sam gave him a dangerous look. "You mean it is the music of a lady and I do not fit that image?"

"Is that what I mean? I did not precisely say those words." His voice held a faintly teasing note to it.

Sam thought he was recalling her appearance in breeches and shirt, and her cheeks warmed at the remembrance of his eyes as they had beheld her. Dratted man. How could she show him she could be a lady? It shouldn't be too difficult, should it? Emma did it all the time. Perhaps she could do something special . . . like . . . "I could be Queen of the May," she murmured aloud.

He chuckled.

She was most angered at his amusement. "Well, indeed I could, if I so chose."

"I was of the opinion the queen was elected. What makes you think they would choose a hoyden like you for the part? Beauty and popularity are a necessity, I thought."

"That does not rule out a hoyden, I believe," snapped Sam. It irked her to be so called by Laverstock.

"With freckles on the nose?" he taunted gently.

Sam rose with a huff and departed for the house before she forgot she was trying to be a lady and crowned Lord Laverstock with her lute.

Emma floated down the stairs looking as though she had not been disturbed one whit by the night's activity. Samantha greeted her absently, then wandered off to locate the snuffbox. One way or the other she had to get to the Dowdeswells' before it was missed.

It was nowhere to be found. After searching all the known hiding places her aunt had favored, Sam leaned against the staircase, contemplating the matter.

"Samantha, have you seen Aunt? I glimpsed her coming back from the barn but she is not around now." Emma paused by the breakfast room door, awaiting a reply.

"No," murmured Sam. The barn? Oh, for pity's sake!

"Where are you going, Samantha? Have you had something to eat? Be careful not to get your gown wet. The grass is still very damp."

Emma's voice drifted out behind her as Sam dashed from the house, forgetting her resolve to be ladylike as she hurried to the barn. Of all places to hide her trinkets, why must Aunt Lavinia choose the barn!

Up near the house, Charles watched as Samantha ran across the lawn toward the barn where her brother kept the glider. What could she want there? Her brother was supervising the clean-up on the estate; there would be no daring flights from the hill today. He might not have given her dash a thought had it not been for the worried, almost guilty expression on her face. What might the young lady be up to now, he wondered. He began to follow her, assuring himself he did so out of curiosity, nothing more.

At the door of the barn he studied the frantic figure that was tearing through everything in sight. She gasped, grabbed something from a high ledge, then turned.

Charles was more than a little intrigued at her suddenly pale face when she espied him. The little freckles on her nose stood out in bold relief against the pallor of her skin. What was she hiding behind her? Her expression was definitely one of guilt.

"Find something you didn't lose?"

4

"I have a matter of the first consequence to attend to."
Sam edged around Lord Laverstock, trying to keep her face toward him while hiding her hands. The snuffbox was vastly pretty, but larger than average in size. Oh, why did they not make gowns with pockets anymore? Had she a pocket, she might have slipped the snuffbox into it, and there would have been no problem whatsoever. "I must go to Squire Dowdeswell's at once."

"Off to fascinate the local gentry? Are you really going to pursue this silly notion of being the May Queen?"

"I do not plan to fascinate anyone. And what is so silly about my being the May Queen?" She successfully slid past him, hiding her hand in the folds of her gown as she walked toward the stables with Laverstock trailing behind. Although there was not a single carriage that could be used on these dismal roads, she could ride Boots over to the squire's. What a pity she had not worn a round gown of sensible blue kerseymere today instead of this frivolous gold muslin. Yet she was determined, regardless.

Something drove him to goad her. "The lovely Emma perhaps might excellently qualify." He shook his head. "Those freckles of yours . . ." His customary reserve seemed to melt away when with this delightful girl. If his London friends could but see and hear him now, they would raise their quizzing glasses in amazement.

"You, sir, are not a gentleman to so remind me of them," she said with spirit. George was coming toward the stables from the opposite direction. Sam hurried toward him, something in her urgency communicating itself to him though she said not a word.

"Where are you off to at this time of the morning? A bit early for calls, is it not? And you not in your riding habit?" George was puzzled at her agitation as well as the look of amusement on Laverstock's face.

"Your sister seeks to capture the interest of the local gentry so she might be named the Queen of the May this year." Laverstock was hard-pressed not to laugh at the thunderstruck expression that crossed George's face.

"And why not?" demanded Samantha. "I believe I could do as well as that whey-faced Mary Edgecombe of last year." Sam gave Laverstock an annoyed look before returning her golden gaze to George. "I have an urgent errand to perform immediately. for Aunt Lavinia." Sam assumed a haughty expression, while hoping her brother would not suggest a servant go in her stead. She planned to request something. What, precisely, she could think of as she rode. "Be so good as to ask a groom to saddle Boots for me."

George gave her an odd look, then turned to motion to one of the grooms standing near. "The last I heard, you as yet had a voice."

"I *am* sorry, brother dear," Sam apologized promptly. "I do not know what possessed me to be so thoughtless. Blame it on my interrupted sleep." She gave him a significant look, hoping he might be aware this was not a normal situation. She hoped to find some way of letting him know that Aunt Lavinia was pilfering again without revealing the scandalous information to the outsider, and failed. Giving up, she hurried to where her horse was being led out. His white stockings, or boots as she had first thought of them, were snowy clean, but by the time she returned, poor Boots would be splattered with mud. Nevertheless, she sighed, she had to get this dratted snuffbox back to the squire's house right away.

The two men watched her ride off, wondering what was really the cause of her unorthodox early-morning call. Not that Sam ever did the expected.

George turned to give Laverstock a concerned look. "She is a funny one. I wonder if she might be serious about this May Queen matter? Or is it all a hum? I confess that I do not understand the female mind."

"I am quite of the opinion that she will do whatever she pleases in that regard," said Laverstock. "But suffice it to say that I would not dare to guess what goes on in that active brain-box of hers." He watched Samantha until she was lost to view.

George turned aside from the thought of his perplexing sister. "Why do we not go up to the house and find us a cup of coffee . . . perhaps laced with a bit of brandy? The damp, y'know."

"Excellent notion," Laverstock agreed.

The two sauntered along the graveled path toward the front door. George cast a glance at the west wing, where repairs were being carried out on the damaged window. "Glad m'father is in London. Busy man, hates to be bothered with this sort of thing. You know him well?"

Laverstock suspected there was more than mere curiosity in George's question. Sensing George was someone he might trust, he replied, "Though I cannot tell you the whole of it, your father has sent me up here for more than to merely get a rest, welcome though that might be."

"I had a hunch it might be something like that. Your being so much younger, and in the War Office, and all."

"Has Sam said anything about me to you? Does she harbor suspicions as well?" Charles wondered precisely what did pass through Samantha's mind when she thought of him. Was he only considered a tease? Or worse yet, a plaguesome stranger?

George frowned and shook his head. "If that widgeon has any odd notions in her head, she will keep them to herself. She isn't one to prattle our business about. No gabble-grinder, she." He continued to think for a bit, then as they entered the front door, he said quietly, "Is there anything I might do to help you?"

Laverstock was coming to have a high regard for young George. Sam might say that there was no earthly use for such a genius, but George was not blind, nor stupid, either. He was not his father's son for nothing. "At present, no. But I will remember your offer should I need it."

"You can count on me," answered George in an undertone while they entered the drawing room.

"Dear boys," fluttered Aunt Lavinia, "such a bother a storm

is. All this breakage is excessively distressing.'' She set aside her embroidery frame after carefully tucking the needle into the fabric, then crossed the room to tug at the bell pull. When Peters entered, she gave him some low-voiced instructions, turning to survey the others when he left. ''Where is Samantha? Emma said something about her going down to the barn.''

George remembered the peculiar look Sam had given him as she said she *must* get to the squire's house and wondered if his dear aunt was connected. She wore a strangely intense expression on her sweet face. ''The stables, I believe. At least, that is where I encountered her. Had a small errand in the village, I think. Was that not what she said, Laverstock?''

Not knowing where the squire resided, Laverstock merely nodded. ''Possibly she intends to seek support for this year's Queen of the May position.''

Aunt Lavinia paused in the act of sitting down on the sofa. She dropped to the cushioned surface with an amazed expression flitting across her face. ''Oh, dear.''

Near the window George ceased contemplating the destruction wrought by the storm to turn toward Laverstock. ''I'll not have it, I tell you!''

''Not have what, cousin George?'' Emma drifted into the room, smoothing down her pale violet muslin gown before seating herself beside her aunt.

''Sam has some maggoty notion of being Queen of the May this year,'' thundered an incensed George. ''She cannot do that! I need her to help me.''

''You cannot be serious, George,'' protested Aunt Lavinia. ''Surely you can manage without Samantha for a day or two.'' Privately, Lavinia thought it would be a very good thing were Samantha to become separated from George and his experimental work. For too long had that dear girl been treated like a young brother. It was time and enough that she come to realize her feminine charms. From the look of that lord from London, there could be a bit of assistance from his direction, given a nudge or two.

At that moment Peters entered with a tray of coffee and assorted cheese samplings. Laverstock accepted a fragrantly steaming cup, adding a dash of brandy from the small cut-glass decanter George handed him.

"I think it should be a fine thing for Samantha to be Queen of the May," said Emma generously. "I fancy that she will do quite well at it, too."

Aunt Lavinia gave her an approving look. "Well said, Emma dear. 'Twould be the making of her, perhaps? What think you, Lord Laverstock?"

Feeling a trifle cornered, Charles sipped his excellent coffee before making a very careful reply. "I can understand that George has come to depend on her, but," he glanced at George as he spoke, "surely you will need to replace her when she is married?"

"Sam . . . married? I had never considered that." George had the look of a man confronted with a distasteful truth.

"What? Is the fair Samantha to be married?" Percival strolled into the room, his deep violet coat in total harmony with a lilac waistcoat and moleskin breeches. "I say, I cannot imagine who she might have selected."

"You see!" countered Aunt Lavinia with glee. "Percival does not find anything peculiar in the idea. We actually were discussing something else, Percival dear."

All heads turned as the front door closed with a bang. A few minutes later a breathless Sam entered to find all faces turned toward her, a speculative expression on each.

Samantha touched her bonnet lightly to make certain that all was proper after her hurried trip. She had caught a glimpse of herself as she entered the house and had had the forethought to ascertain that she was presentable to her aunt and any other person who happened to be around, but she had not considered there might be a gathering.

Observing the thunderous expression on George's face, she inquired, "Is something amiss?"

Desiring to change the subject lest Samantha be put off the entire effort, Lady Lavinia spoke up first. "George was about to show us an experiment of his. His electrifying machine, as I recall. Were you not, George?"

"Huh? Oh, right. Electrifying." He gave his aunt a resigned look before placing his coffee cup on the table.

Sam gave him a skeptical look. "I cannot believe that, for some reason. Emma, might I see you in my room, if you will all excuse us?" Sam nodded to the others, frowning at her brother, who looked about to give her a scold.

"Hurry right back, my dears. Such an interesting afternoon we shall have." Aunt Lavinia gave the girls a complacent smile before she turned to George once again.

After the two young women disappeared up the stairs, George gave his aunt an exasperated look. "Electrifying? Really, Aunt Lavinia. Could you not have thought of something Sam might have readily accepted?"

Percival set his coffee cup on the tray, then picked up a wedge of fine-quality cheddar. "I, for one, think it a vastly amusing idea. I have never seen it done, actually. Do arrange it, George. This is such a dull day."

Trying not to laugh, Laverstock nodded at George. " 'Tis all the crack, you know."

"Come now, George, be a good boy and get that contraption you showed me." Aunt Lavinia wasn't too certain she wanted to participate in the experiment. However, as it had successfully diverted attention from Samantha—at least for the moment— she would try.

Upstairs, Samantha pulled Emma into her room, collapsing dramatically on the chair near the window. "Well, I managed to return the snuffbox Aunt Lavinia took. But the squire had missed it. I tucked it along the edge of the chair where I sat, then pretended to find it. It was a very close thing, I assure you. What a mad dash. It wouldn't do for Aunt to know." She gave a long sigh of relief.

"Oh, dear. Is that why you hurried off in such a flap this morning? I did not know what was amiss." Emma curled up on the chaise longue, tucking her slippered feet beneath her.

"I decided that if you were not aware of what I had to do or where I was going, Aunt could be none the wiser. You know how clever she can be about ferreting information out of one. If she knows that I know, she will merely find another place to hide the items she takes. What *are* we to do, Em?"

"What a coil to be in. If she is discovered we shall all be

disgraced, I just know it." Emma picked up a dainty pillow embroidered by Lavinia with lilies of the valley and pursed her lips as she considered the problem.

"Precisely." Nodding, Sam chewed at her lower lip while also cogitating upon the matter. "We shall simply have to keep watch over her. If she takes off, one of us must be with her."

"I do not mind the visiting, though I know you care not for it. Had she planned it she could not find a better means to get you to pay calls." Emma studied Samantha, then gently queried, "Do you really wish to be Queen of the May this year?"

Sam made a rueful face. "I said that, did I not? What think you of the notion? Am I a total goosecap?"

"I shall do all in my power to assist you, for I decidedly approve." Emma gave an emphatic nod, tucking the pillow behind her.

Perking up, Sam peered at her cousin. "Why?"

"You did say you wish to be a lady and I believe that a queen is a step in that direction. Do you still feel an inclination toward Lord Laverstock?"

"I do not know. He is a tease, and can be quite odious at times." There also was something most smoky about his being here, but Sam said nothing about her suspicions to Emma. "However, if Papa desires me to have the man, I shall be happy to comply. Only . . . I fear Laverstock is not appraised of the matter, as he shows no sign of partiality. I gather I am on my own regarding his lordship. At least the man is not quite as stuffy as he first appeared. Perhaps being with us is mellowing him? We assuredly are not dull."

Emma cleared her throat. "Are you quite certain that it is what your papa meant for you, dear girl? I would not that you mistake the matter."

"Well, Laverstock said he is here due to fatigue and anyone with eyes in his head can see there is not the least thing wrong with him."

Slowly nodding, Emma glanced at the door. "I expect we'd best return to the drawing room. Heaven knows what Aunt will be about if one of us does not keep an eye on her."

"True." Samantha rose to her feet, extending a hand to help Emma. "Thank you for your offer to assist me. I vow you will have a task on your hands, as Aunt Lavinia said. Am I really such a hopeless case?''

Emma didn't miss the wistfulness in Samantha's voice. While not the brightest of creatures, Emma could detect the yearning within Samantha with no difficulty at all. ''Of course you are nothing of the sort. Come, let us see what they are about.''

As the girls rounded the corner of the drawing room, it was to see Peters standing stiffly beside a kneeling George, holding some objects for him. Aunt Lavinia stood on the other side, gingerly clutching a chain. She in turn held tightly to Lord Laverstock's hand, while he held on to Percival.

''Oh, dear,'' muttered Sam.

''Shall you join us, Emma? You as well, Samantha.'' Aunt had ordered, not requested. Samantha accepted the hand Percival offered her, finding herself placed between Lord Laverstock and Percival, rather than being tag end. Emma hesitantly clasped the hand Percival extended just as Alfred entered the room, a look of astonishment crossing his face as he viewed the line of people across the carpeted floor.

''What on earth . . .''

''You might as well be one of us, Alfred,'' urged Samantha. ''Take Emma's hand and complete the line.''

He did as she asked, placing one hand on the fireplace mantel as George requested. George began cranking the cylinder of his friction machine to produce his ''electricity.''

''Oh, dear,'' exclaimed Aunt Lavinia while she waited impatiently.

''I do not feel a thing yet,'' murmured Sam. She spoke too soon. A charge of current shot through her, quite a jolting one. She glanced at Laverstock. He smiled at her, making her totally forget the shock she had just experienced.

Emma had glanced at Alfred, then, as the strong current passed through her, fainted dead away.

''Mercy!'' Aunt Lavinia dropped the chain and began searching for her vinaigrette, while Samantha glared at her brother. He ought to have known better than agree to Aunt Lavinia's silly suggestion.

Alfred had a strange look on his face as he cradled the lovely Emma in his arms. He gathered her up, walking with her to the sofa as though he held a sleeping baby. Carefully placing her down so as she might better recover, he appeared loathe to leave her, rather sitting by her side and chaffing her hands. He called her name softly, though as far as Sam could see it might achieve more if he would shout at her.

Samantha was about to scold him when a shake of the head from Aunt Lavinia stilled her tongue.

"Emma, can you hear me?" Alfred looked up at Aunt Lavinia, clearly worried. "Will she be all right, do you think?"

"Fiddlesticks! Of course, she shall be quite fine. Allow me to tend to her."

Seeing that he had prevented Aunt from ministering to the recumbent Emma, Alfred reddened and jumped up. He turned on George. "See here, George, I can't say that was the best thing to do." Alfred cast a concerned look at Emma, who stirred, coughing slightly from the pungent odor of the vinaigrette. "Females are too delicate for that sort of nonsense."

"Sam is fine. Didn't bother her in the least. Aunt Lavinia either." George was unhappy. Not only had his aunt pressured him into a position he had not wished for in the least, now Emma had made a cake of herself and him as well.

"If you know what to expect, it can be most pleasant, actually." Sam grinned at Alfred, liking this very human side of her cousin. Besides, she might be able to tease him about it, if need be.

"Ohhh," murmured Emma, as she attempted to sit up.

Alfred rushed to her side. "May I get you a glass of water . . . lemonade . . . anything?"

"Water, I think." Emma's voice was faint, her color very pale. Sam decided she looked rather interesting, in a peculiar way.

Peters had reentered the room, having summed up the requirements of the young lady long before anyone thought to send him off for a thing. "Sir?" He held out a tray upon which sat a small pitcher of lemonade, a glass of water, and a damp cloth.

"You are a treasure, Peters." Alfred took the glass of water and offered it to the fragile-looking Emma.

Across the room, Laverstock stood by the window, watching

the scene as it unfolded. He observed Samantha's fascinated gaze. Abandoning his spot, he strolled to where she observed Alfred and Emma.

"Learn anything from that?"

The rich voice so close to her made her jump slightly. "Lord Laverstock! *Must* you do that?"

"Well, did you?" Laverstock had found holding the fair Samantha's hand a rather delightful experience. It had been slim, strong, and yet very soft. When the current had shot through them, she had clasped his hand most tightly. He had found it strangely stirring. That he had paid no attention at all to Emma was missed by him.

Ordinarily, Sam would have ridiculed Emma and Alfred as silly fools. Now she was not quite so certain. "She really is an agreeable girl, you know. And though he is by no means what I would call winning, he has excellent manners . . . when he tries." Sam was a little shaken. Her notions of what she must do altered perceptibly. Could she play the lady to the extent that she fainted? " 'Tis most surprising."

"I think not, Lady Samantha. While Lady Emma is all that is feminine, there are many forms of charm. You do not have so very far to go, if that is what is floating about in your head."

Was she that transparent? "Oh, dear. Do you read minds as well? Is that a talent useful in the War Office?"

"Not necessarily. But it helps other times." Laverstock found the young Samantha vastly amusing. He could see that her father, the Earl of Cranswick, would have a time of it to see her married off.

"I believe I shall continue with my plans for May Queen. Is that a very naughty wish?" She gave him a wary look.

"Alfred mentioned to me there is to be a May King as well. I have not seen such a thing."

"Yes, well, not all villages have one, you know." Sam chewed her bottom lip with vexation. She had not considered that aspect. Who might be selected for her "king"? Providing she obtained the support necessary to be queen?

Percival drifted across the room to confront Samantha and Laverstock. "Quite the most unusual afternoon, what?"

Seizing the opportunity to escape Laverstock and reassess her plans, Samantha slipped from the two gentlemen, leaving after murmuring something vague to her aunt about seeing to Emma's room.

Alone in the peace of Emma's bedroom, Samantha paced about. Why had she not recalled the May King business? How stupid. She well knew what the day would bring. Laverstock did not. The sight of Sam's parading around the village with the king, and all else that was to be done, might well give him a disgust of her. Dear Papa would not be best pleased with her if that occurred. "Drat and double drat," muttered a very upset Samantha. "Whatever shall I do now?"

Emma had recovered rapidly with all the attention focused upon her. When Samantha returned to the drawing room, curious because Emma was not brought upstairs, she found the group assembled with tea being dispensed by her Aunt Lavinia. Emma had pink cheeks and was looking flustered as Alfred urged another biscuit upon her.

Laverstock walked over to join Samantha, a move not unnoticed by Aunt Lavinia. "Feeling more the thing?"

"Oh," said a discomposed Samantha, "I did not feel particularly shaken by the current, you know. It was merely the thought—" Sam stopped. She could hardly reveal to his lordship that she feared being kissed by some local lad who was to be paired with the May Queen. Also, Sam had been very much aware of Lord Laverstock during the electrification experiment. This awareness had been unexpected. Ought she to be feeling like this about Lord Laverstock? It was rather nice to be attracted to the one intended as a husband, she supposed. In fact, it might be a definite asset.

"Your aunt told me something about an experiment with a kite of which she strongly disapproved. Was George testing for electricity with that as well?"

Samantha nodded. "Papa said I might have been killed. I understand, from what Papa said, that a number of people have been killed trying out kites in a thunderstorm. George has promised not to do that one again." She gave Laverstock an ingenuous look, then bestowed her brilliant smile on him, making him blink with its effect. "I own I am vastly relieved."

Laverstock gave George a hard look. "And so you sail across the valley in preference."

Samantha laughed, much amused at his seeming anger. "Well, at least I am dry and relatively safe—until I land, that is. I told George he must change that elevator before I will chance it again. 'Tis a wondrous delight, you know, to sail with the birds. I should like above all things to do it again." She had totally forgotten that to be a lady, one did not partake in such hare-brained schemes.

Laverstock wanted to forbid it. The very idea that she might be killed, or even hurt, on such a daring endeavor was inconceivable! There must be some way he could prevent it from occurring.

Percival joined the two, much to Laverstock's annoyance. "I say, do you know what George plans to do with the flying machine? I heard you mention the elevator needs a spot of work."

"Does all the world and his wife know the ins and outs of George's experiment?" wondered Laverstock aloud.

"Of course not," Samantha said in a soothing way, puzzled at his lordship's seeming irritation. "But Percival is like one of the family. We could scarcely conceal the glider from him."

"I say, dear Samantha, 'tis a pleasure to be here with you." Percival gave her a smile.

"Looking forward to next quarter day, are you Twistleton?" The thrust was unfair, Laverstock supposed, but the young dandy irritated him no end. Why the devil did he have to interrupt when he and Samantha were in such delightful conversation? He frowned, causing Percival to take a step back.

Shrugging, Percival attempted a nonchalant answer. "Well, you know how the thing goes, I daresay. One can only live on tick so long."

"Yes. *Things* tend to catch up with one eventually, do they not?" The purring threat was unmistakable. Percival, though totally at sea as to the reason, decided it best to take his wit and conversation elsewhere.

"I believe you are not a kind man, Lord Laverstock." Samantha tilted her head and gave him an assessing study. "Percival is quite harmless, you know. Aunt Lavinia says the dear boy will come about one of these days, if we have but a bit of patience."

"I doubt I have that much to spare, most generous lady."
Charles refrained from grinning at her with only the greatest of
difficulty.

"I suspect you are bamming me, dear sir. It is not nice to tease
me." She flashed her smile once again before moving toward
where the others were gathered. "Emma, I am so pleased to see
you restored. Another of those biscuits, and I daresay you can
manage without dinner." Samantha giggled as Emma hastily
dropped the latest biscuit pressed upon her by the concerned
Alfred.

"Dreadful man," scolded Emma. "You have me so flustered
I scarce know what I do. I would not wish to miss cook's good
dinner. Shoo, you abominable piece of rascality."

Even George laughed at this sally.

"I am exceedingly pleased to find you have recovered your usual
tongue." Alfred gave Emma an annoyed glare before engaging
George in quiet conversation.

Aunt Lavinia surreptitiously picked up the tea cup Samantha
had set down and began the process she went through to make
her readings. She turned the cup over, studying the inside. Then
she chuckled with glee, darting a waggish glance to where her
niece now sat with Emma. Oh, things were going apace here,
they were.

5

The day began cheerfully enough. It was soft and bright, with a brisk wind from the southwest, a day to make one think of bluebells and roses.

"I believe I shall plant a syringa in the garden. Perhaps two or three. They have such lovely flowers." Aunt Lavinia looked up from the thin catalog of plants she was perusing at the breakfast table.

Emma and Samantha exchanged looks of relief. If Aunt was absorbed with plans for her garden, perhaps she might not be venturing off to the village. They didn't fear a jaunt to Scarborough nearly as much, for she was too cautious to casually pick up anything that took her fancy while in town.

By way of explanation, Emma turned to Laverstock and reminded him, "Aunt is passionately fond of flowers, you see. White flowers, that is."

"Quite so," added Lavinia, beaming a smile at the new addition to the household. "I am exceedingly pleased with the orange trees now blooming in the orangery. White blooms, you know. And such lovely fragrance. It quite overcomes one." Her white cambric cap edged with rows of lace nicely matched her white morning gown with rows of lace marching down the skirt. Above her pink cheeks, shrewd eyes peered out at the assembled group.

Lavinia had always liked to have her family meet at the table of a morning. It seemed so much more sociable than closeting oneself in a bedroom. Of course, Percival was not present, but then, he wasn't precisely family. However, she noted with approval that Lord Laverstock had joined them for breakfast. Ah, he had potential, he did.

"I may go into the village later on today to order these plants." Lavinia noted the swift exchange of looks between her nieces, and smiled to herself. It never did to let them become complacent. And besides, what better way to persuade Samantha to make neighborly social calls. As well, it was such fun collecting all those pretty white things. "Do you think the roads will be passable, George?"

"I believe you may be able to risk a drive come this afternoon." George had not missed the exchange between his sister and Emma. Samantha had slipped into his room last night to tell him of Aunt Lavinia's latest folly. He was fond of the old lady, but she was getting to be a bit of a problem.

"I shall go with you if you do not mind, dear aunt," declared Emma, having decided it was her turn.

At first disappointed, Lavinia brightened as she considered it would leave Samantha in the proximity of Lord Laverstock. "Fine, dear, just fine."

Breakfast concluded, Lavinia rose to drift from the table, catalog in hand.

Emma and Samantha sighed with relief and excused themselves, whisking off to Samantha's bedroom with a whirl of skirts.

Percival sauntered into the breakfast room just as George and Laverstock were about to depart to inspect the glider. "Wonder where the girls were off to in such unseemly haste?"

"Who knows what females get up to, probably gossiping and talking clothes," said Alfred, who had other plans for the day than inspecting the glider. His earlier chat with Laverstock had been interesting. He felt that he had gained his confidence—as much as the gentleman ever gave.

"Somehow I fail to see Samantha fussing over gowns and fripperies," drawled Percival.

Laverstock bristled at the tone of Percival's voice. "I thought Lady Samantha looked quite unexceptionable last evening."

"She is anything but a lady, pardon my saying so, for all that she's m'sister," countered George.

"And who is to blame for that, George, old fellow?" snapped Alfred. "You have kept her in breeches and at your beck and call for as long as I can remember. Has she had an opportunity to turn into a lady?''

Laverstock was ignored as the cousins glared at each other.

"Emma might see to it, given the chance,'' muttered George.

Alfred snorted in disgust. "Emma? She'd swoon first.''

"You were mighty quick to rush to her aid yesterday,'' said Percival, chuckling at the memory of Alfred tenderly fussing over Lady Emma.

Alfred looked as though he might enjoy hitting Percival over the head. Apparently he thought the better of it, turning away.

"I still say it's a bit unfair to blame me for Sam.'' George stood by the door in stubborn refusal to see the truth of the matter.

"See? You even call her by a boy's name,'' said Alfred, quite out of patience with his dense cousin by this moment.

"Well, I mean to say, she tagged after me all the time. What was a body to do?'' George seemed ready to debate the subject indefinitely.

Laverstock decided the best approach was to separate the cousins as quickly as possible, steering George out of the door toward the barn where the glider was housed. If Samantha were to fly again, Laverstock wanted to see to it that the elevator was changed.

George was clearly disgruntled. "I would like to know how I was supposed to keep her out from under my feet all these years. Tried to send her off to London for a Season and she said it was too dangerous there.''

Lord Laverstock blinked in surprise. More dangerous in London than soaring in the sky? Or risking her life on a hilltop in a storm? Samantha was a very confused young lady.

"You'd not stand in her way if she decided to change?'' Laverstock smiled as George paused in the doorway of the barn, a look of horror on his face.

"I don't know what I'd do without her. She understands me, you see.''

"I will never understand George,'' declared Samantha in no uncertain terms. She curled up on the chaise longue. With a critical eye she studied the way in which her dear cousin Emma strolled across the room. "He does not seem to realize that I shall have to marry some day. For I have no wish to remain here to be his slave all my life." That this was a totally new notion she carefully omitted. Prior to Lord Laverstock's arrival at Mayne Court, Samantha had been reasonably content to work with George on all his inventions. She had changed.

"I quite agree with you, Samantha. Perhaps if we can wangle your election as May Queen, it will convince him that he must look on you in a new manner." Emma paused by the window, noting Alfred poking about the orangery. "Whatever is that plaguey man doing now, I wonder?"

Samantha jumped up, brushing away a pesky fly as she peered out the window. "Alfred? Who knows? I daresay he is writing something again. The last time he came he was deep in some notebook his entire visit."

Emma brushed away another fly that had taken refuge in the corner. "What a bother! If the weather were not so nice, the windows would be closed and we should be spared these pests."

"The flies or Alfred?" Sam chuckled at Emma's indignant expression. "I tell you what, we shall swat a few. Just wait until summer, it can be nigh unbearable at times when the wind is right. The pig sties and stables, you know," she said apologetically.

Sam drew a chair to the window, then climbed up on the window ledge to attack the swarm of flies gathered in the upper corner of the window. Emma held out a somewhat battered basket she had found on the floor near the fireplace. "What do you plan to do about the queen business?" said Emma, as she leaned forward to catch a fly.

"Well," panted Sam, stretching up for a hit, "I shall try for it. When we are done with this, why not retire to the orangery and practice being a lady there. Aunt is right, it does smell delightfully this season of the year."

Emma grimaced as she caught another fly, then gave a dubious look in the direction of the orangery where no sight of Alfred was visible. She shrugged. "If you wish."

"There now," said Sam, smiling with satisfaction. "I believe we have murdered enough for the day."

"What horrid language you use, Samantha. That is the first thing you must change if you are to be a lady."

Sighing deeply, Samantha ushered her cousin out of the bedroom and down the stairs. It seemed that being a lady meant giving up nearly everything in the world that was any fun. It was very clear she had a vexing problem that was not going to be solved easily.

"Do you think you can solve the problem?" Laverstock had watched as George studied his plans with an amazing amount of concentration. He had made a few notations near the drawing of the maligned elevator device. Laverstock glanced up with surprise as Percival entered the barn, to be followed by Alfred.

George rolled up his drawings, placing them on his drawing table while observing the others with curious eyes.

"Thought you might want to do something. Moldy old place, this barn," said Percival in an affected manner while he gazed about, wrinkling his nose with distaste at the amount of dust and debris.

"Surprised to see you down here, both of you." Recalling his duties as a host, George suggested, "Perhaps we could go for a ride?"

"Excellent weather," offered Laverstock.

The men nodded agreement and the four strolled to the stables after George carefully locked the barn door, an act noted by Laverstock as well as the others.

"Worried, George?" murmured Alfred.

"When I was in the village t'other day, I heard a rumor that there is some Frenchie nosing about here. Emigré, they said. I never did trust those who came over, even if they said they was fleeing the Terror. Truth of it is, one never knows for sure. He *claims* to be a dancing master. Finally got the new lock installed this morning."

Alfred nodded, deep in thought. At last he spoke, softly, in an undertone not heard by the others. "So you feel your flying machine might actually be of some value, then?"

"I hope so. If Sam will come down off her high ropes, I would like to test it again with a new elevator design."

"Ah." Alfred mounted his horse and said no more.

Shortly the four men were to be seen heading north from the estate.

"Well, what do I do first?" demanded the impatient Samantha.

"We shall work on your walk, I believe. You must not stride as though you still wore those horrible breeches." Emma shuddered delicately at the thought of Samantha so attired.

"Say what you will, they are most comfortable. I suppose women will never be able to be at ease. For if you try to convince me that this shift all creased up underneath my stays is likable, I beg leave to disagree. Not to mention petticoats that flap about the ankles or dresses too restricting below the bust—at times I feel I can scarce breathe. Say you so, and I will declare you to have windmills in your head." Sam gave Emma a defiant look.

Emma couldn't help but smile at her indignant cousin. "But 'tis fashionable, Samantha."

The glare given in return made Emma laugh . . . in a most refined manner, of course.

Sam spent the next hour practicing a ladylike walk and other essentials, such as fluttering eyelashes, inclining the head when given a compliment, and placing the hands together when not actually in use, especially in the lap while seated. A proper curtsy was perhaps the greatest achievement of the day.

"It doesn't do for you to fidget, Samantha," scolded Emma. "When we go out to pay all those necessary calls—which you must do if you are to capture the title of queen—you must comport yourself with charming dignity. Only little children have the fidgets."

Samantha was not attending. She had espied Aunt Lavinia with a gardener. The poor man was toting a large pot of white geraniums and looking rebellious.

"I suspect you had better rescue the gardener from Aunt," urged Sam. Remind her it is time to go to the village or we will have to find another man again. I declare, I cannot keep track of them, for they come and go with depressing regularity.''

Emma agreed, and shortly was to be seen with her aunt, urging that dear lady to attend to her errand in the village. Behind them, the new gardener wiped his brow and returned to his work.

Sam breathed a sigh of relief. Her peace was short-lived.

"How did your morning go?" Lord Laverstock entered the orangery, giving an appreciative sniff as he met the combined fragrance of a half dozen well-developed orange trees in full bloom.

Sam gave him a annoyed look. "Well enough." Deciding she may as well practice on him, Sam bestowed a demure smile. While it was nice, it was not as dazzling as her usual. "Emma is trying to tutor me in my efforts at being queen." Then she curtsied, walked in mincing steps until she was close enough to flutter her eyelashes, and clasped her hands together in an ingenuous fashion. "La, sir, I am truly charmed to know you." She stood quietly while Laverstock seemed to struggle with a cough.

"Quite, er, charming, Lady Samantha. I gather you do not enjoy the niceties of society. But, you know that you must learn such if you are to wed."

Sam perked up at those words. He couldn't be obliquely telling her that he desired her to be a paragon of propriety so they might be married, could he? She shook her head at the silly thought, then turned away to pick up her lute which she had toted along with her. Sam had looked forward to a time alone in which to play a bit of her beloved music.

"This is a pleasant little building." Laverstock strolled about the orangery, finding he did not desire to leave.

"Aunt plans to bring in a hive of bees shortly to encourage the production of some delectable honey. For a time we shall have to forgo the enjoyment of it." Sam wandered toward the door, loathe to depart, yet wanting to play her lute.

"Why not play for me?" Anyone with half an eye could see the lady was wishing to play her instrument and most likely for herself.

"You are doing it once again, Lord Laverstock. Read another's mind, that is." Sam was awed at his ability, if that was what it was.

"No, actually. However, I do seem to know what is on your mind—at times." His gray eyes crinkled up at the corners at the sight of Samantha's dismay. His grin was the sort to place flutters in a hopeful mama's heart.

Sam found his smile enchanting. Her concern melted. If Papa intended this man as her husband, it was perfectly permissable that he read her mind, she supposed. A faint frown creased her brow, then left when she decided to worry about that later. She seated herself beneath one of the orange trees and began to pick out a tune. "This is 'Sweet Suffolk Owl,' a favorite of mine."

Charles leaned against one of the windows as the pretty tune echoed around the high walls of the orangery. Samantha really did look charming seated with the sun caressing her golden-red hair, those strange eyes hidden as she concentrated on her lute. Her voice was clear and sweet, well suited to the haunting old melody.

"Do you know this one?" When he nodded in recollection, Sam insisted, "Join me. 'Tis better when there are two."

She began to play a popular melody, a madrigal still sung from time to time. "Now Is the Month of Maying" rang forth with delightful harmony. Samantha gave him an approving look as their voices blended amazingly well. When the little song was concluded, she sallied forth with another. "Come all Ye Fair and Tender Ladies" brought a smile to those firm lips and Sam found herself watching him while he sang. It was a charming duet, one she quite enjoyed.

She struck a chord, then began "My Thoughts Are Winged with Hope." He fell silent, watching her sweet young face in earnest song. What did she really desire? The May Queen? He would persuade Alfred and George, even Percival, to accompany him into the village to see what might be done to that end. All of a sudden, Charles wished to see Lady Samantha get her heart's wish.

But to accomplish that might require a bit of help in other ways. "Do you dance, Lady Samantha?" he inquired when she completed the music.

Sam frowned at him. He was looking at her as though she was some country bumpkin who had never been exposed to the delicate things of life. Above all, Sam did not like pity. Was he being condescending toward her? Papa would not approve of that. She didn't either, come to think on it. She considered the matter for a few moments.

"La, sir, I fear I have not had the advantage of a French dancing master. You must remember we live in a remote area, not the center of London." She batted her eyelashes at him, hoping Emma had the right of this business. Flirting was something Sam had absolutely no accomplishment in at all. "Perhaps I may engage the gentleman newly come to the village?"

Laverstock coughed, then extended his hand. "Hum that tune you just played and we shall try a few steps in practice." Her reference to the Frenchman might have been accidental, or could there be another reason for her mentioning the man?

Giving him her newly polished curtsy, Samantha then offered her hand, liking the touch of his in spite of her annoyance. He joined in the music, the two of them humming the melody as he led her through the steps of a country dance, he explaining from time to time what the other dancers would be doing as they went along.

Sam stumbled, she turned the wrong direction. Her toes refused to point out, as was proper during the dancing. And her arms . . . well, her arms seemed to go at right angles, rather than the accepted oval position, all on their own accord. She possessed about as much grace as a lumbering cow.

A very confused Laverstock strove valiantly to correct the young lady. How could anyone who seemed to have such fluidity of movement otherwise turn into such an awkward creature while attempting to dance? He would have wagered she would perform her dancing with agility and skill. It shook him to be proven so wrong. He was determined to see her creditably equipped to cope at the next assembly or ball.

"Look at me," the long-suffering man demanded. "You must never watch your feet—or mine, for that matter. I gather you spend your time at the local dances either looking on or playing cards with the dowagers." His patience had never been so sorely tested.

"That was an unkind remark, sir," said Sam in a soft voice that wobbled treacherously, like she might burst into tears.

Alarmed at the alteration in Lady Samantha, Laverstock offered a change. "Allow me to try a variation. A pairing in couples is the latest thing. Perhaps with my hand on your waist to lead you, the dance may prove easier."

Having his hand slide about her waist was a dangerous mistake, she thought. It had been difficult enough before to think what she must do. Now her mental processes were as though George's electrifying machine had been applied to them, all shattered to pieces.

Leading Samantha across the orangery floor, weaving around the potted trees with deftness and grace, Lord Laverstock instructed her on the latest craze to hit Almack's. It quite delighted Sam. She bit back a smile as they performed the intricate little steps in a variation of a contredanse.

They stopped, Lord Laverstock studying the demure face not far from his for a moment. "When I was in Vienna they were performing a newly developed dance. It is called the waltz. While it is not accepted at Almack's, it shall be one day, for it is charming. Shall we try it?"

Without waiting for an answer, he again placed his left hand at her waist, while the other hand lightly clasped her right. He instructed her to place her left hand at his shoulder. Then he whistled a merry tune and off they went around the room at a rapid pace. He whirled her about, turning, weaving with dexterity.

Sam was enchanted. While she expected her aunt would think it a scandalous dance, she thought it was vastly delightful. To have a gentleman's hand just so and her own sweetly placed in his care for the duration of the dance was most different from all the other dances. He gazed into her eyes with a tender expression and drew her closer to that tall muscular body she so admired.

"I trust there is a reasonable explanation for this." Lady Emma stood in the doorway to the orangery, Alfred behind her, both with astonished expressions on their faces.

Breaking away from his lordship, Sam turned to meet her cousin's concerned gaze. Flushing a delicate pink, Samantha gave her two cousins a guarded look. "Nothing much, actually."

"Practicing dancing," added Lord Laverstock with his most loftly address.

Emma threw him a bewildered glance. She was about to speak when Sam rushed in with a question.

"How did your trip to the village go, Emma? Nothing occurred?" She darted a look at Laverstock, then back to where Emma stood, now more perplexed than ever.

"Ah, no, nothing at all." Emma's confused glance darted from Lord Laverstock to Samantha. It was plain she wondered what had been going on.

"Emma, you sly thing. You have forgotten your momentous meeting." Alfred leaned against an orangery window, chuckling when Emma bloomed a becoming rose color.

"You, dear cousin, ought to be punished for something. Give me a few moments and I shall have a tidy list." Emma glared at Alfred as though she would dearly adore to drop a bucket full of water over his head.

Samantha threw up her hands with impatience. "What happened?"

Emma cleared her throat. "I was introduced, while at the Moores' for a visit, to an interesting gentleman. He is a French emigré and lately come to visit the area."

"A dancing master?" queried Laverstock with great forbearance.

Again bewildered, Emma struggled on. "I believe he did mention something to that effect, sir. But," and she turned to Samantha with this bit of information, "he is prodigiously handsome and exhibits such fine manners, good enough for an Englishman. Unlike other men who shall remain nameless." She gave Alfred another frosty look, then turned her back to him. "I cannot imagine why Alfred thinks I need to have a shadow along with me. I was quite well able to care for your aunt while we were gone."

"The visit went well?" Samantha asked with caution.

"Oh, my, yes," answered Alfred, ignoring the stiff back so close to him. "We even put in a good word for you, Samantha. Why, if that Mrs. Moore ever stops talking long enough for anyone to ask a question it will be amazing. I believe that by tomorrow night not a soul in the village—as well as the manor houses in the area—will but be aware you would make an excellent queen."

"You were careful? I would not wish to be thought coming." Samantha ignored the choking sound close to her ear. Lord Laverstock seemed to have a distinct difficulty at times.

"We were all that was discreet. You know how Aunt Lavinia is." Emma raised her brows in a significant manner.

Desiring to know all that had not been said, Samantha looked at Emma and gestured. "Why do we not go up to the house and call for a pot of tea? Then I can hear all the details you have omitted." Samantha picked up her lute from where it had rested against an orange tree and sidled toward the door. "Gentlemen, we bid you good day. Oh, and thank you again, Lord Laverstock." Then, with the most graceful of movements, Sam swept a curtsy and walked from the orangery. A very puzzled Emma trailed behind.

Alfred turned to Laverstock, a calculating look in his eyes. "I would very much like to know what was going on when Lady Emma and I entered this place. If you have compromised my sweet widgeon of a cousin, I unfortunately shall be obliged to do something. Precisely just what, I would rather not consider."

"Nothing to worry you. I was attempting to teach Lady Samantha how to dance a few of the more simple steps. My, she is sadly lacking. I wonder if that fellow might actually *be* a French dancing master?"

Alfred cast Laverstock a disbelieving look. "You tried to teach Sam how to dance?" He momentarily forgot he had scolded George for using that name earlier.

"Is it forbidden?" Laverstock was genuinely puzzled when Alfred's shoulders now shook with his laughter.

"Oh, help," moaned Alfred, gasping for breath. "Lady

Samantha is one of the most accomplished dancers I
know . . . at least when it comes to country dances. I doubt
she knows any of the new steps you may have picked up. But
she is light on her feet and possesses a lively sense of rhythm,
quite the most delightful of partners.''

Urging Alfred out of the orangery and along the path in the
general direction of the barn, Laverstock gave a rueful glance
toward the house. "I have the feeling that I have just been played
for a fool.''

"Welcome, dear fellow, to the exclusive club of those who
have annoyed Samantha over the years. She has a plaguey sense
of humor.'' Alfred chuckled once again, giving Laverstock
another grin. "You were lucky. The last man who irritated her
was nearly smothered with a bucket of weed blossoms over his
head.''

"I can see I shall have to be extremely careful when it comes
to that young lady. But, I tell you now, my friend, that she can
think again if she believes to best me.''

Alfred gave him a dubious look. It was clear he had a different
opinion.

"Now, tell me about this emigré. Why do you suppose he
has come so far from London, where his fellow emigrés linger?
What sort of game does he play?'' The two became engrossed
in conversation, soon joined by George and a curious Percival.

"Samantha, what manner of game are you at now?'' demanded Emma as the two settled in the back parlor with a pot
of tea and fresh cream cakes.

"I vow I believe my papa has made a mistake. There is no
way I can consider that odious man as a husband. He thinks
me some sort of peagoose who cannot dance, nor have the least
notion of what is proper! I may need a bit of tutoring, but I
know I am not beyond hope. Agreed?'' Sam flounced about
in her chair, biting into a cream cake as though she were
snapping at Laverstock himself. "Perhaps I shall engage that
French dancing master, as long as he happens to be in the

village. There must be some way in which I can teach Lord Laverstock a thing or three.''

"Samantha . . .'' cautioned Emma.

"I know not how, but I vow I shall do it,'' declared the incensed Samantha.

6

Samantha carried her vow in the back of her mind wherever she went the rest of the day. It had irritated—no, more than that, it had angered her that Lord Laverstock thought her such a green girl that dancing would be beyond her.

His opinion had also given her pause. She considered each of her actions and concluded, somewhat irrationally, that he could be right, at least about some of the things she did. Flying was most improper, she agreed—wistfully. Yet, she considered the insipid pleasures granted to most women and shuddered. Whatever was she to do?

Her father had always told her that the most important thing was to be yourself. Sam brightened at that thought. If her papa believed most firmly in that dictum, it would only stand to reason that the man he chose for his dear little Sam would as well. Of course. Naturally. Maybe?

Not sure of anything at this point, Sam sank into a gloom that immediately infected the entire household. Maids, wondering what displeased the normally sunny Lady Samantha, crept furtively down halls. The footmen tried to remain unseen. The cook, when informed Lady Samantha had ignored her sole in lobster sauce, threw a tantrum to strike fear into the hearts of the entire staff.

Next morning, Emma, quite unknowingly, saved the deteriorating situation from total disaster. "Samantha, did you know they are to begin the decorating of the maypole soon? The ribands have been ordered from Scarborough. I expect we had best drive into the village to secure your election."

Giving Emma a pleased smile, Samantha nodded her agreement and shortly was seen with a happy expression on her face, wondering how she might manage the thing. The May

King matter bothered her not a little. Precisely who would be selected could not be known. Here in the village it was usually a person of prominence. Most everyone had had at least one turn, for the community was not all that large. Samantha could not like the idea that the fat son of the squire would be chosen again. He was too short to dance well and ate far too much garlic. To imagine him at her side garbed in white and wearing a crown of flowers and ribands was simply horrid. She wrinkled her nose with distaste at the very notion, and continued to consider the matter. When her grand idea struck her all of a heap, she said not a word to anyone, but smiled secretively, her eyes sparkling with mirth.

The roads were found to be in excellent order. A warm, drying wind had prevented the ruts from getting too deep. Samantha and Emma drove along in the carriage with no great amount of jouncing while planning just who they might best visit.

" 'Tis a wonderful day," said Emma enthusiastically.

"Yes, how nice to be by ourselves for a change. I vow that while company is lovely for a time, it can be wearying." That she considered Emma to be family and not company was, in a way, a high compliment from Samantha.

Sam sighed, thinking of the presently elusive Lord Laverstock. He spent all his days with George. How that was going to help him win her hand was beyond her. Perhaps she might contrive some special entertainments. If only she were more clever at that sort of thing.

"Especially Alfred. I should very much like to know what he is about." Emma frowned, turning to Samantha with a concerned expression. "I saw lights last night."

"Did you now?" Samantha debated for a few minutes before deciding to confide, "I did too. When I went to draw my draperies, I tried to see what it might be. 'Tis not fire, we know that. I had not thought myself a coward, but I confess I have no desire to prowl about in the dark."

"It frightens me, Samantha. I cannot like the thought of someone . . . or something wandering about in the house. What if it comes for one of us?" Emma shivered delicately and moved a trifle closer to Sam.

Sam's tender heart went out to her dear, if oversensitive, cousin. "I will not have you losing sleep over the matter," Sam declared stoutly. "The very next time we see a light I shall do something about it."

Emma drew back in alarm. "Never say you intend to look out there yourself!"

Sam, who had had no such notion, nodded and airily replied, "Of course. Ghosts may sound frightening, but they rarely actually *do* anything, you know," she stated, as though she were an expert on the subject. She wished her heart could be more sanguine about the matter. After all, she had no actual knowledge of what a ghost really did do while performing those silly moans and flutterings. Best not consider it.

The carriage had entered the village, and the first call was to Mrs. Moore. Samantha found visiting a tedious task. She had yet to master the art of polite pleasantries that conveyed much yet said nothing. She brightened at the sight of Mr. Moore, a man of uncommon sense. He had often come to watch George while they had tested glider shapes. While he had no advice to offer, he did not ridicule, and for that she admired him greatly. Sam attempted a demure smile, receiving the reward of a few kind words in return.

Emma kept Mrs. Moore occupied. The good lady's tongue wagged full spate and Emma had little to do other than listen. She had confided to Sam that it was sometimes hard not to nod off while the dear lady rambled on.

From the Moores' they traveled to the Holcrofts' and from there to the Dowdeswells'. Samantha was beginning to feel more comfortable about the queen business. Judging from the sparks she had observed in various male eyes, she would have the gentlemen's support, and they were the ones who controlled the village. It was comforting to know she could also count on the discreet help of the ladies, who all pitied the motherless girl with only that strange, though quite genteel, aunt to guide her. These three were the crucial calls; all hinged upon their support.

When Emma and Samantha stopped the carriage in the village green, they saw the maypole stretched out across the broad area edged by tall trees. A young man carried a heap of holly and ivy intended for decorating the pole.

"Oh," cried Samantha, "it will be a lovely sight. Only think how it will look once the greenery, the ribands, and flowers adorn it. Then we can await the performance of the Jack-in-the-Green as well. I wonder who it will be this year? He is excessively funny, you know. He always frightens the children with his comical dancing about. Oh, I can scarce wait."

"You say that every year, I suspect. I am happy that I can be with you." Emma studied her hands discreetly folded in her lap, slowly smoothing the fine silk of her white gloves over her fingers.

Suddenly sober, Samantha turned to place an impetuous hand over Emma's restless fingers, giving them a gentle, comforting squeeze. "I imagine you miss your dear parents greatly. We shall try to make it up to you." She impulsively reached over to give her cousin a brief hug before getting down from the carriage to inspect the work to be done.

Samantha looked like a spring bloom in her gold-colored muslin spotted with white. Her chip straw bonnet had a pretty green bow tied pertly beneath her chin and she carried a matching green parasol. She tilted this at a flirtatious angle, smiling at each and every person she met with infectious gaiety.

"I vow you shall be May Queen without another word said," whispered Emma as they strolled to the far side of the green. "There is not a lad around here but what has fallen over his feet admiring you. Take care or they will shoo you away lest nothing get done this day in the village."

"Oh, pooh," said Samantha with unassuming good nature. She gave her cousin an amused look, not believing a word she said. "What a great tease you are."

"I do believe that is Percival coming toward us. What can he be doing in the village at this hour of the day? For that matter, what can he find to occupy him in such an unprepossessing place as this?" Emma's tone was dry and a touch acerbic. Though she tolerated the dandy, she was sometimes annoyed by his disinterest in life.

Samantha exchanged glances with Emma, both silently agreeing that Percival could be a distinct pain at times. Yet he was everywhere accepted and well enough liked.

He made an elegant leg. "Fair ladies, I am delighted to come upon you in this benighted village. 'Tis vastly wearying to seek amusement where none is to be found.'' He affected a broad sigh.

"Beware, dear Percival,'' said Samantha, trying not to giggle like some foolish maid. "If someone should hear you, you might find the Jack-in-the-Green seeking you out.''

The dandy shuddered delicately. Attired in fawn pantaloons with a pale blue velvet coat, Percival looked a world apart from the sturdy village lads bustling past the trio in the shade of a tall elm by the edge of the green.

"It takes someone with strong shoulders to carry that wicker framework around all day. Once they put the ivy and holly over it, I expect it ceases to be light in weight.'' Samantha chuckled at Percival's expression of distaste when she had mentioned the cagelike affair the Jack always wore on May Day. "Never fear, you will not likely be asked.''

"I cannot see why you desire to be part of this so-called celebration,'' Percival rejoined. "In town—London, that is— the chimney sweeps have taken over the day and it is positively revolting. Not exactly the sort of thing to give tone to Society, what? Of course, there is that persistent story of the lad who was taken from his mother and was found again among the sweeps.''

At Samantha's look of amazement, Percival preened a bit and continued, "So 'tis said. Mind you, I do not believe a word of it. But the story goes that the boy was stolen from his parents while in infancy, trained in chimney-sweeping, then one day sent to sweep the chimney of his mother's bedroom. Rather hot and tired, he climbed into the very bed he had so often slept in when a little one, and there he was discovered by his mother, who recognized him. Every May Day after that, she is supposed to offer a fine dinner for all sweeps who present themselves at her door,'' he said with a sniff.

"But surely there is a Jack or a May Queen!'' declared a fascinated Samantha.

Percival shrugged. "No Green to amount to much, and a sad rattle of a queen. Some fat milkmaid with a dirty dress and tattered ribands cavorts down the street with the sweeps a-battering on some pans quite horribly. If there is a Lord of May, he is naught but some fellow dressed in tawdry finery.''

"Shame on you, Twistleton. Telling such tales to the tender ears of innocents.'' Lord Laverstock, appearing from the direction of the village blacksmith, looked down his nose at the shorter, more slender Percival with a disdainful air. Percival seemed to shrink in size before that look.

"Well, 'tis only the truth and you but know it,'' insisted Percival, defending his words with more bravado than sense.

Glancing from the superior countenance of Lord Laverstock to the slightly resentful face of the younger dandy, Emma moved to Percival's side. "Perhaps you can have a look at our Jack-of-the-Green's frame to see how it compares with the one you saw in town. Did you actually see such a procession? I vow, it quite makes me shudder with the thought of such clamor.'' She placed one delicate hand on Percival's arm and the two strolled off across the green. He seemed pleased at her attention, for he had cheered up immensely at her words.

"Peagoose,'' murmured Samantha affectionately as her cousin left. Turning to Lord Laverstock, she curtsied, then added, "Emma is ever the peacemaker.'' Sam gave him a considering look. "I had no idea you intended to visit our humble village this day, milord.''

"Did you not? I came with George. While you have been busy garnering support, your brother and I have been at work on the glider.'' He placed her slender hand on his arm and began to stroll about the green, watching the arrangements for the coming maypole with idle curiosity. "I find myself reluctantly fascinated by these preparations. I gather from what was said just now that in the village you still celebrate the May after the old fashion.''

"Yes, we still do—as I suspect they may in many a village yet. 'Tis quite harmless, I assure you.'' She glanced up at him, very much aware of the firm arm beneath her light touch. "What is George doing in the village? Finding bits and pieces he needs for the glider? I shall be glad once the elevator is replaced.''

"You shan't be flying again.'' He uttered these words with the assurance of a man who had never been crossed.

Samantha took exception to this glimmer of dictatorship. "Since there is no one else to fly, I daresay I shall do so.'' Then she remembered she was trying to act the lady while around this man. Or need she bother? He really confused her terribly.

Lord Laverstock came to a halt on the near side of the green, unmindful of the watching eyes of those supposedly at work. He possessed that aristocratic oblivion to anything he chose to disregard. He covered Samantha's hand with his own, ignoring the pleasant feeling it gave him.

"I believe that if your father knew what was going on up here it would displease him very much."

This had not occurred to Samantha. "Oh, dear, do you really?" She studied him a moment, then rashly tossed her chances of a fine husband out the window. "Are you always so stuffy? My, but you must be tedious to live with."

Laverstock froze with hauteur, looking at Samantha as though he had not heard aright. Then he really looked at her. Those sparkling golden eyes were tilted with mirth. That pert little nose so finely dusted with freckles was wrinkled up as though making fun of him. He observed the charming curl that had escaped from her bonnet and now twined about her slim neck. Strangely enough, his fingers knew a desire to trace it, not wring her neck, as had been his very first inclination at her saucy words. What a very lovely creature. He shook his head in dismay.

"I believe we had better return you to your aunt." The effect of his restrained words was amazing.

"What? Is my aunt come to the village with you?" Samantha was clearly upset. She withdrew her hand from Lord Laverstock's arm. "Where is she, sir?"

"I believe we left her at the Holcrofts'." Her sudden alteration in mood was puzzling, but then, she was like quicksilver.

"Oh, dear," exclaimed Samantha. "Excuse me," she murmured, much concerned. Aunt Lavinia loose in the Holcrofts' drawing room without a watchful eye upon her was to be avoided at all costs.

Samantha darted away from Lord Laverstock without one flutter of an eyelash or a shy twirl of a parasol. Instead, she nearly fled from the green in the direction of the Holcrofts' lovely old house. It was the first time in his life that Lord Laverstock had been so deserted.

His lordship became conscious of the amused stares of the locals. With an annoyed sigh he strode from the green toward the shop where George had said he would be. Really, women could be so bothersome.

He made his way along the road, avoiding a stray dog without really seeing it, stepping over a gap in the paving stones before one of the shops with automatic care.

He had been sent here to observe. He was to seek information, not become entangled with a madcap girl possessing golden-red hair that flamed with a life of its own. And those very speaking eyes of hers when she pronounced him tedious. Was he? He had always considered himself to be a proper gentleman, and had accepted the deference due his position with little regard for whether it was mere formality or given with friendship. After all, in his world a great deal of life had to do with formalities.

But not in hers. Lady Samantha was all spontaneity, laughter, and delicious fun. When she attempted to come across the proper miss, he could almost feel her natural instincts aching to burst forth in some ridiculous remark or outrageous action.

And why did he care one way or the other? Her father had indicated a concern, but fathers often did that sort of thing. Though the earl had not requested Charles to intercede, there had been a hint in his voice of something.

Glancing about, Charles wondered where that French emigré was lurking about. It was highly curious that such a stranger should appear in the village just now. Dashed strange, actually. Charles was so deep in thought he totally missed the blacksmith's place where George was discussing a special type of hinge. Fortunately, an alert eye caught sight of him and a quick chase by a young apprentice saved him an embarrassing spate of questions from George.

Breathless in her hurry—oh, why did Aunt have to choose this day to pay a visit?—Sam skidded to a halt as she saw that lady coming toward her, a beatific smile on her face.

Samantha's heart sank. She was too late. That smile, so very angelic, could mean only one thing. Aunt had struck once again.

From behind Samantha came Emma and Percival. As they

met, Alfred exited from the stationer's shop, much astounded to see the assembled party.

"I gather everyone decided to leave the house today."

"I say," said Percival, "George and Laverstock are down the road a bit. What say we join them, Alfred old fellow?"

That Percival seemed anxious to part from her company bothered Emma not one whit. She was trying to figure out why Samantha was wildly signaling her behind the men's backs.

Lady Lavinia watched the two men stroll down the lane with a curious expression. "I wonder what Alfred was doing in the stationer's shop? He seems to go through a goodly amount of paper nowadays. And why is Percival so interested in whatever George is doing? He is far more in need of searching for a rich wife. I am persuaded he cannot know of your dowry, dear Emma."

Not overly concerned with her aunt's implication that Percival ought to pay her court, Emma guided her along the lane toward the Blue Lion Inn, where she hoped to discover what was amiss. Sam trailed behind, deep in thought.

Soon Aunt Lavinia was seated in the Blue Lion's best parlor, the innkeeper's wife serving her with tea and scones. Emma drew Samantha aside and gestured to the window as though discussing the pot of red geraniums. "Please do inform me what that nonsense with the hands was all about."

"She has done it again. Lord Laverstock told me he left Aunt at the Holcrofts' house. Did you not see the look on her face when she joined us? 'Twas positively gleeful. How shall I manage this time, I wonder?" Samantha sighed. After a suitable lapse of time, she rose, fumbling with her reticule.

"Excuse me, dear aunt, I just remembered an errand. Ribands . . ." she added vaguely. Samantha slipped from the room without waiting for a reply. She passed through the common room and entry, only to bump into a gentleman in the act of entering the inn. He was a stranger to these parts, dressed in a fine blue coat and gray pantaloons, with very elegant shoes on his feet.

"Pardon, mamzelle." He bowed and scurried up the stairs to where Sam concluded he must be staying.

The Frenchman. And wandering about the village? He had

come from the same direction where she now saw George and Lord Laverstock standing. Sam went the opposite way. If she was to succeed, she best see the greatest gossips.

Samantha did find it possible to make her suggestion regarding the King of the May to the appropriate people, returning to the carriages in good time. When she joined the others to return to Mayne Court, she was well pleased with that aspect of their jaunt into the village. If only Aunt had not claimed she needed more silks for her embroidery work and made the trip as well. Sam suspected that it was all a hum, and that dear Auntie had simply wished to do a bit of ''borrowing,'' as Sam preferred to call it. To call it what it really was—stealing—was too serious. That implied punishment was needed. As long as Samantha continued to return the items no damage was done, was there? The thing that worried her was the thought that one day her aunt might ''borrow'' something that Sam didn't know about. She shook her head at Emma, murmuring, ''We must do better at watching Aunt.''

Emma nodded thoughtfully, wondering if Samantha had considered what would happen once Sam and George married. For it was preordained that they both would be required to enter that state. Perhaps they might find some nice relative who could be trusted to assume the vigilance of Aunt Lavinia. George was too absent-minded. Who would think to look upon that innocent-seeming face that she possessed itchy fingers?

It was a merry group that entered the gates and drove up the neatly graveled road to the house. Sam watched as Emma was handed down by Percival. She also noted the curious attention paid to that courtesy by none other than Alfred. He had a sour look to his face, like he had tasted an unripe plum.

''May I?''

Sam was jolted from her speculations by that faintly husky, rather deep voice. She gave Lord Laverstock an annoyed glance. ''You do have a way of sneaking up on a person. However, I expect that is a needed requirement in the War Office. Has anyone ever complained?'' She accepted his help from the carriage, leaving her hand on his arm where he placed it. Although she might be out of reason cross with him, he was their guest. He might think her a hoyden, but she knew full well the proprieties that were due. She merely ignored them at times when they got in her way.

Charles gave her an amused look. "I am unaware that it is a requirement, though possibly it would be useful if one were sent off to spy or the like."

"Did you see the Frenchman in the village? I vow he was rather noticeable. I am persuaded there is something smoky about his presence here, although there are a number of young ladies who might be in need of dancing lessons." She slanted a narrow look at him, recalling the scene in the orangery. "But then, there are those who might say the same of you—that you are here for odd reasons, that is. For you must know, you look not in the least in need of recuperation." She gave him a candid look followed by one of those blazing smiles she was wont to surprise him with, the kind that sent a sinking sensation to the pit of his stomach.

Her artless disclosure did not amuse him. Ignoring that radiant smile, he inquired, "What makes you think his behavior out of line?"

"Well, a dancing master, I ask you! I find it difficult to accept he would come to *our* village on a whim. We are so few here, you know. He stays at the Blue Lion. You must have observed him, for he passed by you when you must have been leaving the blacksmith's. He entered the inn just when I was about to leave. I ought to request he give me a few lessons. Would you say I might benefit from his services?" She gave Laverstock a dangerous smile.

"I cannot say he caught my eye, though George and I were rather deep in discussion. The fellow may be quite innocent. I doubt if he could teach you any steps you don't already know, my lady," he said. At her glance, he added, "Alfred told me." The last thing he wanted was to have the daring Lady Samantha involved in this hunt. Then, hoping to change the direction of her thoughts from the Frenchman, he added. "It seems to me you spent a very busy morning." If he intended to discover what she had been about, he was doomed to disappointment.

"Yes," Sam replied complacently. "I was quite busy." Her satisfied tone gave him a sense of unease, for some odd reason. Especially when it was accompanied by that overly smug look she wore as she floated up the stairs. It quite reminded him of the time his cat had eaten his mother's pet canary, then wiped the feathers from its mouth with a bland expression on its face.

Dinner went very well, if one ignored the dark looks from Alfred when Percival paid Emma nice attentions. Emma accepted them with her usual calm air, disregarding those sullens, as she later referred to them, to Samantha. Actually, Emma was finding the entire situation rather amusing. Alfred had always fought with her over one thing or another. He was unable to quarrel over Percival at the table. She could only anticipate a good row when Alfred managed to get her alone.

The very thought of a rousing battle was something to relish. Alfred would have to accept that Emma was perfectly capable of telling when a man was after her dowry and when he truly cared for her as a person. And Percival didn't fall into either category. Emma suspected the dandy merely wished to have a bit of fun.

Samantha ate every bit of her sole with lobster sauce, earning her a smile from the cook if she but knew it. Sam found all this dashing about hungry work.

The ladies assembled in the drawing room, Aunt Lavinia bringing a look of dismay to Sam's face when she gently waved a delicate white fan before her.

Turning to Emma, Sam nodded her head toward her aunt. "Warm, isn't it? Hardly need a fire this evening, true, Aunt Lavinia?"

"True. I find a fan always helpful. One never knows when one might be overcome with heat." Aunt continued to wave the fan about, seeming to ignore the exchanged glances between her nieces.

Sam walked to the window, wondering when her aunt might slip away to stash the fan to keep it from being recovered. Staring off toward the barn where the glider was housed, Sam considered where the most likely hiding place might be.

The arrival of the gentlemen brought a temporary halt to her speculations. She waited impatiently for the time to go up to bed; the sky remained light far too long these days. Her aunt usually loathed going to bed before necessary. However, this evening she had other things on her mind and went up early. Sam followed after tucking George's key in a pocket.

As soon as the house became dark, Aunt Lavinia was espied tiptoeing from her room by a waiting Sam. The old lady crept from the house—carefully avoiding the steps which creaked— followed shortly by her niece. Sam might have tried to peer through one of the barn windows, but she knew full well that they were obscured with years of grime.

She bided her time, listening carefully to the steps within. When all was quiet, and the ghostly form of her aunt slipped from a rarely used rear door of the barn and disappeared from sight, Sam entered from the now, unlocked main door, stumbling over a piece of board before she lit her lanthorn.

Aunt was getting most clever; it took quite some time to locate the fan.

Outside the barn, Charles watched that flickering light with growing concern. He had noticed Lady Samantha's restlessness that evening, coupled with longing glances at the door. Obviously she had better things to do than play her lute or engage in card games. But what?

He simply could not suspect *her* of traitorous activities, not with her avowed interest in Wellington and all. So what was she involved in that required such questionable behavior? He would have to note her every movement from this moment on. That keeping a close eye on the exquisite Lady Samantha was no hardship in the least, he totally ignored.

7

Samantha shivered as she crept from the barn, thankful beyond measure she had found the dainty white fan. Fortunately, Aunt Lavinia had wrapped it in silver tissue before stashing it in the loft, which had made it easy to spot. Sam hoped it would be a long time before she had to climb up that ladder again while holding a lanthorn. She shuddered with the very thought.

It was a fine spring night out, a bit dampish but not overcool. An owl hooted in the distance and glowworms were dancing near the west wing of the house. Sam thought with delight of the times she and her brother had collected the greenish-glowing insects during childhood midsummer nights. When at their most brilliant it was possible to read just a little if one gathered several at a time.

Sam stopped dead. Glowworms? 'Twas the wrong time of year for them, much too early. Looking once again, she realized the light was fixed and there was no green tinge to it. It had to be the spirit. Or ghost. Or more likely the person prowling about the holland-shrouded state rooms. Light would tend to shatter into little fragments when coming between the slats of the closed blinds, wouldn't it?

She wondered if Emma had peered out in the darkness and seen that light. Emma would be frightened. Something would have to be done about the "ghost." It simply would not do to have her sensitive cousin so terribly upset. She could very well develop a nervous fever or something.

Quickly firming her resolve, Sam dashed to the house, tip-toeing up to her room to hide the fan carefully away so she might return it on the morrow. Then she smoothed down her breeches, which had been far better for climbing around in the barn than

87

the nuisance of a gown, and tucked in her shirt once again. Taking a deep breath, she returned to the hall, then silently crept down the staircase, avoiding all those boards that groaned and squeaked.

The corridor to the west wing was gloomy, for there were no windows to permit light of any sort to enter. Sam swallowed with care and proceeded into the darkness, hesitantly making her way. She had brought her candle and tinder box along, but one could scarcely hunt for spirits, or ghosts, or . . . intruders while bearing a bright light!

Charles had watched the mad dash to the house with great puzzlement. If she felt afraid, it was an odd time to show it. When he had followed her to the barn, she had sauntered along as though it was midday and she on a stroll. Then he saw the light flash in the west wing and began to wonder what was going on. He followed Lady Samantha with a growing concern. There was something afoot and he meant to see what it might be.

Upstairs, Emma peered out her window, clutching at the draperies with a trembling hand. Straining her ears, she caught the soft click of Samantha's door. Since Emma had most carefully left hers ajar, the sound came to her with unusual clarity. Samantha, dear, brave Samantha, was going to challenge the ghost for her cousin. Well, Emma decided courageously, Sam was not going to face it (or them) alone. And so the timid Emma tightened the sash on her dressing gown and went out her door and down the stairs. She ignored the magnified squeaks where she forgot about the old boards. Somehow she doubted if Samantha was listening for those. Intent on going to Samantha's assistance—though what help she might possibly be didn't occur to her—Emma bravely overlooked the rustling noises and strange thumps in the night. There were shadows in the central hall that seemed to move before her and it took firm resolution to proceed. It was merely Samantha, Emma assured herself with great flutterings in her heart. She clasped her hands together in a somewhat prayerful attitude and headed down the long, exceedingly dark hall.

* * *

Percival had been pacing about his room. It was too early to go to sleep. He was bored, and wishing he were back in London, when he had heard the noise. He recognized the sound of the squeaky old stairs; he had been annoyed at them often enough while on visits, especially when a schoolboy and larking about. Someone was up and about! In this house? Could dear little Samantha be up to a lark of some sort? He grinned in a most undandified manner, his superior ways gone for the moment. He removed his sleeping cap and brushed down his elegant dressing gown of burgundy brocade, then walked to the door slipping a spare candle and the tinder box into his pocket. Though he might desire darkness now, a light could be welcome later. He stepped out into the hall and went quietly down the stairs, avoiding as many of the noisy stair treads as he could recall.

Samantha paused by the first of the state rooms, thankful she had at least reached it. The hall had seemed much longer than she remembered. Far darker, too. It seemed to her that her heart pounded so loudly she would scarcely hear a noise should there be one. She ran a nervous tongue over extremely dry lips, then cracked open the door with great stealth . . . and found no sign that anyone—ghost or otherwise—was inside. She took a calming breath, sagging against the wall a moment while she gathered her courage to continue.

Not bothering to close the door entirely, she continued on down the hall. She had decided it best to keep one hand trailing along on the wall. With total darkness around her it was impossible to see a thing. She kept hoping to find that elusive light.

The next door yielded the same results. Discouraged, Sam froze as she heard a sound behind her. She flattened herself against the wall and strained to hear if another might follow, while wondering what that noise might have been. Taking a deep breath to soothe her frayed nerves, she wondered if she could detect a ghost if one were there. She was certain she had heard a muttered curse. *That* could not possibly have been a ghost. Or did ghosts find that sort of thing necessary? She listened intently, conscious of the rapid beat of her heart, the rustle of her clothing magnified each time she moved.

Silence. Sam drew a cautious breath and continued along the wall, groping for the next door. At last she felt the door lever dig into her side and she stopped again.

The door creaked slightly as Samantha opened it. She vowed to remind Peters to oil the hinges as she gingerly stepped into the room. There was something different in here, she could sense it immediately. The smell. Sam could quite definitely detect the odor of burning wax . . . and a recently snuffed out candle.

She carefully stepped inside, closing the door softly behind her. Annoyed that she had barely missed the ghostly apparition, or whatever haunted this place, Sam groped about until she found the fireplace mantel, then placed her candle down. Striking the tinder was not a simple matter when attempted in darkness, but she managed due to long practice. The candle flared into brilliance and she searched the room, then drew in her breath.

"*Alfred*?" Sam was glad she had placed the candle on the mantel for she most assuredly would have dropped it at the sight of her cousin dressed in black and crouched in the corner of the room.

He gave her a disgusted look, then left his niche to approach her. "I might have known you would come bumbling in here. What are you doing up at this hour? And," he added after looking at the breeches and shirt, "why garbed in those clothes?"

"How like you to question *me* when it is *you* who are behaving in a highly suspicious manner. Why are you here in the middle of the night?" Sam demanded, speaking softly as though it were necessary.

"Shh," he cautioned. He glanced at the door, hastily putting out the candle. "Someone is coming."

Sam wrinkled her nose at the acrid smell from the snuffed out candle, then tensed as she too heard a noise. Someone had bumped up against the door lever. Her hand slid up to her throat in apprehension. The pounding of her heart seemed so loud

Alfred surely must hear it too. Beside her, Alfred readied the tinder box. He intended to light a candle as quickly as possible.

The door inched open. Sam blessed the unoiled hinges that permitted her to know just how far it now stood. Whoever it was entered the room. It appeared not to be a ghost or spirit. Ghosts wouldn't need to open a door, would they? Didn't they merely pass straight through the wood?

Alfred struck at the tinder, and shortly the light from his candle revealed the figure of a man also garbed in solid black.

"Lord Laverstock! What are you doing here?" Sam thought quickly, "What brought you down in the night . . . dressed just like Alfred?" She gave the two men a frowning look.

Just as Lord Laverstock was about to reply, Alfred shushed them both. With a resigned sigh, he gestured at the door behind Laverstock. "I believe we are to be joined."

Laverstock quickly moved to one side, alert and wary.

The door again inched open, a white-capped head peered around, then Emma stepped inside, shutting the door to lean against it with astonishment. "Gracious! Whatever are you all doing down here in the middle of the night?"

"I saw a light and decided it was time to find out what was going on out here." Samantha looked at Lord Laverstock. "And you, sir?" She was more curious about him than Alfred. Had he followed her to the barn? Did he suspect Aunt Lavinia of her pilfering habits? What might happen to her dear aunt if she were found out? Others were hung for far lesser crimes. Samantha bit at her lower lip as she waited for his answer.

Laverstock cleared his throat, deciding the least said, the better. "I found sleep elusive and decided to take a stroll. When I saw a light out here, it seemed wise to investigate, especially after the remarks about fire the other night."

Relaxing for a moment, Sam then turned on Alfred. "Now it is your turn to explain. Will you please tell us why you have been frightening us half out of our wits with your spooky light in the night?" Sam had not been all that afraid, but she knew full well that Emma had. What sort of maggoty notion had Alfred picked up now?

"I came about the family ghost." Alfred seemed most

reluctant to continue and Sam walked over to stand before him, glaring up at him with the threat of promised retribution in her eyes if he failed to complete his story.

"Very well," he said, sighing with disgust. "I do a bit of writing now and again—to help the coffers when they get low, you see. I had the idea of writing a ghost story and thought that if I might find a real one, it would make jolly good reading. I knew the story of our family ghost, for Aunt Lavinia has complained about it often enough. So I came up here with the hope of luring it out for a visitation. Or whatever it is that ghosts do."

"I don't believe this one is ever seen," said Samantha thoughtfully. "It merely enters the room and supposedly ministers to a person asleep on that bed over there as though it was some sort of nurse or maid. The last person to sleep in the bed grumbled about being awakened in the night by a hand soothing his brow . . . only no one was there. The bed has not been slept in since."

"I ought to have been in the bed, obviously." Alfred quickly strode to the bed and plopped himself across it, coughing at the gentle rise of dust that enveloped him.

"I am happy that Samantha was in no real danger," murmured a subdued Emma.

"You mean you hazarded this dark hallway to assist me?" squeaked Sam, much taken by the gesture of her normally timid cousin. "Oh, I am proud of you, dear girl."

"Shh," cautioned Lord Laverstock, wondering if that was the true reason behind Alfred's nighttime perambulations. Charles was not all that convinced that Alfred needed to write for money. However, he might prowl about in the night seeking to filch George's plans, then copy them out here in an undisturbed part of the house under the guise of seeking ghosts. Had he decided to contact the Frenchman in the village to sell the plans? Granted, the glider had not been given the final test of being attached to a balloon and dropped from a high altitude, but Charles suspected the scheme would work. And if it did, the enemy would pay a tidy sum to have those plans. Wellington had been succeeding all too well in his campaigns as of late to please the French. *If* Alfred actually needed money, it would be an easy way to get it. Hadn't Lady Lavinia said something about Alfred's receiving a large sum of money in the near future? Charles resolved to watch Alfred closely. Yet Charles had to admit that Alfred seemed unlikely a candidate for spy. His nature was remarkably open—for a writer of gothic tales, that is.

A thump against the wall was followed by a hasty twist of the lever. The door was pushed open with little regard that someone might be on the other side. Lord Laverstock got a bang on his head as Percival rushed into the room. "What is going on here? I say, Samantha, what are you up to this time?"

Alfred sat up in the bed, sneezing at the disturbed dust which filtered into the air about him. "I swear, is there anyone left abed?"

Explanations came from a surprising source. Emma stepped forward to place a calming hand on Percival's sleeve. "Alfred is doing research for a story he plans to write. Did you know he is published? I am very greatly impressed. He is going to create a gothic tale! Is it not vastly diverting?"

"Gothic tale?" exclaimed an astounded Percival.

Samantha had been watching Lord Laverstock all the while, wondering just how much of his account was true. She then observed his head had taken more of a blow than she first believed and hastened to his side. She brushed away his hand, taking a better look at the swelling lump on his temple. "Light the rest of the candles, please. Lord Laverstock has been hurt. Though I fail to see how the door did such damage." Standing on tiptoe, she smoothed his hair back and motioned him to a chair Alfred had uncovered.

Charles felt like a fool, though he knew his mishap could have happened to anyone. "I was following Lady Samantha when I crashed into a door which she left ajar. A second bump on the head in roughly the same area did the trick." He winced as Samantha gently touched the site of his injury.

Deciding he needed an application of a cool cloth, Samantha shooed the others back to their rooms, then led him up the stairs, all the while talking in a calm manner, as though her heart wasn't doing strange antics while she guided him along the hallway.

Pausing at the door to his room, she decided that what with

the injury to his head there was little danger he might attempt to take advantage of her, whatever that meant. Aunt Lavinia was always saying tantalizing things like that and then never explaining them. Just once, Sam thought wistfully, she wished Aunt would follow through with one of her admonitions and do a bit of explaining.

Leaving the door wide open, Sam urged Lord Laverstock to a chair by his bed, lit two more candles, then bent down to study the wound. "My, that is a sizable lump. We shall have to hope there is no concussion. It is indeed a nasty bruise."

Sam was not totally convinced that Lord Laverstock had merely been out for a walk in the middle of the night. For one thing, it was an odd time to take a stroll. And further, he was dressed all in black, just like Alfred. Her mind skittered to a halt. Was he mixed up in something with Cousin Alfred? It would bear close watching. She took a careful look in his eyes, hoping to see the truth therein.

"Pity you don't have some ice to apply to that bump on your head. 'Tis the best remedy I know," came a voice from behind them.

Charles glanced over to see Alfred lounging against the door jamb, a curiously intent expression on his face.

His remark brought Sam's head around sharply, barely missing another collision with Lord Laverstock's injury.

"Really, Alfred, have you not caused enough problems this night?" snapped a sorely tried Samantha. "If you wish to go out to the ice house and crawl down to fetch a chunk of ice at this hour, you are more than welcome."

Alfred bestowed a scornful look on her, then crossed the room to pull the bell. Within a remarkably short time, one of the maids rushed around the corner, her sleepy eyes widening as they absorbed the scene before her.

"We wish some ice for his lordship's wound. If you will have the goodness to see to it immediately, it would be a great help." Alfred turned away from her, assuming his wish would be seen to without further ado.

"Yes, sir." The maid bobbed a curtsy, then scurried from the room, her mind agog at the strange doings of the Quality . . . in the middle of the night, yet.

"Really, Alfred," Sam said once more. "Allow me to remind you that I am the one who resides in this house."

"Never mind about that. I want to know what you were doing dressed up in those old breeches of George's and wandering about the house at this hour."

As Charles wished to know precisely the same thing, he watched Samantha's face with great interest. It was entrancingly close to his and he could easily have counted the scattering of freckles across that pert little nose of hers if he so chose. Instead, he met her eyes, those strange pale amber eyes, so large and glowing from within like fire-lit jewels. They reminded him of the set of family topaz his mother had never cared to wear, declaring the jewels to be difficult in color. Charles could see them shimmering about Samantha's throat and on her ears, capturing the color of those unusual eyes.

"I was most definitely not wandering about." Sam tore her gaze from Lord Laverstock's with a struggle. He had utterly beautiful gray eyes, so dark and soft, with intriguing depths. What went on behind them? She backed away from him, unable to cope with the peculiar emotions creeping through her at her proximity to this man. "I told you. I saw those dratted lights and decided to calm Emma's fears about them once and for all."

"Did you not consider it could be the family ghost?"

"While I was making my way to the west wing I remembered the old story—that ghost never needed a light, it merely appeared. Right out of nothing." Sam shivered with the thought of an apparition suddenly popping up before her. "I must say, I am delighted it did not come. I do not believe I should like it one bit."

"That still does not explain the breeches. Why do you have such apparel? What are you up to, Sam?" Alfred walked close to his little cousin as though to intimidate her by his height and size.

Not afraid of Alfred in the least, Sam tilted her head, glaring up at him. "I use them when I'm helping George. It would be a great nuisance to bother with a skirt when gliding across the valley in his flying-machine. If I crashed, it would be downright annoying."

Alfred turned to Lord Laverstock, his concern plain to see.

"I cannot believe George actually permits her to maneuver his glider!"

"I have watched her do so." Charles managed to shrug his shoulders without moving his head in the least.

"I am certain Alfred can cope with the ice since he seems so terribly knowledgeable," Sam inserted, anxious to be away before Alfred questioned her further. "I believe I shall crawl into my bed. I am extremely fatigued. Good night, gentlemen." With that, Samantha marched regally out of the room, head high.

The two men exchanged amused looks. Alfred accepted the bowl of ice when a breathless footman entered the room with it. Placing the bowl to one side, he took the ice, applying it most gingerly against the rising lump on Laverstock's head.

"Sorry about all this. You must think we are a rather queer lot." Alfred used his handkerchief to mop up the drops of water as they rolled down that noble forehead.

"I must confess I somewhat doubted your story about the writing." Lord Laverstock winced when Alfred momentarily pressed the ice a bit harder.

"Perhaps you might be more familiar with the name Lord Hardly." Alfred's voice was hesitant, almost apologetic.

A raised eyebrow accompanied by a low whistle was the initial reaction to the surprising news. "And your family does not know about this? I have read two of your novels. Quite good, actually."

Shifting uncomfortably, Alfred mopped up more water from the slowly melting ice before replying. "Thank you for the kind words. No, I have not explained to them. It seemed to me that our family had quite enough eccentrics as it was."

"The *non de plume*? A play on words, I expect. Because you never anticipate inheriting the title?" Charles decided he had had enough of the ice and firmly took it from Alfred, dropping the remains back into the bowl.

"Just so. Most perceptive of you. I doubt if anyone else has figured that one out." Alfred chuckled with appreciation.

Frowning, Charles gave Alfred a thoughtful look. It seemed his theory regarding that young man had just gone out the window. But that still left someone who prowled about the barn in search of . . . the plans? His mind jumped to Lady Samantha and her nighttime meandering. What *had* she been doing in the barn earlier that evening? With a key. She had most cleverly left his room before the truth could be found out. He would have to maintain a close watch on that lady.

"Well, old man, we'd best seek our beds before there is no need." Laverstock extended his hand. "I do thank you for the ice application. I believe my head is much improved."

Both men wasted little time on the niceties of bedtime ritual, falling onto their respective beds with as little fuss as possible.

Charles's sleep was most restless. Between his aching head and the unsettled state of his mind, the night was not a good one.

When Samantha entered the breakfast room the following morning she found Emma the only occupant.

"Is he better?" Emma's lovely brown eyes were full of concern.

"I inquired but found he is still asleep." Sam loaded a plate with as much food as she thought she might stomach this morning although it was nearly noon. She yawned, then added, "I do hope the poor man does not have the concussion."

Emma frowned in alarm. "How you can calmly sit down to eat while that dear man may be in dire straits is more than I can see."

"Nothing I can do about it." Sam proceeded to bite into her muffin.

George strolled into the room. He glanced at his sister, noting the smudges beneath her eyes. He then looked at Emma, observing she also had what might be called interesting shadows beneath hers.

"What has been going on about here? You two really ought not stay up half the night reading those novels." Not waiting for a reply, he continued his perusal of the room. "None of the others down as yet? Thought at least Laverstock might be up come this hour."

Samantha decided George had best be told. "There was a bit of a to-do last night. Emma and I thought we saw a ghost— well, at least we saw lights in the west wing and you know that old story about a ghost there. We went to investigate, Lord

Laverstock and Percival followed us. We found Alfred, not a ghost.''

"Whatever was Alfred doing in the old state rooms?'' asked an extremely curious George.

Clearing her throat first, Emma answered him in her soft, clear voice. "He was doing research. He is a writer, you see, and wished to explore the subject of ghosts for a novel he plans to write."

"Never say so!"

"Never say what?'' inquired Aunt Lavinia as she whisked herself around the corner, carrying a lovely bouquet of white lilacs in her arms.

Leaving the others to explain, Samantha slipped from the room and up the stairs to retrieve the fan from its hiding place. Concealing it in the reticule that matched her primrose jaconet gown, she went down the back stairs to avoid possibly seeing the others, then out to the stables.

It would never do to go calling while riding Boots as before. She knew her limitations. Instead, Samantha ordered the whiskey made ready, sending for one of the maids to go with her. How fortunate she could manage a morning call; the village was quite accustomed to her vagaries. In short order she was driving the smart little vehicle down the graveled road from the Court, the tissue-wrapped fan securely in her reticule. She only hoped it might be possible to tuck the offending article along the cushion of a chair. Really, what was she to do with Aunt Lavinia?

It proved quite simple to replace the fan at the Holcrofts'. Since Mrs. Holcroft was extremely absent-minded, she had attributed the missing fan to a lapse of memory. When Samantha delved along the cushion and exclaimed over finding the fan, the lady was most gratified. She insisted on a prolonged visit, declaring Samantha simply must see her garden.

Sam felt an utter fraud.

A gentle breeze was blowing when she left the Holcrofts'. It served to cool her flushed cheeks. She feared she was not suited for a life of deception.

"Lady Samantha! I am surprised to see you out and about so early this morning. I trust you slept well?''

"Lord Laverstock! You startled me." Sam thought of the fan she had fortunately disposed of at the house behind her and gave a relieved smile.

She looked guilty, thought the gentleman who faced her on the pathway. How would he discover the truth? One could scarcely torture so lovely a creature.

From across the street, Percival watched as the elegant lord extended his arm for Samantha. She placed her dainty hand carefully upon it, then gave him an entrancing smile. She would never do so for him, groused Percival sourly. No, it had to be a broad-shouldered man with a great deal of money. Percival glanced down the street to the village green where the maypole still lay. Not far from it stood the wicker frame used by the clown of the celebration, the Jack-of-the-Green. Samantha had said the Jack needed to be strong to carry the load.

Setting off along the walkway, Percival strode toward the green, a purposeful look in his eyes.

8

L ord Laverstock was frustrated in his attempts to discover precisely what Lady Samantha had been doing the night before—by the approach of the local squire and his son. The genial squire, tall and spare of frame, was a great contrast to his rotund son, William Dowdeswell, who stood quietly beside him, casting knowing glances at Samantha.

She made the introductions with a pretty politeness Charles could only admire. The chit did not lack for manners when she chose to use them, it seemed.

"Welcome to our little village, sir. We are indeed pleased to have you with us for a visit." The squire gave them a cheerful look that thanked Samantha for bringing this fortunate event about. "We selected Lady Samantha as our queen by unanimous consent. We understand you are to be among us for a number of days, and we would deem it a great honor if you would consent to be our May King this year. Since Lady Samantha has been elected this year's queen, we felt it only fitting that her guest join in the celebrations with her." He harumphed and added, with a somewhat apologetic smile, " 'Tis a simple ceremony, but one that stretches back into antiquity, unlike the present doings in London and other large cities. I am told the sweeps have taken over this happy day there."

Charles looked down at the winsome face beside him. Her eyes glowed with what could only be described as sheer delight. He could almost sense her desire to laugh with joy. He would not be so cruel as to deny her such a modest pleasure. Thus the elegant lord from the most hallowed sublimity of London Society found himself nodding his assent to making an utter fool of himself—for he possessed the sinking feeling that it would come to that before the celebration was over.

"The honor is all mine, I assure you." With those few words he sealed his fate.

"The fiddler will be Daniel Johnston, as is custom, and the identity of our Jack will be a secret." At Laverstock's obvious puzzlement, the squire added, "No one knows for sure when the idea of the Jack-in-the-Green originated; some say as far back as heathen days. Here, for us, he is a comical character and as such delights the little ones with his teasing and cavorting about the street. He is a happy part of our little procession, along with the king and queen, and the fiddler. You and the lady will, of course, preside over the maypole, the morris dances, and the archery contests which will mark the day."

Samantha chuckled softly, adding, "You must not forget the children who join in the walk about the village." Turning to face Charles, she continued, "In our village it is our duty to gather charity alms for the village church. The little tots enjoy becoming a part of the procession after we have ruled for the day." She prudently omitted the business about the kissing after each contribution. It was entirely possible that the locals would overlook that bit of nonsense in view of the exalted position of their May King this year.

"Along with much waving of ribands and flags among other things," inserted William with a sly grin.

"And then we all return to the village green for tea and cakes," Samantha concluded with a satisfied nod of her head, thankful she didn't have to contend with William.

"Sounds enchanting," murmured Charles with a wry twist of his mouth. He gave a polite bow to the squire and his son, then urged Samantha along the pathway away from where the maid patiently waited in the little carriage.

"Was this your idea?" he demanded in a pleasant tone as though inquiring about the display of ribands in the window of the village shop they now passed.

"My idea?" echoed Samantha in what she hoped was an innocent voice. "I did not even know that I am to be the queen until just now when the good squire mentioned it. How might I have arranged such a thing?" She was grateful her cottage bonnet concealed whatever expression she had on her face at the moment. She feared she might give the thing away could he see her face. She had, in fact, been fairly certain.

He shook his head. "I do not know for sure, but I have a feeling that you know something of the matter."

"I near forgot to inquire about your poor head this morning. I do not see any sign of the bump of last evening. It is better?" Samantha sympathetically studied his forehead.

Impatiently he replied, "Fine, fine. Now as to the other matter—"

"Here comes Percival," Samantha cried with not a little relief. She would far rather Lord Laverstock not know of her hand in these doings. "I am surprised to see him out and about at such an early hour of the day. I vow he usually sleeps much later . . . and after being up so late too." She quite forgot the time of day. Samantha cast a curious look at Percival, wondering what brought the pleased expression to his face. He was normally given to a supercilious sneer, unless he forgot himself and behaved naturally. Now he appeared rather smug about something.

"I say, lovely day out, what?" He executed a bow with an exquisite grace that sent the vicar's wife, who was strolling on the opposite side of the street, into transports of admiration.

"I am to be the May Queen this year Percy—" cried Samantha, edging toward her carriage with the devout hope she might return to Mayne Court before Aunt Lavinia discovered the fan was missing.

Not wanting to go into a discussion of his part in the festivities, Charles jumped into the conversation. "I thought perhaps we all might enjoy an outing in this fine weather. I consulted with Lady Lavinia, after I discovered from a maid you had gone. She agreed with me. We are to meet in some meadow near a brook she assured me you would know, Lady Samantha. I felt the fresh air would be most restorative." Lord Laverstock gave her an expectant look while awaiting the usual cries of delight it was his custom to receive when making such a suggestion. In his experience, young ladies enjoyed capturing him for an afternoon in a rustic setting. It seemed to bring forth the coquette in the meekest of girls. He had to admit he was curious to see how Samantha reacted to such a situation.

The dismayed expression that crossed Sam's face was almost

comical . . . and not in the least flattering to the dignified lord from the city.

She knew precisely the spot to which Aunt Lavinia alluded. It was quite the most charming of places, with a gentle stream tumbling over rocks creating pools where one might find a small trout or carp should one desire to fish. Beneath the spreading branches of a great beech Samantha often sat with her lute, playing for the birds, she laughingly told her brother.

But . . . she wasn't certain she wished to share this precious spot with the others. Then, thinking herself to be the poorest of hostesses, she nodded. "Of course I know just where it is. If you follow me, I shall lead you there directly."

She gave Lord Laverstock a cautious smile when he assisted her into the little carriage. Taking the reins in hand she set off toward the gathering place with mixed emotions, darting glances at Laverstock, who rode alongside. Percy jogged along behind them.

They were greeted by a flustered Emma, a somewhat subdued Alfred, a good-natured, if mildly bored George, and a placid Aunt Lavinia. She had read her tea leaves and felt she knew exactly what the day would bring.

Laverstock handed over the care of his horse to the groom who attended Lady Lavinia's carriage, then joined George, drawing him aside from the others. "Did you check the contents of the barn this morning, as I suggested?"

"Aye, that I did. Nary a thing missing. You must be mistaken in what you imagined you saw. I did lock it, you know. Other than some additional straw on the floor, nothing was altered in the place. The plans were just where I put them, down to the string I placed across the roll to see if they were touched. If someone did indeed get into the barn last night, he was not after the plans."

Unbeknown to these two gentlemen, Percival had walked close to them, close enough to overhear every word spoken. "Oh, I say, I hope there is nothing amiss. If I can be of any assistance, count on me."

Laverstock gave the dandy a considering look, then gravely replied, " 'Tis nothing serious, Twistleton."

"I got the distinct impression there was a problem. Now see

here, George, I can carry my weight as well as the rest of you. Be a good fellow and let me help. If you fear someone snitching the plans, surely you can post a guard at the barn.'' Percival gave him an earnest look as he spoke.

George exchanged a glance with Laverstock. "It might come to that.''

"Count on me to do my share. I'm accustomed to late hours, you know, old boy. Wouldn't be any hardship for me to stay awake.'' Following that sally Percival nodded with great amiability and strolled off to chat with Lady Lavinia.

"Why do I have misgivings about him,'' complained George to his newfound friend. For all that he knew Percival, he found his present attitude puzzling.

"We'd best be more careful where we discuss this. It was far too easy for Twistleton to overhear what we said. Not that I actually distrust the fellow, you understand. But one always wonders about a possible motive in a person hard-pressed for funds. Have you heard any more of his problems?'' Charles questioned idly while he studied the loose cluster of people gathered in the dappled shade of the tall beeches. He could pretend to believe Twistleton innocent of involvement, but inwardly Charles felt the dandy to be up to his neck in some manner of chicanery. But what? Charles hoped that by seeming to be unsuspecting, he could lead Twistleton to expose his intent.

"No,'' murmured George as the two men walked back to where the others were positioned by the stream. "He has said nothing to me about it.''

Beneath the gently waving branches of her favorite beech tree Samantha helped spread out a cloth for the nuncheon Aunt Lavinia insisted they all must enjoy.

"There is something that quite famishes a person when one is in the open air.'' Lavinia held her furled parasol firmly in one hand while she directed everyone about her. In her bonnet, tied with crisp white riband and decorated with bunches of oversized white silk roses, Aunt looked a picture of ladylike grace. She pointed her umbrella, white and decorated with roses to match those on her bonnet, and said to Emma, "Tend to the biscuits, dear girl.''

Glancing to see what her aunt wished, Emma turned to fetch

the desired item. She was wearing a pretty cherry striped cambric decorated with knots of green ribands and a neat little bonnet having bows of cherry and green above the brim. And she seemed most conscious that Alfred was watching every move she made today.

"May I help you, cousin Emma?" His gesture was courteous, bordering on something more gallant.

"We are not related, you know," the flustered Emma blurted out.

"I am well aware of that, you may be sure. However, I have been given to think of you that way in the past." Alfred bestowed a small grin on her, further discomposing her. He then assisted her to the little open phaeton where a number of edibles yet remained. Standing by her side, he watched with a half-smile at her confused motions as she searched for the biscuits. It was very unlike the usually calm and orderly young lady he knew.

"And now?" queried Emma, turning toward him holding a little tin of biscuits in her hands while her heart seemed to come to a halt.

"And now," he concluded, "I do not. Come, let us bring the rest of these good things to where the others are waiting for us." He gathered several small packages, then gestured for Emma to precede him.

"Oh," cried Emma, her face turning a delicate pink, "how silly of me. Of course." And she picked up several more little items, carrying them to where Aunt Lavinia watched with narrow-eyed acuity.

Samantha was delighted to find her lute had been brought along. She rescued it from the pile of cushions Aunt had ordered and strolled down to sit by the bank a little apart from the others. She found a rock just the right size, dropping a cushion on top of it before carefully seating herself.

She was shortly joined by her brother, who settled down beside her, for once careful of his pantaloons.

He spoke in a voice he hoped could not be overheard. "I believe I have solved the problem of the elevator and rudder. Once I construct it, are you willing to go up again?"

"What a question. Of course I will take the glider up once

more if you wish.'' She slanted a teasing glance at him from beneath the brim of her bonnet. First brushing down her delicate primrose muslin, she then traced a pattern on her lute, watching George's face. "Unless our dear papa's friend talks you out of it. Do you think you could teach the youngest groom to be your assistant? I believe we are of a similar weight and height.''

George gave his usual shrug when confronted with an unanswerable question. "We can only hope Papa does not catch wind of it. I intend to keep at work on the glider until I am convinced it will operate properly. Contrary to what you believe, I have no desire to see that pretty neck of yours broken.'' A look of alarm spread across her face and George cursed himself for his thoughtless remark.

"I told you I will not take chances,'' whispered Sam furiously. "Although I dearly wish to help, if you cannot give me reasonable assurances I shall be safe, I will not go up.'' She struck a loud chord on her lute and gave him her most contrary look.

"Now, see here, Sam, I need you, and maybe Wellington does as well. If this works as I hope, it could save the lives of many English soldiers.'' George at his most persuasive could beat Samantha any day.

"Well, put so well I can scarce refuse, can I?'' She began to play a pretty air when she observed Alfred approaching. "Alfred,'' she murmured aside to George.

Turning from his now-persuaded sister, George rose to stand facing his cousin. "Hullo. Finished helping Emma? I thought you might tip her into the stream like you used to do.''

"No,'' drawled an amused Alfred, "I have grown out of those boyish pranks, I hope. And Lady Emma has grown up far too nicely. How does the flying machine come along? Having any trouble with the changes? If you need any help . . . keeping guard or the like, do not hesitate to call on me.'' With those words he strolled off to accept a plate of various delicacies from Emma, whose cheeks still bloomed a lovely tint of pink.

"Interesting.'' Laverstock paused behind George to watch Alfred. "That is the second offer of help in posting guard by the barn. You are fairly inundated. Shall I offer mine as well? Might as well make the number complete.''

"How true. I say, did I tell you? I believe I have solved the

elevator design. I can show you later if you like." George
gestured upstream, and the two ambled away, deep in conversation.

Samantha watched them leave with mixed emotions. She
hadn't wanted Lord Laverstock to see her favorite place at first.
But now he was here, she perversely wished he would sit and
chat with her, not wander off with George to discuss the glider.
What would Lord Laverstock say when it became necessary for
her to take off across the valley once more?

Well, he couldn't stop her. He was no relation and had
absolutely no authority over her, not even from her father. And
given his nonchalant attitude toward her, she could scarcely
consider him an applicant for her hand.

What would he say, or more importantly, do, on May Day
when it became apparent he was supposed to kiss her? Her
cheeks grew warm at the very thought.

Her reflections were interrupted as Aunt Lavinia called them
all back to where she was seated on a high cushion—like some
pasha, Samantha thought with amusement. The older lady
picked up the tea pot, a simple but beautiful piece of white
Rockingham with a double twisted handle, and poured out
steaming tea while ordering Emma to hand around cakes and
other delicacies.

George had suggested to Cook that she include papery slices
of ham on white bread and pickled cucumbers as well. He saw
to it the men sampled this delight.

Picking up her plate, that appeared to be a piece of primrose
leaf molded in white, Samantha allowed her lute to slide to the
ground while she concentrated on a few bites of food. She wasn't
all that hungry. The realization that she had achieved her desire
to be the May Queen was still fresh in her mind, but now a
disconcerting doubt hovered there as well. Was she really
pleased? Her scheme might rebound on her to cause dreadful
trouble. Just what form that trouble might assume, she preferred
not to consider. She turned to her aunt. "I almost forgot to tell
you that I found out in the village this morning I am to be May
Queen." That she had neglected to share the good news said
much for the state of her mind.

Aunt Lavinia nodded, totally unsurprised. "I knew it, for the tea leaves told me so this morning. I hope it goes well.'' She watched Sam with smiling eyes, but said no more.

Alfred challenged the other men to a fishing contest, and was immediately accepted. The four picked up the simple poles Alfred had rigged up to test their skills, each heading for the best possible spot.

Her plate and tea cup set aside, Samantha gathered up her lute, but merely sat watching the men while she meditated on her situation. Aunt Lavinia wandered off to inspect some white flowers she'd espied.

''I doubt they will catch very much of anything in that little stream. However, it does give me a chance to chat with you.'' Emma dropped two cushions on the ground, then neatly arranged herself on them before studying Samantha. ''Are you pleased? Or is something else on your mind?''

''How does one know when one is in love, Emma? Must one feel that way before getting married?''

Startled by this totally unexpected question, Emma thought for a moment, then gave a dainty shrug. ''Only your own feelings could determine such an important point.'' Then, as though expressing her own inner conflicts, she added, ''I believe the possible evil from marrying where there is no love is far greater than remaining on the shelf. Think of a lifetime with a man one can barely tolerate.'' She looked at the four men by the stream, all handsome in individual ways. ''You have met so few young men, you do not really know what you are capable of feeling. Who knows what you might encounter should you venture to London for that Season Aunt has been wishing for you. What temptation might come your way were you to marry prematurely, and then discover that perfect mate in a different man? That would be a great tragedy, would it not?'' Emma pulled up a strand of grass, fiddling with it while she watched Samantha's reaction to her words.

Soft notes from her lute floated across the sylvan glade to mingle with the songs of the birds. ''What a wise woman you are, dear Emma. I fear I have become quite taken with a gentleman, and''—Samantha sighed most woefully—''I strongly suspect he does not care for me in the least.'' Sam looked up at Emma from beneath her sooty lashes, giving her cousin a wry grin. "I am now quite certain I was mistaken about my papa's plans. There has been not the least indication that Lord Laverstock sees me in any way other than as Papa's daughter and George's sister. As a matter of fact, I suspect he considers me a dratted nuisance."

Looking at the men, Emma thought back over the past few days and shook her head. "I would not be so assured of that, my dear cousin. It may be that the gentleman in question believes he feels concern when it is actually a deeper emotion. I understand that at times it takes a man some while before he is aware of what is in his heart. They are perhaps not as in tune with their emotions as we are."

"And less likely to heed them as well?" Sam mulled this idea over in her mind, plucking the notes of a popular melody on her lute.

Just then, Aunt Lavinia called out for assistance, and Emma hastened to her side, leaving Samantha alone.

It was very peaceful if one ignored the jovial banter between the gentlemen along the bank of the stream. She leaned against the trunk of the tree behind her to look up into the leafy expanse over her head. There was a yellow wagtail up there, she was sure she had spotted its bright yellow face through the leaves. It must have just arrived for the summer and would soon be nesting.

Giving up on the elusive bird, she glanced at the far bank where columbine bloomed, the dainty foliage fluttering in the faint breeze. Bending her head, she concentrated on an intricate bit of fingering she had invented for the tune she now began.

"Clever. You really are quite good at that, aren't you."

The music abruptly halted. Sam gave a resigned look into Laverstock's face, shaking her head at him. "Perhaps you might warn me of your approach, just once? If it would not be too much trouble. I daresay your training in spy work or whatever it is that you do in London has prepared you to move about silently. *I* find it most disconcerting. What happened to the fishing contest?"

Appropriating the cushions left behind by Emma, Charles eased himself down so he might watch the primrose-clad figure so entrancingly absorbed in her old-fashioned lute. Dressed a bit differently she could easily come from a previous century. Except he didn't like the thought of concealing that glorious hair beneath one of those conical hennens.

"I gave up. Your brother tells me he intends to test the glider again once he completes the changes to the elevator." Charles stared at the far bank, his mind seeing the craft with its precious cargo skimming across the sky to crash on the other side of the valley, so close to where he had stood transfixed, totally fascinated. What if she was hurt this time . . . or worse? "Do you plan to assist him?"

Sam bit her lip at the deadly calm voice. If he intended to be intimidating, he was near the mark. What to say? She wished she might please him, she wanted more than anything to do so. But she could not disappoint her brother. And what about Lord Wellington? If he could possibly use the agility of the glider to improve his knowledge of troop movements, wasn't she duty-bound to help?

Cautiously, she nodded her head, then gave voice to what she knew would anger Lord Laverstock. "I do." She wouldn't explain, nor would she seek his approval. He had made it clear he didn't seek that right.

"You little fool," he snapped, rising quickly lest he reach out to shake that slender body until she submitted to his will. He was stunned with the force of his feelings. "You risk your neck again . . . for what?"

"Because I believe in my brother and have faith he will succeed. He says he needs me." Samantha also rose, gathered the cushions in her arms, then turned from him and walked across to return them to the phaeton. She swallowed bitter tears. How unfair she should have to choose like this. But it had to be this way, for many reasons.

Another problem reared its head as she caught sight of her aunt. That lady must have discovered the fan missing. How long would it be before she collected some other frippery she fancied? Wishing to get away from the others for a bit, Sam suddenly decided it was time to seek some expert help.

Crossing to her aunt, she softly explained, "I must return to the village, dear Aunt. I ought to see about a fitting for my May Queen gown. At least, I should select the fabric and pattern.

As well, I had intended this morning to buy the silks you mentioned yesterday that you needed, but I forgot. I am persuaded that if I go promptly, I shall accomplish my errands and be back at the Court in a trice.''

Aunt Lavinia had observed the angry exchange of words beneath the beech tree and noted the high color that still clung to Samantha's cheeks. "If you wish. I should be grateful for the silks, dear girl. And Samantha . . . I am pleased about the May Queen selection. I feel you will do quite well.''

Sam nodded, having a good deal more misgivings than she cared to admit at this point. In moments, with her maid clinging to the seat, she briskly tooled her little shiny black whiskey from the picnic spot, carefully ignoring Lord Laverstock though she was quite conscious of his watching gaze. Behind her, the sounds of the party grew ever fainter as she urged the horse toward the village.

When she made her way down the main street toward the far end where she suspected she might discover the men she wished to consult, she still fumed at the unjustice in the world.

"Miss," ventured a very concerned maid, "ought ye be going this way? 'Tis a most improper area, down 'ere.''

"I know," admitted Samantha. "I need some information. I wish you to say nothing of this to anyone. Do you understand? No one.'' With those words they entered the yard of the other, less reputable inn in the village, where the more unsavory elements of the community hung about.

Samantha handed the ribbons to a poorly dressed groom, wondering if her rig would be safe. Then she bravely made her way to a cluster of men, determined to get the information she desired. Warily, her gaze darted from one to another.

"The more ye looks, the less ye'll like it, missy," chuckled a particularly grimy individual. He glanced at the man next to him, who gave a sharp bark of laughter.

"If you please, I should like some information." Sam drew back a trifle at the suddenly hostile faces, and bravely continued. "I wish to know how to steal something in reverse—that is, return an item without the owner being any the wiser.''

The man who had spoken gave her a crooked grin, revealing two missing teeth. "Yer don' mean ter say! I ain't had much

of a need fer such. Don' know.'' He glanced at the man next
to him and they began a discussion that was totally incompre-
hensible to Samantha.

The man who had appointed himself spokesman presented
their conclusions. He seemed to understand how difficult it was
for Samantha to comprehend their speech for he spoke slowly
and more plainly to her. "It be like this, missy. Yer sneaks
it in and puts it down in an unlikely spot. An they finds it, they
thinks they's been wrong.''

Curious to perhaps glean other ideas from these remarkable
men, Sam asked another question. Surprised that a lady of
quality showed no distaste and little fear, she rose in their
esteem. Their respect was revealed in suddenly doffed caps and
careful speech.

Across the road a tall figure leaned forward in his saddle to
scrutinize the scene before him. So this was the place Lady
Samantha was to get the fabric and pattern for her May Queen
dress? Lord Laverstock wondered why she sought out these low
types.

They seemed to respect her, which was a distinct relief. He
wished to remain concealed to discover what she might do next;
he did not want to dash to her rescue—though of course he
would, if necessary. Odd, he had wanted to trust her so very
much. Though he thought her a little fool for complying with
her brother's need to test the glider, he admired her loyalty.
Which made the situation across the street utterly incompre-
hensible.

Why?

He withdrew into the shadows when she returned to her little
carriage to join the obviously trembling maid and wheel back
down the central street of the village. He slowly followed,
hanging back yet keeping her in view.

She stopped at a village shop, the very one he and she had
passed earlier that day. It didn't take her long to exit with a
small packet that she handed to the maid to hold. From there
she went to a discreet little stone house with a white painted
sign that indicated the dressmaker was to be found within.

It took her longer here. Charles found his horse wasn't the
only one to become restless. It gave him time aplenty to mull

over the peculiar scene with the men he figured to be thieves or worse. How did she possess the courage to approach them? It must have been very serious indeed. What business had she had with them?

When Samantha left the little house, then set her carriage off in the direction of the Court, Laverstock returned to the inn at the outer end of the village to ask a few questions. He got no answers.

Apparently the men had decided the little lady was to be protected, even from herself. What was afoot? How could he find out? It would seem there was a connection to George's plans in some manner. But what? And with whom?

Charles slowly rode his fine black horse back along the road leading to Mayne Court, deep in thought. He would have to get as close to Lady Samantha Mayne as possible. But how best to accomplish that? That was the now crucial question.

9

E mma hesitantly tapped on Samantha's door, slipping inside at her cousin's beckoning voice.

Preoccupied with the multitude of her own troubles, Sam at first did not perceive the worried expression on Emma's sweet face. Since not a brown curl was out of place, nor did Emma wear a frown, Sam's lack of observance could be forgiven. A worried expression sat on her own piquant face, one hand rubbed her brow.

"You can see I *must* help George, can you not, dear Emma?" Samantha beseeched her cousin, giving voice to internal arguments. Sam's topmost concern was revealed the moment she spoke. "Lord Laverstock seems to think me the fool. If so, then I must be, for I refuse to disappoint George after all his hard work. 'Tis not so simple a matter to train someone to take my place as one might think."

She took a long look out the window before continuing, sketching a gesture of frustration as she considered another of her many problems. "I believe I have found a way to circumvent Aunt Lavinia as regards the return of the pretties she purloins. I sought a bit of advice while in the village." At the look of alarm that crossed Emma's face, Samantha reassured her. "I mentioned no names, nor the reason I sought the help."

"Oh, dear, were any nieces faced with such problems as we?" Emma clasped her hands before her, plumping herself on the cozy little chair near the window with a sigh. It was then that Samantha noticed the abstracted air and troubled eyes.

"What else is bothering you?" Sam didn't believe in roundaboutation. It wasted time.

" 'Tis Alfred," Emma confessed. "I scarce know what to

114

make of him lately. He has changed greatly, as you can undoubtedly see for yourself. He is no longer the boy I knew. I could not believe it when I discovered he is a well-known writer. To think he has been penning those gothic tales all this time. That he is in reality Lord Hardly! I am amazed!'' She studied her hands a moment, then peered up at Samantha, her soft brown eyes shining with what seemed to be hope. In an offhand manner, she added, ''He treats me quite differently now, as you may have noticed. Though I must say, his behavior is rather confusing. I suspect he is drawn to me . . . yet he keeps his distance. Why?''

''Just because he no longer teases you nor nudges you into the stream does not mean he has formed a lasting passion for you,'' retorted the practical Sam. At the sudden crumpling of Emma's face, Sam dropped down beside her, heedless of the lovely amber silk dress she wore in anticipation of dinner. ''Oh, dear, I have overset you. 'Tis my thoughtless tongue. Truly, I did not realize you hold a tendre for my cousin. For he is not your cousin, is he?'' stated Samantha, now her attention had been drawn to the matter.

''He told me he is aware of that fact,'' sniffed Emma into a dainty scrap of lace and cambric. ''I am a goosecap to bother my head or yours about such a silly notion. Only . . . Alfred has become an attractive man since I last saw him. It confuses me that he pays me certain attentions, but no more. Am I repulsive to him?''

Samantha shook her head. ''What a pack of arrant nonsense! You are the loveliest of creatures to be found. Indeed, I could wish I had your creamy skin and not my horrid freckles. If there is an impediment to his attraction for you I will try to uncover what it might be. Rest assured, it has nothing whatever to do with your beauty or charm, for those you have in abundance. If I know that chuckleheaded cousin of mine, it is something stupid.''

''Now, Samantha,'' cautioned Emma.

''Never fear. I shan't do or say anything to put you to the blush. Come, let us go down for dinner. All that fresh air has given me an appetite.''

With a coaxing smile on her enchanting face, Samantha held out her hand to Emma, drawing her from her chair with a gentle tug. "Alfred will be down there with the others, I expect. Smile and laugh and let me do the detective work."

Emma cast a wary glance at her vivacious cousin, following her down the stairs to the drawing room with more than a few misgivings. But Samantha's lively countenance betrayed none of the thoughts that spun around behind it.

Alfred and George were conversing quietly in the corner while Percival chatted with Aunt Lavinia. Lord Laverstock was nowhere to be seen.

Aunt Lavinia was first to catch sight of the two girls.

"How lovely. Like two flowers in bloom. Emma is like a white rose and Samantha is a tiger flower."

"Right down to the spots on the petals," murmured the low voice behind Sam.

She spun around to find Laverstock perilously close to her. Hastily, she backed up, nearly stumbling over the footstool Aunt Lavinia kept to ease her tired feet. "One of these days you shall be repaid, I do not know how, but you shall. What cat feet you have." Sam tried her best to look angry but failed miserably. "Allow me to remind you that I requested you not to do that again."

"But you look so charming when you are startled."

The note of amusement in his voice was enough to send her into strong hysterics, Samantha decided. She compressed her lips lest she utter the words that longed to skip off her tongue. "I wonder if tiger flowers bite and scratch?"

Her idle tone was not in the least deceiving to the man who stood close enough to catch the softly spoken words. He slowly backed away, much to the entertainment of Aunt Lavinia, who had observed the byplay with interested eyes.

Emma deplored her cousin's wayward tongue, and had taken refuge near the fireplace where a small blaze curled its smoke up the chimney in spite of the mild temperatures outside. It seemed Aunt Lavinia believed most firmly in the necessity of fending off the night vapors.

"Did you enjoy the afternoon, Lady Emma?" Alfred strolled

up to where Emma stood supposedly examining the carving on the mantel.

"I did." She turned to face him, cautiously studying his face. "Why the formality of a sudden, Alfred?" she asked boldly. "We have known each other since leading strings days. Surely I rate more highly than such distance upon your part." She gave him a vexed and slightly puzzled look. It was all of a piece with his attitude toward her since they had faced each other in the state room that night. He had very subtly changed.

"That is it precisely." He bestowed one of his enigmatic smiles upon her, turning to greet Lord Laverstock with what Emma suspected was relief.

She excused herself after a few moments of polite chitchat, wandering to Samantha's side. "Alfred is of a certainty most peculiar. When I asked him if I did not rate more highly than such Turkish treatment, he merely agreed!"

"Hmm," replied Sam in a rather abstracted manner. Try as she could to wrap herself in Emma's concern, Sam found it difficult to ignore the feelings Lord Laverstock created within her. If Emma possessed a tendre for Alfred, what were the emotions Samantha discovered whenever Lord Laverstock chanced to come close to her?

"I had the nicest visit with Mrs. Wyndham this afternoon after you went to the village, Samantha. Emma and I paused there on the way home. George and the others rode on ahead so there was no reason why we ought not pay our respects, was there?" Aunt Lavinia uttered these innocent words as she rose to extend her hand to Lord Laverstock upon the butler's announcement of dinner.

Samantha turned to Emma, horror clearly flashing across her face before she schooled her features. "Did she . . . ?"

"I do not know," whispered Emma, "I forgot to tell you about that," then she smiled at Percival, her dinner partner for the evening.

"Oh, dear," murmured Samantha as Alfred joined her.

"Trouble, cousin?" His voice mocked her concerns and she glared at him.

"If you but knew all my difficulties, you would be kinder."

She glanced at Laverstock, then Emma, followed by an unhappy look at George, and finally she gazed at Aunt Lavinia. Why did it seem that all the woes of the world were dumped onto her slim shoulders? At least it felt as though they were.

Dinner was a peculiar meal. George attempted to talk with Laverstock, who was trying to ascertain what Samantha was saying to Alfred. In turn, Samantha was attempting to probe Alfred's reasoning while Emma strained to overhear their conversation as Percival regaled her with an amusing tale from London Society. Aunt Lavinia held a handkerchief to her mouth, a white one lavishly embroidered with roses, and chuckled at the goings-on.

Samantha suddenly ceased her inquisition of Alfred as she espied the handkerchief in her aunt's hands. She would be very much surprised if that item had been in her aunt's possession before today. One thing she had to give Aunt Lavinia, she did have lovely taste.

"What a pretty handkerchief, dear Aunt. New, I believe?" Sam's dulcet voice betrayed none of her inner trepidations.

"A little thing I picked up recently. I saw it and simply had to have it." Aunt Lavinia waved the article about in the air with a pleased smile.

While those words might sound innocent enough to anyone else, they rang with grim foreboding in Sam's ears. Aunt had done it again. "Picked up" had a slightly different meaning when applied to Aunt. She had purloined that exquisite handkerchief from the Wyndham household this afternoon. And now it was up to Sam to get it back there. She hadn't planned upon putting her newly acquired information to use so soon.

Catching Emma's apologetic look, Sam merely shrugged and turned her attention to her meal. Alfred and his peculiar thinking would have to wait while Samantha figured out how to deposit the handkerchief in a spot guaranteed to assure its being found . . . at the Wyndhams', of course.

Following the meal Samantha and Emma trailed after Aunt Lavinia, leaving the men to their port and conversation. In the drawing room, Aunt settled onto her usual place on the sofa, then looked at the girls. "I would that you play for us this

evening. You both look so charming in your pretty gowns while
at your instruments. Something lively, please.''

Bowing to her request, the girls set aside their worries and
commenced to play a gay little air. It was to this sound that
the men entered the room some time later.

"Delightful," commented Lord Laverstock at the conclusion
of the music.

Emma took the opportunity to leave the piano, strolling across
the room with Percival to stand near the fireplace. Alfred
frowned in evident displeasure but did nothing about the
twosome, turning to George instead. While puzzling out the
behavior of the assorted relatives, Samantha missed the approach
of Laverstock.

"I believe you promised me a game of backgammon, Lady
Samantha.''

"Hmm?" murmured Sam, engrossed in the perplexing
motives behind Alfred's actions, or lack of them.

Charles raised an eyebrow in rueful acknowledgement of her
lack of artifice where he was concerned. Accustomed to the
flutterings of London ladies, it was a distinct change to be
ignored. He couldn't say he cared much for the feeling. A man
of his rank and wealth expected a certain amount of attention.
It was quite clear Lady Samantha wasn't aware of his due. Then,
realizing the pretentiousness of his thoughts, he smiled.
"Backgammon?"

"Oh, yes, of course, if you wish," replied Samantha with
an unflattering lack of enthusiasm.

Charles followed her to the game table where he drew up a
dainty chair, while she set out the board and removed the black
and white men and the dice from the drawer. Sam won the
opening throw.

What was going on inside that delectable head? Charles
wondered. Beneath that red-gold cap of curls something was
astir, most assuredly. She really was a lovely young thing, he
mused. Those unusual eyes enchanted him, their color changing
from amber to gold with her moods. And those little freckles
he enjoyed teasing her about were charming, really. That petal-
soft skin, freckles notwithstanding, was such many women

would crave. He longed to caress it, and run his hands through those fire-kissed curls. Her hair had to be pure silk. Even in the poor light of this room, it glimmered, shining with health and a luminosity all of its own. She was lovely, bright, and sparkling. And she was up to something underhanded, of that he was sure. While she kept her thoughts to herself, she could not totally conceal her feelings. They were revealed in her eyes. And now those eyes held a mystery.

"Your turn, I believe." Sam sighed with barely concealed impatience. Really, if the dratted man desired to play, the least he might do was pay attention. She had been sitting at this table waiting for him to make a move for an age and he stared at her as though she had soot on her nose or something. The expression in his eyes had caused flutters deep within her again. It was developing into a very peculiar sensation. Most unsettling. She best try to ignore it.

"Clever move," said Charles, after a chagrined look at the board. With her double-six opening throw Samantha had taken two of his men and placed them in her home table as far as they would go. The best he could manage was to bring home two men from the five in his outer table.

Sam was in luck and again got a double six when she threw the dice from her box. She filled both bar points, placing two men on each. With each throw of the dice her luck continued to hold. It was plain to her that his lordship was not playing his best.

"I say, Laverstock, she is beating you to flinders," said Percival as he paused to look over Laverstock's shoulder. He tittered at the amusing notion of a nonpareil like Laverstock going down to defeat at the hands of a young miss.

"Go away, Percy, do," murmured Samantha. "The game is not finished yet."

He left the table in a decided huff after bestowing a narrow look on the red-gold head bent over the table in concentration. Whatever his thoughts might be, they did not appear to be pleasant.

Aunt Lavinia observed the interplay and sat quietly with a speculative expression on her face. This situation would definitely require a reading of her tea leaves. She gave a loving pat to the elegant scrap of embroidered Swiss linen on her lap, smiling with remembered pleasure.

Laverstock shook his head in amusement. His preoccupation with the charms of his adversary had wiped out the concentration for which he was famous. It would be a good thing if he could keep her unaware of his attraction. But then, with her guileless manner, perhaps she wouldn't notice. Then he caught sight of Aunt Lavinia and knew that while Lady Samantha might be untutored in the art of dalliance, her good aunt was well up to snuff. Well, he wasn't here to court the young lady. He had best scout about tonight to see what action might be abroad.

"Do you wish to concede, sir?" Samantha gave her opponent a wide-eyed stare.

"Not in the least." He made a valiant effort to recoup his losses but to no avail. It seemed that although Lady Samantha had not the benefit of a London Season to teach her how to flirt, she had learned to play backgammon very well.

So much for his desire to remain close to Lady Samantha. In so doing, he had allowed her to beat him quite soundly, probably making himself look like a fool in the process. He waited for a caustic comment from her.

"Well, that is a start at any rate," she said softly. A smile illuminated her face, her golden eyes blazed with mirth.

"A start?" He was at a loss to imagine what she meant by that cryptic comment.

"I said I would pay you back one way or another, did I not?" She laughed delightedly at his dismayed expression.

"Perhaps I would fare better were I to take on your brother? He is apparently the clever one in the family." Charles wasn't sure how he kept a straight face as he uttered the words, but he managed somehow.

"Oh, pooh. George is a genius at flying, but he is no earthly good to anyone. And as to brilliant, well, he grew up thinking Charlemagne was a member of the family. He referred to him as old Charlie Mayne." She was disconcerted when Lord Laverstock threw back his head in laughter.

"Tea, everyone," announced Lady Lavinia. She fluttered the

exquisite white handkerchief about as she directed Samantha
to the low table where Peters had set out a bountiful spread.
Supposedly this would compensate for the early dinner. The
Londoners must be accustomed to dining at a later hour.

Samantha eyed the lavish display of cakes and wondered a
little at her aunt. Lavinia's intent became clear when she drained
her tea cup and turned it over on the saucer. Aunt planned to
read her tea leaves for some reason. It seemed to Sam that she
had been doing it a great deal of late.

Alfred broke off his discussion of coastal wind and weather
conditions to stroll over to where Samantha poured tea. He
caught sight of Aunt Lavinia and paused. "Reading again, dear
Aunt?"

She gave him an impatient look, then concentrated on her cup
without answering.

Gliding over to stand close, but not too close, to Alfred,
Emma glanced at the fancy white handkerchief lying between
Aunt Lavinia and Samantha. She gave Samantha a significant
look, then a faint nod of her head. Bless her cousin, she was
quick off the mark. The handkerchief surreptitiously disappeared
beneath the folds of Samantha's gown. Emma admired the way
her cousin managed it so smoothly, her hands quickly returning
to the tea pot with scarcely a pause.

Only Lord Laverstock appeared to catch the byplay between
the two girls. Evidently, Lady Samantha was gifted with a slight
of hand that opened all manner of speculation. He puzzled over
it, then turned his attention to Alfred, when that young man
sat down next to Lady Samantha and proceeded to chat in a low
voice that was most difficult to overhear.

Samantha was delighted at the opportunity to quiz Alfred,
the only problem being that Alfred wasn't revealing one thing
that she didn't know already. Drat the man. The least he might
do was cooperate when she wanted information.

"What do the tea leaves tell you, Aunt?" inquired Emma.
She too had noticed how often Aunt was resorting to readings
lately.

"There is a web in the bottom of my cup," replied Aunt
Lavinia, her voice and manner vague, a frown creasing her
brow.

Samantha caught those words and exchanged a meaningful look with Emma. Aunt was caught in an intrigue not of her own choosing and it was bothering her. If it worried Aunt, it most certainly disturbed Samantha.

Percival asked for a reading as well, but the others declined, perhaps affected by the web which had shown up in Lavinia's cup.

Rising to leave, Samantha was stopped in her steps by her aunt's voice. "Would you give me my pretty handkerchief, dear girl? It seems to be caught in your dress somehow or other." The vagueness was still present, but Samantha knew that her aunt was aware Sam had tried to spirit the stolen item away. Double drat! Now she would have a beastly time uncovering the hiding place for such a small thing.

Later, up in her room, Samantha paced back and forth, finally deciding she had best take a look about to see if there was indeed some manner of intrigue going on that she didn't know about—other than her Aunt's hiding of that handkerchief.

Once her mind was decided, she acted swiftly. From the bottom drawer of her clothes chest she pulled her breeches and shirt. Hetty might not approve of the attire but she always saw to it that it was kept clean, Sam noticed with amusement. Snuffing out her candle, she cautiously made her way to the window, staring out at the darkness with a searching gaze.

At last assured the house had subsided into nighttime silence, she groped her way to her door. How thankful she was that Alfred had given up his prowling in the state rooms.

In the pocket of George's old breeches were tucked candle and tinderbox, not to mention the key she had borrowed again. She would need illumination to locate that scrap of pretty linen.

The stairs were negotiated with her customary caution. Instead of using the front door, she went out by a small side door and was soon crossing the lawn toward the barn. She had observed Aunt Lavinia heading this way earlier. It had taken restraint to remain in her room rather than confront Aunt with an accusation and demand. Experience had taught that neither was to be considered. Aunt simply refused to accept that her behavior was wrong, nor would she agree to stop. Sam had tried that once. Now she merely waited. Sometimes she wondered if Aunt hadn't made a game of it.

A sea breeze cooled the night air. Sam shivered, whether from a chill or a peculiar feeling, she didn't know. It was quite odd, but she had a sensation of being watched, though she could have sworn everyone had gone to bed ages ago. Certainly, there were no lights to be seen at the house.

The barn loomed up ahead and she heard the call of an owl. Rubbing her arms, she wished there was another way of fetching the dratted items Aunt Lavinia took.

From the shadows of a great oak, Lord Laverstock observed Lady Samantha's movements with tight-lipped anger. As she neared the barn, he stealthily slipped from behind the tree to follow her. What had she in mind? The plans? He realized that he had greatly hoped that she was not involved in a clandestine operation. Who was her partner? Alfred? She had chatted with him in a most confidential manner during tea. She certainly never spent any time with Percival Twistleton. But then, that dandy would scarcely dirty his hands with any nefarious doings. Or would he?

He heard the click of the lock, then the door swung open, and she slipped inside. Darting ahead, Charles caught it before it totally closed. He held it with care lest she be aware of another's presence. He wanted to make certain she found the plans before he confronted her. Surely it must be the most distasteful job he had faced in a long time.

Samantha stopped inside the door to withdraw the candle and tinderbox. Once she could see, she espied the lanthorn hanging on the wall and lit that before blowing out her candle. The lanthorn was a good deal safer to use than a candle and provided reasonable light for her purposes. Ignoring the clutter on George's workbench, she set to work, trying to decide precisely where her aunt might have concealed the dratted handkerchief.

Something white caught her eye and she climbed up on a stool to discover what it might be. Tucked atop a beam was a lovely white-bound book, a copy of Alfred's latest gothic tale. Sam giggled at the thought of such a pristine cover for the lurid story within. Now . . . why on earth was it here? Had her aunt sneaked it from the house? But surely Alfred would have given her a copy had she desired one. Shaking her head in puzzlement, Sam climbed down to continue her search.

Suddenly her gaze strayed to the workbench. There, at the very back and half hidden by some of George's papers, was the handkerchief. How silly! Surely her aunt might know it would be seen by George first thing in the morning. Then she reconsidered. Knowing George, a pair of silk stockings could be draped across his plans and he would merely push them aside. George had singular powers of concentration. Most singular.

Sam dragged the stool over to the workbench, then climbed up, stretching her slender arm as far as she could. Aunt had done well. Sighing, Sam put one hand alongside George's set of plans for the glider (really he ought to keep them in a safer place than the workbench, given the Frenchman in the village, and all) and reached out.

"In a spot of bother, are you?"

The crash was awesome, coming in the silence of the night as it did.

Sam glared at Lord Laverstock from the floor of the barn, noting as she did his black attire from head to toe. A few paces back and he would blend into the inky darkness without a trace. Pushing aside the stool, she rose to her knees, then abruptly sat down and gazed at him with disconcerting directness. "You again. You do have a way of turning up when I least expect you. Come to think of it, perhaps I ought to anticipate you when I do not . . . or something of the sort," she muttered, confusing her listener no end. "What are you doing in the barn at this hour and in those clothes?" she demanded, causing Laverstock to stare at her in utter bafflement.

"I believe I am the one who ought to be asking why you are disturbing your brother's plans," he countered.

"George's plans?" Now it was Samantha's turn to be bewildered. "What do his plans have to do with this? That is not the reason why I am here. Why are you here? And at such an hour? I made sure you were fast asleep before I left. You are *not* asleep," she accused.

The girl had lost her senses . . . or else she was extremely clever. "Tell me what you were about in here. Does it have something to do with the Frenchman in the village?"

Sam clambered to her feet, wincing as her injured posterior let itself be known. She probably would feel it tomorrow. Gingerly, she rubbed the worst of the area while staring at Lord Laverstock. What a pity he seemed daft in the head. She had become quite fond of the man. He certainly was the most attractive man she was likely to see in these parts. Perhaps Aunt had a point about the necessity of a Season in London.

"Lady Samantha." He stepped forward to confront her and Samantha found herself backed up against the workbench. One of George's tools poked her in the back and she shifted to find a better spot.

"You might tell. I could never bear that." She studied that handsome countenance, wondering how much he suspected.

"I swear, if you will give up this wild scheme, I will carry the secret to my grave." Charles felt if he could get her to confess, he could perhaps save her from her intended crime. He found he very much desired an innocent Samantha.

"Well, it is not *that* serious." She reflected a moment and shook her head, "then again, perhaps it is. I would never wish to hurt Aunt, you see. I fear she might be put in the stocks or something of that kind, and no relative of ours has ever done such a thing." Sam edged away from his disturbing presence, giving him her most earnest look.

Charles rubbed his hand across his face, then gazed at Samantha with his confusion mirrored in his eyes. "What is it you seek out here?"

"You promise you will not tell?" At his reassuring nod, she took a deep breath and revealed the awful secret. "Aunt Lavinia likes to filch things that take her fancy. I came out here tonight to recover this elegant handkerchief and found a book as well. I was reaching for the handkerchief when you frightened me half out of my wits. You really should not do things like that, you know," she confided.

Lord Laverstock leaned up against the bench in relief, then froze, pulling Lady Samantha against him. There was a sound at the door. Quickly, he covered her mouth with his hand, not trusting her to keep silent. She stiffened in fear. He turned them to face the noise as a light flickered outside. Someone was coming.

10

T he door creaked open and a lanthorn shattered the dark with its light. A figure stepped inside, then held the lamp up so his face was seen. He seemed taken aback to discover who was in the barn before him.

Laverstock dropped his hand from Lady Samantha's mouth and she sagged with relief. Charles remained alert and did not step away from her, desiring to offer her protection if needed. There seemed something decidedly odd about Twistleton's showing up at this time of night.

" 'Tis but Percival," said a very relieved Samantha. She stifled her desire to scold Laverstock for silencing her in such a rough manner. His rock-solid presence had been most comforting, she reluctantly confessed to herself.

"I say, you two, what is going on? I chanced to look out my window—couldn't sleep, you know—and saw a light down here. Curious, couldn't fathom what might be doing. This is a deuced odd place to hold a tryst, Laverstock." The look he cast at Lord Laverstock was anything but friendly.

Drawing further away from her foe-turned-guardian, Samantha shook her head at the family friend. "It is not as you might think, Percival. I am *not* here for a tryst with Lord Laverstock. Indeed, I had no notion he might appear. Took me quite by surprise." She absently rubbed that sore portion of her anatomy, darting a black look at his elegant lordship before casting a searching gaze at the dandy.

Percival strolled closer to the pair, both of whom looked remarkably guilty of something. "Good thing I ain't given to blackmail. I guess there might be a few souls amused by this scene." His eyes narrowed, perhaps in mirth, and then again, perhaps in speculation.

128

Samantha considered that peculiar smile. She thought she was acquainted with all of Percy's odd starts, but that smile and his expression were new.

Not desiring to reveal his concern, Charles shrugged, stepped away from Samantha, and sauntered toward the door, guiding Percival along with him. "Not really, old boy." Over his shoulder he tossed a word to her. "Be a love and put out the lanthorn when you come along, will you Samantha? And do not forget to lock up behind you." He dared not look behind him. The dagger-drawn look sent his way would undoubtedly be bone-chilling.

Sam watched the two men leave the barn with mixed emotions. Rather than spitting angry—which she had a right to be, mind you—she was extremely thoughtful. How Lord Laverstock would talk his way out of this predicament, she didn't know, but she was certain he would. No, she had something quite different on her mind. Something she must mull over, and hope to discuss with Lord Laverstock in the morning.

Gathering up the book and handkerchief, she lit her small candle, put out the lanthorn and hung it up on its nail, then exited the barn, locking the door tightly behind her. The night seemed darker, chillier than before. How she missed the comfort of Lord Laverstock—only as another person, she assured herself.

The candle held tightly in her hand was nearly dropped when a soft, very male voice came from behind her, startling her nearly out of her wits.

"What was that all about, Sam?"

"Alfred! What a fright you gave me. Did *you* have trouble sleeping as well?" Pulling her poise together Samantha offered the book to him. "I believe this is yours. Inscribe it to Aunt, will you? I suspect she would like that."

"You are evading the issue, Sam. Were you secretly meeting Laverstock? I saw how you eyed him this evening. Your papa would not care for any havey-cavey business, missy." He tried to sound the stern parent to her.

"Alfred . . . this is the outside of enough. I cannot tell you why I was in the barn, but safe to say the reason as innocent as a newborn babe. Almost," she amended, recalling the means by which the items came to be in the barn. Although it was not really a barn anymore, not having held animals for ages. "At any rate, it is very likely that Lord Laverstock wishes me to Jericho at this point. For whatever it was that brought him here is doubtless gone by this time."

"Hmm," murmured Alfred, seeming not convinced in the least. "With your father in London, George ought to be looking after you better than he does. You have been allowed to go your own way too often, dear cousin."

Anger rising within, Samantha halted, giving him a haughty stare which was totally lost in the darkness, unfortunately. "You may think what you like, but I get along quite nicely, thank you."

"And a husband? How will you marry well in this remote place with only George and Aunt Lavinia to attend to your future? I fear your father forgets about you." Genuine concern tinged his voice, touching Samantha in a vulnerable spot.

"Leave be, Alfred." Sam spoke softly in a gruff tone, a trace of her emotions revealed. That she was developing a sensitivity on the subject could be heard most plainly.

As they neared the house, Samantha put out her candle, preferring not to call attention to them any more than necessary. Who else might be looking out windows or lurking in shadows this night? "I am becoming a believer in your gothic tales, the way things have gone lately. This evening has taken at least a year off my life."

"I heard a crash. What happened?" Alfred assisted Samantha along the gravel path and up the steps to the side door he, too, had used. They stepped inside the house to find one hall candle lit, the house in silence. Lord Laverstock and Percival were not to be seen.

"I fell." Samantha liked her cousin, but she felt there was something smoky about his being out near the barn. All his talk about her future had deflected questions about his presence. Percival, then Alfred. What was going on about Mayne Court that she didn't know? It certainly intrigued her. Samantha dearly loved a mystery.

"So I gather." He glanced at the dusty seat of Sam's breeches. "It shows. Better get up to bed before Aunt Lavinia senses

;omeone is up and about.'' He stood by the stairs, waiting until Samantha had reached the top before going to the library.

Lord Laverstock turned from the fireplace where a small fire had been recently stirred up to a respectable blaze for a coolish night. ''She is safe inside? You think she will remain?''

Shrugging his shoulders, Alfred joined Laverstock. ''No telling, but I think she is satisfied to go to bed. I believe we both frightened her well and good.''

''I hope so. That young lady is entirely too venturesome. What she requires is a firm hand to keep her from harm's way.'' Laverstock gestured to a slender bottle of port. ''I helped myself.'' Alfred poured himself a glass, then the two drew up chairs by the fireside and sipped while gathering thoughts.

''Percival?'' Charles was becoming more and more convinced that the dandy had a traitorous scheme up his sleeve, but to find out what it might be . . .

Alfred shook his head. ''I cannot see him in the role, somehow, in spite of his needing funds till next quarter day. I would not like to think an old school friend to be a traitor. No, we must look elsewhere.''

''Lady Samantha seems to have an excuse.'' Laverstock studied the remaining port in his glass before transferring his gaze to his fellow investigator. He hoped his trust in Alfred was not misplaced. He had never erred in judgment of a man before, but there was always a first time.

''She would not confide in me . . . her own cousin. It is a rare mark of accord that she tells you. I'll not ask you to break her confidence, but I am glad she is innocent.''

''Oh, I didn't say that. Just that she has nothing to do with George's plans. Lady Samantha has her own problems apart from ours.'' He drained his port, then rose to splash a bit more in the glass.

''What does George say?'' Alfred found his liking for the faintly stuffy lord growing with each association. While he usually kept his thoughts to himself one felt instinctively that he was rock-solid dependable, a man to trust.

Finishing off his wine, Charles placed the glass on the table. ''George is a most remarkable young man. While a genius at his gliders and the like, he is curiously uninformed about the remainder of the world.'' He thought of ''Charlie Mayne'' and smiled. ''He can be depended upon if need be, however, if we can but impress upon him the necessity of security. The plans ought to be concealed, as well as locking that door.''

Alfred joined him as they returned to the hall and quietly walked up the stairs together. At the door leading to Alfred's room, they paused. Charles placed a hand on Alfred's shoulder. ''We shall see what the morrow brings. Perhaps we shall be fortunate. I hope so.''

Charles continued on down the hall, pausing outside Lady Samantha's room. Satisfied there was no light and that all was peaceful within, he went to his bed and finally slept. If his dreams were filled with a sleek tiger who roared, then purred at him, a golden-eyed animal with tawny hair and freckles on a pert nose, it would have been understandable.

Aunt Lavinia was most distracted next morning. She fluttered about the breakfast room, not settling to her usual tea and toast. Samantha found her there peering out of the window.

''Is there a problem, dear aunt?'' She hurried to slip an arm about the woman who had been mother and friend to her during all her growing-up years.

''Samantha, I fear we have a thief in the house. My handkerchief, the one your father sent to me, is missing. I did so adore it.'' Aunt dabbed at her eyes with a scrap of plain linen.

''Papa sent it?'' Sam asked in fading tones. ''Oh, dear. I thought you said you just picked it up because you simply had to have it. I saw it last night.'' Sam wasn't sure whether to credit this explanation or not.

''Yes, stuck to your dress for some peculiar reason. I have noticed things disappearing from time to time, so I took it to the barn, where I have hidden other valuables in the past. It was gone this morning when I decided to retrieve it. Gone! As to the other, I merely said that, you know. I did not wish Emma to be upset that she has gotten nothing from her parents. The girl is so sensitive.''

Aunt Lavinia's voice broke on these words and Samantha

turned away in dismay. Could that dainty white handkerchief actually have been a present from Papa? She couldn't recall any parcels coming to the house, but then, she was not always about.

"I shall see what I can do after I have broken my fast. I seem to be extra hungry this morning." Samantha decided she would quiz Peters—he always knew when parcels came—and if it was true, replace the handkerchief by the method suggested to her.

"Have you seen Percival this morning?" Aunt queried.

"No. I have not seen Emma, either. No one other than you. Why?"

"I read his tea leaves last night. I was of a mind not to tell him his future. I did not like what I saw in the least." Aunt seated herself next to Samantha, peering at her with an intent gaze.

"Percival? Surely you jest? I know of no one more harmless." Samantha chuckled as she indulged herself in an excellent breakfast.

"I have changed my opinion of that young man. Percival is like a jewel-bright frog sitting in the sun on a lily pad. His eyes do not miss a thing." Aunt Lavinia sipped from her tea cup, then took a dainty bite of toast before staring off into the distance.

Samantha gave her aunt an indulgent smile. "Dear ma'am, you know Percy does not have a thought in his head save the pattern of his waistcoat." Then her thoughts strayed to his appearance last night and the curious circumstance she knew regarding it. Did Percy watch the others while preparing to strike out at them? The very notion was preposterous. Was it not?

Polishing off her substantial breakfast in record time, she determined to seek out Lord Laverstock at the first opportunity. This came sooner than she expected. As she rounded the corner from the breakfast room on her way to find Peters, she bumped into the gentleman. Crashed might be a more apt description of the encounter.

"Ah, you are beginning to discover that it does not always pay to be so silent." Her smile at Lord Laverstock was sugar-sweet. Then she became serious, casting a wary glance about the spacious hall. "I must talk with you," she whispered, stepping as close to him as she dared.

Charles took one look at the intent little face so near to him, and ushered her to the library down the hall. "What is it?" He was normally not so terse, but he was devilishly sharp-set this morning. Traipsing about in the night made an fellow hungry. Even the sight of Lady Samantha in a golden gown and looking like a ray of purest sunshine didn't help.

"Last night Percival said he saw a light from his window. That is quite impossible, given the fact that his room is on the far side of the house and the windows face the opposite direction! Most peculiar, I should think. Is he up to something sneaky? And if so . . . what? Aunt said his tea reading of yesterday quite disturbed her. She would not tell me what it was! In fact, I do not believe she told *him* the whole of it. All she revealed was that she could not like it."

"Hmm," replied a thoughtful Lord Laverstock. He turned from the lovely vision of spring to pace about the room. Sam began to wander toward the window, narrowly averting a second crash when he suddenly stopped. "There are a number of things about young Twistleton that do not add up to a pleasing account. However, since we have nothing solid to pin upon him all we can do for the moment is watch and wait."

Samantha nodded sagely. "Of course. I shall do my best to keep alert in his regard. And you . . . you will take care, will you not? Aunt indicated she feared Percy for some odd reason. I wish she would confide in me instead of having some mistaken notion of protecting me."

"There are times when it is not in the best interest to maintain silence." He began to guide Lady Samantha toward the door, intent upon satisfying his hunger.

"Then why will you not tell me why you are here? I decided long ago it was not to court me. You have not the least aspect of a lover, you know. It stands to reason that there is another reason entirely." She peered up at him with an intense stare.

He coughed into a swiftly raised hand. The chit was most disconcerting. Had she actually thought he came up here to court her? Taking a look at the delectable face and form, he realized it was not all that repulsive an idea.

"There are other times when the least said, the better." He gazed into those golden pools that peered so entreatingly up at him, and deliberated how much to reveal. "Very well. Lord Cranswick, your father, has had a report there may be a spy in this vicinity. He sent me up here to check into the story, if there be any truth to it. Since George told me of the disturbance in the barn, we have been keeping watch on the place. Only you manage to interfere with our plans with annoying regularity. Could your aunt not find some other place to hide her purloined articles? Dash it all, a man cannot handle two plots at one time."

Sam thought his frustration actually rather charming, in an attractively boyish, and decidedly unstuffy, way.

"You need an assistant. I shall help you," she stated with decision. She offered her hand to him. "Partners?" She could not help but be pleased at the bemused expression on his face as he accepted her suggestion. The touch of his hand was warm, firm, and very agreeable. Bestowing one of her most beguiling smiles on the gentleman, Samantha then left the library in search of Emma.

Charles stood where she left him for a moment. Never in all the years in the service of his country had he been so nonplused. He preferred to work alone, or with men. Women only complicated things. He rubbed the back of his neck as he strolled to the breakfast room. There, over a breakfast as hearty as the one Samantha had consumed, he considered his plight. Lord Cranswick had not informed him of the dangers to be found in this job, the greatest of these being Lady Samantha. A fellow might expect a villain, but an enchantress with golden eyes?

"Emma? Are you up and about?" Samantha rapped on her cousin's door, then poked a curious head inside. Emma was cozily ensconced in her bed, pillows propped up behind her, while she sipped her morning chocolate.

"Join me, cousin. What plan you today?" Emma finished her chocolate, then leaned back against her pillows.

"I must try on my queen's dress. The festival day is fast approaching and I desire to look my best. Do you think Lord Laverstock will mind wearing white as well?"

Emma paused as she slid from her bed, giving Samantha a cautious look. "What do you mean?"

"I thought you knew. Lord Laverstock is to be May King. I expect you have been preoccupied. 'Tis no secret.'' This was announced with a good deal more nonchalance than Samantha felt.

"Never say so. How very droll. Does he know . . . everything to do with the position?'' Emma pulled on her wrapper, then joined Samantha by the window. Samantha had fixed her gaze on Percival, who was wandering about the garden.

"Hmm?'' Samantha recovered her attention and turned to smile at Emma. "No, but he will find out, will he not?'' She giggled with her usual glee and Emma smiled.

"You are a wicked girl."

"I know.'' Samantha twirled about, recalling the pleasure of serious conversation with Lord Laverstock. George never took her to heart, and it had been such a delight to have Lord Laverstock listen so intently. Though, to be honest, she really did believe Percival was acting in a most peculiar manner.

"When you are dressed and have had a bite to eat we shall drive into the village to have my last fitting. I wonder if I ought to inform Lord Laverstock about his garb yet?'' Sam walked to the door, suddenly recalling she must find Peters and quiz him about parcels.

"Oh, yes. The sooner, the better, I should say.'' Emma watched with misgivings as her younger cousin left the room.

Samantha hummed a little tune as she tripped down the stairs and went hunting for Peters. A conversation with him was most illuminating. It seemed a parcel had indeed been delivered to her aunt. That the dear lady had kept the information to herself was rather disturbing.

Back up in her bedroom, Sam retrieved the handkerchief from where she had hidden it the night before, then returned to the barn. Here she placed it in the most obvious place she could think of before departing in a rush. It would not do for Aunt to discover her anywhere near the scene of the reappearance.

In the breakfast room, she found Lord Laverstock preparing to quit the table. "Sir? I neglected to inform you of a minor matter.''

One glance at the innocent-looking face and Charles inhaled a cautious breath as he rose from the table to join her by the door. "And that is?"

"You are to dress in white for the festival." At his momentary flash of dismay, she added in defense, "It is customary. It is merely a costume."

He had been right. The day was going to make a total fool of him. He could envision himself decked in some silly outfit, draped with flowers, no doubt, and looking like a damned idiot. "What is the costume like?"

"It is styled after clothing of old; fifteenth century, I venture to guess. My dress is a simple gown; high waist, tight long sleeves, and full skirt."

"With a very low neck?" he inquired, a shade of amusement in his tone.

"With a very low neck," she agreed, not daring to meet his eyes. "I believe your costume is to have doublet and hose—the usual sort of thing."

The image of himself in a padded doublet, skin-tight hose, and tall boots with pointed toes was enough to make him wish he was far away. However, a gentleman did not go back on his word, and, after all, it was but for a day. "Where do I pick up this garb?"

Samantha sighed with relief. He was not going to be disagreeable about the matter. "I shall write you the directions at once. You would get the best choice by going to Scarborough this morning. I presume you do not fuss as to fit, as Percival might. Yet even George cares about his appearance."

Being compared to the dandy and the carelessly dressed genius was not a pleasant thing. It piqued his manly pride to realize that Samantha evidently did not consider him desirable. All the ladies in London had certainly fussed over him. Or was it his position and wealth they sought? he wondered. It was evident that Lady Samantha would not esteem those qualities as much as a man's individual excellence. She appeared to place much value on the person, not what he possessed. He found the notion appealing.

At this point Emma came down the stairs, hurrying up to Samantha. She curtsied to Lord Laverstock before addressing her cousin. "Alfred has said he will drive us into the village. I expect Aunt will come as well."

Did Alfred go with them to keep an eye on Sam's activities, or did he merely wish for Emma's company? Samantha nodded. "Have a bit to eat before we go. You will surely faint if you do not eat."

Emma shot a knowing look at her cousin before excusing herself and slipping away to the breakfast room.

"I believe I shall join the group," Laverstock said in a cool tone. "Perhaps after Alfred has accompanied you ladies to the dressmaker's shop, he can ride with me to Scarborough?"

"Saints forgive me, Samantha. The handkerchief was in the barn after all. I cannot see how I overlooked it. 'Tis no doubt a sign of my age." Aunt Lavinia came into the house waving the scrap of embroidered linen with a pleased expression on her face. A key dangled from her other hand.

There was no way that Samantha might have refrained from glancing at Lord Laverstock. The exchange was unnoticed by a fluttering Aunt Lavinia, but Sam felt the most uncommon lurch in her heart. His dark gray eyes were intent with shared concern, leaving Samantha nearly lightheaded with some strange emotion she could not identify. She would try to explain all to him later.

Shortly, Alfred and Emma joined the three in the hall and they all strolled to the waiting carriage and horses. Percival rode up to join them followed by George.

Laverstock frowned at the sight of the last person to join them.

Interpreting the concern briefly revealed, George rode over to where Laverstock now sat astride his horse. Leaning toward him, George spoke softly, "The plans are stowed and the barn locked. All should be well while we are gone. I have a fancy to check over Samantha's gown. Alfred tells me I have been remiss in that direction." He straightened, and took a good look at his younger sister in the carriage. "She has indeed grown up this past year. I expect one of these days Father will send up word of an impending marriage for her."

Lord Laverstock wore a serious face as the party left Mayne Court for the village. The very idea of Lady Samantha's being united with some stranger she had never even seen was

repugnant, never mind that it was an accustomed arrangement.
What if her father considered title and wealth, not giving thought
to Samantha's unusual sparkling nature?

Emma chattered away to Samantha and Alfred, who rode quite
close to the carriage. If Samantha was preoccupied, none took
notice, except perhaps Aunt Lavinia. But that dear lady was
unusually observant, her eyes not missing the expression on any
one of the faces about her. Truly, she had not been so diverted
for many years.

At the village dressmaker's shop, Samantha disappeared to
try on her costume while the others milled about in the tiny front
room of the place. Charles refused to leave for Scarborough.
"I feel I ought to see what Lady Samantha will be wearing
before I choose my costume. I would wish to find something
appropriate."

He caught sight of an altered awareness in Percival's eyes,
and turned to see Lady Samantha framed in the doorway. His
breath was caught somewhere in his chest. Never had he seen
anything quite so lovely.

Samantha entered the room feeling unaccountably shy and
not a little self-conscious. The tiny bodice of the silver tissue
dress hugged her curves rather daringly, she thought. And the
rounded neck was cut very low across her breasts. Rather
scandalous, was it not? The long, tight sleeves—the tips nearly
covering her hands—were not uncomfortable, but felt strange.
The full, heavy skirt, lined with white stiffener, swung about
in a disconcerting manner as she moved forward to where the
others stood in silence.

"I expect I ought to have some sort of headdress, but I much
doubt if I can cope with such a thing. I remember seeing one
on a tapestry at Mayne Court. They could not have been very
comfortable to wear." Anxiously, she sought the eyes of each
of the people in the room.

Percival peered at her with his usual narrow-eyed speculation.
Emma smiled, shaking her head in bemusement. George
appeared dumbstruck, while Aunt Lavinia seemed pleased.
Alfred looked as though he was trying not to laugh, the dratted
man. And Lord Laverstock—Sam turned to him last—studied

her with the air of one making a decision about something.

"You need a necklace, my dear," offered Aunt Lavinia. "Something wide and jeweled. I recall a piece belonging to your mother. When we return to the Court I shall find it for you. I believe it will be just the thing. 'Tis gold studded with topaz, quite right for your coloring." Aunt sighed, apparently with happy memories.

The vision in silver had stunned Charles. Could the little hoyden of the glider be this exquisite woman before him? She was breathtaking, so feminine and dainty. She had appeared lovely before, but not like this. He watched her pirouette about, the folds of the skirt belling out about her. She should not cover her glorious hair. It served as a brilliant foil for the gauzy dress. When the jewels were added, she would outshine anyone. What did it matter what he wore? With Lady Samantha at his side, who would see him? He met Alfred's amused gaze with resignation.

"You shall be the loveliest May Queen the village has ever had, Lady Samantha," Charles said, feeling his poor words sadly inadequate. "I count myself honored to be your escort for the day."

The lady seemed pleased, however. She grinned at him and curtsied. "Thank you, sir. I hope that you may feel the same by the end of the day."

Alfred laughed at that, then ushered the men from the dressmaker's. "We'd best get on our way now that you know what it is you must seek. Percy and George will come along with us. Did she give you directions?" He glanced at the proferred slip of paper, nodded with satisfaction, and the four set off toward the city of Scarborough.

Samantha tried to turn her eyes from their departure, but failed. Absently, she said to her aunt, "You feel it is proper?"

"Since when have you ever worried about such?" Seeing Samantha's crestfallen face, Aunt Lavinia added, "I feel 'tis lovely and faithful to the period. Mrs. Bates is a finer seamstress than I suspected."

Just then, Samantha caught sight of the Frenchman strolling past. Had he signaled to one of the four men on horseback as they rode off toward Scarborough? And if he had, which one?

11

"**Y**ou must be jesting! You don't mean to say I am to wear this damned thing!" Charles exploded as he gazed at his reflection in the mirror of the costume shop.

An enterprising tailor had set up a small side shop especially for festival affairs and costume balls, which seemed to be more popular than ever. With luck, he was sometimes able to purchase the contents of an attic chest, at other times he improvised. Today, the tailor beamed with pride at the man in the dressing area. A frown flashed in his eyes, quickly veiled, as he listened to the annoyed words.

Alfred attempted to soothe his new friend. "You look very handsome in the outfit, Laverstock. Not every man has legs as good as yours."

Charles glanced at the skin-tight, waist-high hose that seemed damned indecent to him, then the well-padded doublet with long sleeves and high neck. He accepted the long jerkin from the tailor and slipped it on, his ire fading as he realized the overgarment would conceal the most objectionable part of his attire. Reaching to mid-thigh, the white velvet was banded in a tawny fur Charles thought would compliment Lady Samantha very nicely.

"I suppose it will do," he grumbled, totally unlike his usual polite self. Apparently the tailor was prepared for the May Day festivities, as there were any number of white costumes available. Some looked ancient, others, like this one, were newly made. He turned to the tailor, nodding his assent. "Very well done. I shall take it."

Shortly after, the four men left the shop and wandered down toward the shore. Alfred looked about with keen eyes, motioning to Charles. "See the castle from here? Not much left of it now,

I'm afraid. Must have been a splendid place when Henry II used it for a time.''

Laverstock looked up to the ruins standing high on the headland, dominating the bay. The remains of the impressive keep rose above the tumbled stones of the curtain and barbican. ''It looks the sort of castle that would be complete with a dungeon and all the ghosts you could want.'' He slanted a crooked grin at Alfred and George laughed.

''I heard something last night,'' said George. ''Was that you hunting our poor old ghost again?'' He looked at the other two, then glanced to where Percival stood not far away. George decided to refrain from further comment, considering the guarded expression in Laverstock's eyes. It was impossible to tell if Percy had heard what they said or not. While unconvinced his old friend was suspect, Laverstock had raised a question.

''No, but I may try again one of these dark nights.'' Alfred chuckled. ''If you can keep that sister of yours in her room, that is. She has a way of upsetting things. I keep telling you that you must do better by her.'' He nudged George before looking to Lord Laverstock for confirmation.

Percival turned and walked over to join them. He gave Laverstock a curious look, before commenting, ''Samantha is a bit high-spirited, but a man could easily tame her.''

Deciding to say nothing, Charles wondered what method Twistleton favored for taming a young woman. Swatting with a scented handkerchief, no doubt.

''All the same, I shouldn't like to be wandering about that castle in the dark,'' muttered Alfred.

''Aye,'' agreed Laverstock. ''I seem to recall a number of deaths associated with the place. Doubtless you could take your pick of historical ghosts there. Let's see, George Fox, for one, if I recall from my history. How about you, George?''

George clapped Alfred on the back and chuckled at Laverstock. ''Alfred, here, can tell you I am no lover of history.''

Recalling the family's story of Charlie Mayne, Alfred grinned back at George, then added in a more serious vein, ''There is a postern down below. I suspect many a person has crept out through that small gate to slip away to the water's edge where a boat might carry him or her across the sea. Convenient exit, especially if you were in a hurry to leave.''

''I imagine it would be handy for a smuggler—if you could locate the postern from the outside, that is. Dashed hard to find, that gate,'' added George, remembering a summer's visit to the castle some years ago.

''Seems rather dank and nasty if you ask me,'' muttered Percival, sniffing in disdain.

Alfred gave Percy a twinkling look. ''Aye. There is a deep well in the upper bailey; bottomless, they say. Handy spot to drop unwanted cargo . . . or persons, if so inclined. Who knows how many bodies lie in the depths of that castle?''

Giving an affected shudder, Percival turned away from the sight of the castle and its haunting aspect.

The four wandered off in search of an inn where they could slake their thirst and perhaps have a bit of cheese and bread before returning to Mayne Court for dinner.

The delicate silver tissue dress was hung up by a notably pleased Hetty. ''About time you come over the lady, Missy,'' she pronounced with the familiarity of a servant of long standing. ''Been good to see you wearin' those pretty gowns your papa sends up from town, too.''

''I vow 'tis a lovely creation. Although I could never consider such a public appearance as being the May Queen, I somewhat envy you, Samantha.'' Emma's voice was wistful as she fingered the fabric of the skirt.

''What troubles you, dear Emma? I expect it must have to do with Alfred. Is he ghost hunting again? Or merely ignoring you?'' Samantha attempted to tease, but her words had not the desired effect.

Emma bowed her head, clasping her hands before her. ''Will you try to find out what his problem is? You said you would.'' She crossed to stand by the window, looking out to the road which led from the village. ''I wonder when they will return?''

''Scarborough is a longish ride, but if I know the four of them, they will make short work of the miles. No more than a few hours and they will be here, I should say. If I can separate Alfred from the others, I will do my best to uncover the truth of the matter. Do you wish to know what that might be, regardless?''

"Trust you to carve to the bone," said Emma with a rueful compression of her lips.

"There are times when it is for the best. Very well, then. So be it." Samantha gave a decisive nod, then went to the door, towing Emma along with her. Hetty watched them depart with a fond smile.

The two girls sauntered down the stairs, each much absorbed in her own thoughts.

Samantha had turned her reflections to Lord Laverstock. He had seemed pleased with her gown, or—more likely—had he simply been reconciled? His behavior was decidedly odd, however. Downright smoky, if you considered his turning up at the barn last night.

Could he really be here to find a spy? Did her father actually suspect there was one locally? Just because the new dancing master was a Frenchman did not mean he was a spy. Perhaps she ought to take a few lessons? She could acquire a bit of polish along with the newest steps, and maybe discover something of value? After the May Day festival she would tend to the matter.

But why send a stuffy man like Laverstock? Was it because no one would ever believe Laverstock was the sort to be a spy hunter? He had certainly not been obvious in his purpose since his arrival. Jaunts about the countryside, trips to the village, and those midnight trysts—or whatever they were—at the barn where George kept his plans. What did Laverstock intend? To trap the man with the plans in hand? If so, her appearance last night must have annoyed him considerably.

If they could but work together in this effort, she could know what was intended. And if she had refrained from telling him all, she had no doubt that he in turn would tell her only what was necessary. Men seemed to have so little regard for women's brains. They treated a woman as though her mind were inferior.

Deciding that it was no use to wander restlessly about the house, Samantha decided on a course of action.

"I believe I shall go back to the village to inspect the maypole. Do you wish to come along?" Sam asked her cousin. She ignored the threatening clouds on the horizon. They might not reach the vicinity until tonight.

"I promised Aunt I would check on the maids this afternoon. It is becoming more difficult for Hetty to see if the girls do their work properly."

Shrugging off the feeling that she ought to be doing the same, Samantha nodded, then sped down the stairs and out to the stables, where she ordered the small whiskey hitched up. Shortly, she tooled along the lane, one of the maids seated alongside her in uneasy silence.

The maypole looked ready to set up on the center of the green. Painted in the traditional red, white, and blue stripes, it would soar impressively in the sky when erected. Long ribands had been attached to the top and several young men, together with a pair of sturdy horses, prepared to bring it about. Samantha watched in the sheltered safety from her seat in the whiskey.

Had it been but a few days since she had strolled down the village street with Lord Laverstock? Each day seemed to be crammed with so much activity. Not to mention the nights, she added in reflection.

As she sat in the shade of one of the elms that skirted the edge of the green, she saw Lord Laverstock, George, Alfred, and Percival come dashing along the road from Scarborough. They were on the far side of the green, unaware that she watched them. She had judged them rightly; they looked as though they had traveled hard and fast.

Lord Laverstock spoke briefly to Alfred, then wheeled away from the others, heading down the main street of the village. Alfred motioned to Percival and George, and the three set off in the direction of the Court. Sam had not been observed, having decided to remain discreetly in the shadows.

Samantha handed the reins to the maid, then clambered down from the carriage. "I shan't be but a moment. I recollect I need a paper of pins." As an excuse, it was rather poor, but the maid accepted it meekly.

Sam hurried along the street, ducking into doors, turning her back, bending her head so her bonnet might conceal her face. She doubted he would notice her bonnet. Men seldom paid attention to such details. At least George did not. At last she saw Laverstock vault from his horse, handing the reins to a groom outside the Blue Lion Inn.

The inn! This was where the Frenchman was staying. Did Laverstock seek information . . . or did he meet with the spy to plot? She could not accept the thought of that. Her dear papa would not have anything to do with that kind of man. Besides . . . she liked Lord Laverstock . . . far too well.

Samantha leaned against the wall, ignoring the curious look of a passerby. When she had extended her hand in trust, asking they be partners, she hadn't considered this. Since there was no manner in which she might get close to the inn to do a bit of her own inquiry, Samantha returned to where she had left the whiskey.

A gentle, misty rain began to fall, and Sam hurried the horse along—the road could get such nasty ruts when wet.

It was about a quarter of a mile from home that the carriage became stuck. There was nothing to do but get down and lead the dratted horse and carriage through the mud that rapidly formed in the soft earth. Previous ruts were becoming even deeper. Really, someone ought to invent a better road. Now, that was something George might do that would be of real service.

Sam handed the reins to the maid, then climbed down. A poke at a stone freed the whiskey. Her umbrella in one hand, the other hand at the horse's head, Sam plodded along the road, sorry she had left the pleasant house for her restless curiosity. Had she not taken it into her head to follow Lord Laverstock to the inn, she could have been tucked cozily by a window, looking out at the rain, instead of struggling through it. "Oh, drat!" she exclaimed, as her slipper was lost in a puddle.

She spotted a stick, stopped the horse, retrieved her sodden slipper, and slipped it on. A soggy slipper was better than nothing at all on her foot.

The sound of a horse splashing through the forming puddles brought her head around. "Ah, Lord Laverstock," she called, as he rode up to join her. "This time you could not be silent. I heard you coming."

"You have a problem?" The look she bestowed on him was far from a sweet smile. More like an acid bath, he decided.

"No. I always walk the horse through the mud like this. 'Tis such a jolly thing to do on a rainy day." She was annoyed to see he did nothing other than observe her plodding along in the rain, her increasingly wet umbrella in one hand, her soggy slippers making peculiar noises with each step she took. If only she'd had the foresight to wear her half-boots when she had hurried from the house.

"I make no doubt I will catch an inflammation of the lungs ere long if I keep at this much more," she said with a disgusted tone.

"It does you credit you leave your maid in the carriage." The young girl huddled under a sensible cloak and hood. Apparently she was better prepared than her mistress. He observed a shed not far from the road and rode to Samantha's side. Leaning over, he scooped her up beside him, then took the reins to lead the horse and carriage off the muddy road.

The shed was partly open on one side, but it afforded protection from the rain and slight breeze. Samantha shivered, wondering if it was Lord Laverstock's touch or merely the damp that affected her.

Laverstock helped the maid from the carriage, then took a rug to wrap about Lady Samantha. "Your bonnet is quite ruined," he observed.

Sam pulled it off and tossed it aside. "How right you are. Fortunately, it is not one I cared much for." She raised her gaze to meet his. His hands felt warm, right through the wool of the rug. What was he thinking? That she had gotten herself into another pickle? She must certainly give him a disgust of her. Sam looked away from him in dismay.

The rain had become more of a drizzle. Laverstock studied the now averted face. What was in her head? Something was clearly bothering her. Had she seen him while she was in the village? It was possible. He decided to say nothing for the moment. The maid had ears and a tongue that probably could wag with the best.

Samantha's red-gold hair was the only thing that looked warm in the gray, misted landscape. It glowed as though lit with a fire of its own. Charles took a lingering look at the vibrant face and hair, then prudently decided he'd best get help before they all took cold. She was far too tempting.

"I'll go to the stables. There ought to be someone there who can fetch the carriage.'' He left her side with reluctance. There was something about the little hoyden that continually drew him. He managed to mount his horse and turned toward the Court. ''You will be all right?''

Samantha glanced up to where he sat astride his horse, water now dripping from his hat, his parcel tucked inside a leather satchel the only thing between them that was likely to be dry. ''I shall manage, thank you,'' she said stiffly.

He failed to answer, but tore off toward the stables, splashing through assorted puddles. Drat the man. The maid sneezed loudly. Sam huddled close to her, realizing that Lord Laverstock had considered the health of both young women by leaving them together rather than taking Sam up before him. She wished she could feel more grateful.

When one of the grooms came dashing across the puddle-dotted road to assist Samantha, she revised her hasty opinion of Lord Laverstock. She hurriedly mounted the horse he had ridden, and lost no time getting home, while the maid and groom were left to deal with the carriage and the rutted road. That the groom would have them all snug and dry within a short while, Samantha had no doubt.

Within minutes she was at the stables, handing the reins to another groom, then hustling up the steps and into the blessedly warm and dry interior of the house.

The first person she saw was Laverstock. ''I must thank you for your help, sir.'' She didn't trust herself to say more, rather she whisked up to her room to change to warm clothes, then—mindful of her commission—hunt out her cousin Alfred.

She shortly discovered Alfred poking about the state rooms, thanks to the eagle eye of Peters, who saw a great deal more of what went on in the house than anyone realized. Sam entered the state bedroom to find him peering behind a portrait on the far wall.

''What do you expect to find there, if anything?'' Samantha sought to engage Alfred in conversation, hoping to bring him around to the subject of Emma.

''There must be something to substantiate the tales that have

been passed down through the family these past generations.
I intend to leave no stone, or picture, unturned." Alfred turned
a quizzical eye to his cousin.

Samantha seated herself on a marble bench after brushing it
off. Two of the maids had just done the annual cleaning of the
room, so the dust was minimal. Sam hugged her shawl about
her, thankful for a warm gown and stockings that, while not
fashionable, were comforting to chilled feet. This room was
faintly damp and chilly.

"Do you suppose the ghosts would object if we lit a fire in
here?" Samantha watched Alfred continue to prowl.

"I expect it would be good for the furnishings . . . and you.
You look as though a blizzard were raging outside. What
brought that about?" Alfred gave her an amused glance before
he began exploring the exquisitely carved wood paneling.
Acanthus brackets and scrolls framed the portraits hung on the
walls; a flowing pattern of richly carved shells and palm fronds
decorated the surface over the doors and around the cornices.

Deciding action to be preferable to huddling, Samantha
crossed to the fireplace, found the tinder box, then started a
small blaze. She knelt on the hearth, rather liking the cozy
warmth. Rain beat against the window panes, a puff of smoke
came out every now and again, bringing the pungent scent of
burning apple wood into the room. She turned to face Alfred,
enjoying the heat on her back.

"You know how restless I can be at times. I decided to take
a ride into the village to see how the maypole progressed." She
reflected, "With this rain, they will not get it up today."

He paused his inspection, giving her a searching look. "You
were in the village about the time we returned from Scarborough?"

Avoiding his probing gaze, Samantha turned to poke at the
fire. "I may have been."

"No games, Sam."

"Then what are you about with Emma?" She swiftly turned
to glare at him. "You have her most confused, you know. One
moment you are fawning over her, the next you treat her as
though she was beyond the moon."

Leaning against the wall decorated with fine examples of the York school of wood carvers, Alfred crossed his arms to study his cousin. "You are changing the subject."

"So are you. I dearly love Emma, and I do not care for the manner in which you treat her." Sam studied him in return, searching his face for some clue to his feelings. Had her words been precipitate?"

"Did she ask you to speak to me?"

"How presumptuous of you, to assume she might be that concerned about such a thing." Sam glanced away, knowing full well she was a poor dissembler.

He left the wall to draw closer to where she knelt on the hearth. Sighing with the futility of his interest, he said, "You may as well know the whole of it. I am well and truly captured by the fair lady. I have been for some time. But, Samantha, consider this—she is of a higher rank, the daughter of an earl and titled. I am but a younger son of a younger son."

"And no title? Pooh! As if that would bother a woman as fine as Emma. You have an income as large as *she* might wish. Supplemented by your writing, I daresay it is quite handsome. Though there is no title, there is some money. It has been my observation that genteel money is to be preferred to titled impoverishment."

"The sudden expert." He strolled about the room, seemingly studying the divisions in the paneling. "There are unexpected breaks in the wood here. I wonder why?"

"Pray, do not evade the issue. What do you intend to do about it, now that you know a lack of title does not bar the way to Emma's heart?"

"That is for me to know, and you to wait to discover, my inquisitive little cousin." Alfred chuckled at her look of annoyance.

"Bah! You and your silly ghosts." Samantha rose from the hearth and flounced toward the door. She paused as a sound came from the other side, somewhere in the hall. She glanced back to meet Alfred's gaze, then hesitantly moved to reach for the lever. As it turned before she could touch it, Samantha backed away, retreating to a safe distance.

"Silly?" taunted Alfred softly.

"Of course not," whispered Samantha.

The door slowly opened and Lord Laverstock stepped inside, raising his brows at the sight of a dismayed Samantha and a highly amused Alfred. Charles gave them a tentative smile. "Nothing amiss, I trust? Your butler said you were to be found in these parts. I checked the room next door first." Turning to Samantha, he inquired, "You are none the worst for your wetting? In the future it might be best to heed the clouds."

"I keep telling George that she needs a closer watch on her," murmured Alfred. "Who knows what she may get up to next? As if being the May Queen weren't enough."

Laverstock turned a shrewd gaze upon Alfred. "Is there something I ought to know before then?"

Shrugging, Alfred threw Sam a taunting look, as though to imply that if she would interfere in his life, he could in hers. "I am certain she has told you about the morris dancers, the archery contests, and the procession to gather alms for the church?"

"She has." Charles had a feeling all had not been said about the subject. "And?"

"Did she happen to mention that the king must kiss the queen at each donation?" When Laverstock assumed a startled expression, Alfred laughed.

It was a rather nasty little laugh, Samantha thought. "Well, if you do not require me here, I'd best be going. George wishes to talk to me about the next test of the glider. I did mention I may go up tomorrow, weather permitting?" Samantha batted those long, sooty lashes at the two surprised men and sashayed sideways toward the door, intending to open it swiftly so she might leave while the leaving was good. She was not quite fast enough.

Lord Laverstock proved he must be adept as a fencer, for his footwork was excellent. He rested his hand on the door panel, preventing Samantha from the exit she had thought rather clever.

"You consent to this . . . this spectacle?"

Sam couldn't decide what his tone of voice meant. Did he

disapprove or was he merely curious? "Of course," she replied with far more outward confidence than she inwardly felt. "It is for a worthy cause, and surly a peck on the cheek is not so scandalous."

Her eyelashes hadn't saved her the first time, perhaps they might do better now? She tried and met no success.

Crossing his arms before him in mock displeasure, Charles began to enjoy himself. So the chit thought he could be handled so tamely, did she? "I wonder at your temerity, Lady Samantha. Surely you do not expect a man to settle for a mere peck on the cheek."

"Why not?" she demanded in her usual forthright manner. Samantha seldom practiced feminine wiles and hers were sadly rusty.

He shrugged—so very elegantly, she thought with growing unease. This was not going precisely as she had envisioned.

"It would be a slur upon my masculinity, to be sure. Right, Alfred?" He made the query without looking at the other man. Indeed, it seemed to Samantha that his eyes fair bored a hole in her.

"Oh, pooh," she said, hoping to bluff her way out the door. "I am not such a ninny-hammer as to believe that taradiddle."

Alfred wandered away to examine some carving on the farthest side of the room.

Charles decided this young miss was badly in need of a lesson. He stepped forward suddenly to clasp her arms, looking down into those golden-amber eyes so wide with apprehension. "And then again, perhaps we are in need of a bit of practice. Something tells me you have not a wealth of experience in this business of kissing."

"No!" Samantha tried to break free, then stood still, reaching the conclusion it was best not to make an undignified struggle.

"I thought not," Charles whispered, amused to see the pretty cream-tinted cheeks suffused with deep peach-pink. He bent his head, intending to take a mere taste of a kiss. It was then that all his preconceived notions of kisses were shattered.

The touch of her lips was as sweet as ripe berries, heady as fine champagne. Samantha's very innocence was stirring. A delightful scent enveloped her, like lilies after a rain. Her slender body for a moment yielded against his, and he knew that Samantha was most definitely the greatest danger he faced, here or anywhere.

He lifted his head to gaze down at her, the taste of her lingering to tantalize him. Alfred cleared his throat, but neither Samantha nor Charles heard him.

"I believe we shall do quite well . . . if you are not put to the blush every time." His voice was soft and almost caressing.

Samantha gave him a wary look. Her heart was bound to return to normal soon, and surely her legs must still function. "That remains to be seen, does it not? Now, I had best seek out George. And remind me to see if Emma can wear my dress . . . just in case something happens to me when I go up in the glider. You may not have to worry about your performance—at least not with me." She tossed him what she hoped was a saucy look, then made good her escape.

Behind her, Laverstock turned to Alfred, an expression of utter frustration on his face. "She would not!"

"Indeed she would."

12

"Men can be so tiresome," Sam announced the following morning as she trod the rain-washed path to where she was to meet George for the test of the newly designed elevator.

Emma, having decided to brave the sight of Samantha soaring across the valley, was walking alongside her. She smiled and answered, "Oh, I think not."

"But then," Sam countered, "you do not have a brother seemingly bent on breaking your neck."

"True. No brother at all, as a matter of fact. Will Alfred be there to assist George?" Emma's attempt at nonchalance failed with the newly perceptive Samantha.

She frowned. That had been up in the air, as of last night. "I have a sinking feeling that George will have both Alfred and Lord Laverstock at his side today. They seemed remarkably curious. I expect Percy is still lolling in bed." Sam was not best pleased at the unsettling notion of Lord Laverstock anywhere in sight. His brief kiss had turned her world upside down, and she had not yet righted her tumbled emotions.

"I fail to see why you must wear those horrid breeches and shirt today. Could you not manage to guide the craft while wearing something a little more . . . ladylike?" Emma had sensed the unspoken, that her fun-loving, adventuresome cousin had developed a tendre for Lord Laverstock. Emma considered it highly unlikely that the elegant marquess would seriously consider a hoyden in breeches as his future marchioness.

Shaking her head, Sam chuckled, refusing to admit that she quite liked the idea of appearing before Lord Laverstock in something more feminine. While playing her lute last evening, she had felt that she looked most unexceptionable in her peacock

green jaconet gown trimmed with embroidery. Yet Lord Laverstock had ignored her all evening to chat with George and Alfred
about the possibilities of good weather and the prospects for
the proper operation of the newly designed elevator. Percival
had attempted to soothe her sensibilities with pleasant
compliments and kind words about her music, but Samantha
had found it difficult not to glare past him at the men on the
far side of the room.

Drat it all! *She* was the one who would pilot the soaring craft.
She ought to have been consulted instead of being treated like
someone lacking the wit to comprehend air flow and levers and
the like. It was she who had felt the tug of the wind, maneuvered
the direction of the glider, while the men remained safely on
the ground.

Samantha had tried to direct her gaze elsewhere than at the
three men near the fireplace last night, but it had been difficult.
Lord Laverstock had looked exceptionally handsome in his buff
breeches, claret silk vest, and deep blue coat. He (or his valet)
had a clever way with a cravat that George would do well to
emulate.

Now, George, Alfred, and Laverstock stood by the craft
examining the wheels. George was evidently explaining their
design and construction. To save weight, they were fashioned
of thin layers of tough wood that had been wound around each
other on a cylindrical form, then cemented with some kind of
special glue, something George had obtained from a ship
builder. When they were dry, George had fixed these hoops
to a light axle by thin wires. He had told Samantha the tension
enabled these wheels to be stronger than other, heavier wheels.
Although she was not totally convinced, she admitted the new
wheels had done well when she landed so precipitously on her
first flight.

"Halloo," called out Emma, bringing the combined gaze of
the men around to where the two girls walked toward them.
George grinned and waved an arm. He looked happy, assured.
Samantha felt terribly proud of him. She would have been
immeasurably more pleased had Lord Laverstock been absent.

Never before had Samantha felt so conspicious in her
breeches. With each step she now took, she was aware of how

they clung to her thighs, hugged the gentle curve of her hips, nipped in at her tiny waist. Lavinia had cried they were most immodest. And so they probably were.

Well, Samantha shrugged inwardly, once Lord Laverstock discovered whether or not a French spy dwelt in their midst, he would be gone, and life could revert to what it had been. But she knew in her heart that was not true. Nothing could ever be the same again. He had kissed her with gentleness, yet with a depth of feeling that shattered her fond ideas of her future.

"How does it look?" Samantha cast an expert eye over the elevator, dismissing from her thoughts the effect of her attire. The new shape of the elevator appeared capable of providing good control of height. She ran a tentative finger over the curved prow of iron, supposed to ease the shock of landing. This was a decided improvement over plain wood. She knew only too well how wood could splinter.

George turned back to run a hand over the glider's upper surface, thumping a finger against the smooth fabric. "So you see," he concluded what must have been his explanation, "it was in the Cayley article that I read four years ago in *Nicholson's Journal* that I got the idea to build this." He patted the taut canvas sail with a fond hand. "That is where I learned the importance of lightness. And why," he glanced at Samantha, "we are forced to use Sam today. She is light in weight, and intelligent enough to pilot properly."

"Nicely said, brother, dear. I must take care not to let that extravagant praise go to my head." Samantha walked away from the group to check the inner part of the craft, where she soon would sit once more. Running a finger along one of the bracing wires, she calmed her annoyance.

"He means well, you know," Alfred said over her shoulder. " 'Tis not in George to mince words, nor give praise lightly. If he says you are intelligent, you can accept it as truly meant."

Samantha turned to bestow a rueful smile on her cousin. "I know his words are kindly intended. I truly do care about him and his work." She glanced across the valley, then down at her attire. "I fear I am not a very proper female, am I? 'Tis a wonder I am not shunned. At times I . . . I wish that things could be a bit different.'' She pressed her lips together as though she had said too much.

This intriguing subject was dropped as the other men joined them beside the glider. Samantha stepped away as the men prepared for the launch.

The delicate-looking craft was pushed into place, then Samantha climbed inside and gave the assembled group a brave smile. Why was it she felt so tremulous this time? Emma's attendance made no difference. Aunt Lavinia waved her white handkerchief—no doubt the new one—from the other side of the valley. It was the presence of Lord Laverstock that made her altered feelings, she admitted. She tried to concentrate on George's instructions.

The sun touched Sam's hair with gold before she had tucked it under the silly jockey cap once again. She took a deep breath, then called to George. ''I am as ready as I shall ever be. You may as well tow me now. And you,'' she pointed to Lord Laverstock, ''you can go to the far side to catch the bits and pieces.''

Charles took a step toward her, then checked himself upon seeing her wide grin and twinkling eyes. The minx. If she but knew how her words had hit him like a blow. He ran down the hill and up the other side in record time. He would wait here and catch her in his arms, if need be. She would not die if he could help it.

The wind was gentle, the flow of air just right. The men pulled on the strong ropes until the glider bounced over the turf toward the edge of the hill.

Emma sat down rather hard as she watched, fear touching her tender, sensible heart. She had wanted to protest, to remind them that if the good Lord had wished them to fly like birds, they would have been given wings. But she couldn't. Samantha had flown before; she would again. Understanding what propelled her daring cousin was beyond Emma. She could only pray that again Samantha would emerge alive and her usual sparkling self. Emma hadn't missed the frequent, annoyed glances of last evening, nor who received them. Poor Samantha. She was doomed to a broken heart, even if she survived the flight.

Sam was aloft, flying like a bit of thistledown above the valley. It was like one of those Chinese kites George loved so much, only this "kite" had a woman on board. She soared high—at least fifty feet in the air—startling a number of curious sea gulls who screeched and darted away toward the east.

The new elevator worked perfectly. Samantha felt a growing sense of power as she controlled the direction and angle of flight. Up! To the side! Down! Everything was as George had hoped.

Her feeling of elation grew as she drifted over the valley observing her brother standing tall, waving proudly at her. Alfred and a silly Emma waltzed over the daisy-speckled grass. Aunt Lavinia waved her fluttering scrap of white in the air. She had assured Samantha that all would go well, she had read it in the tea leaves this morning as she had on the day of that first flight.

Only Lord Laverstock seemed reluctant to celebrate and Samantha gave him high marks for his caution. Had he sensed her fear that this time she might not fare so well in her landing? Samantha felt in her bones it was the most dangerous time for her. Last time she had been shaken up. What would happen this time?

She was skimming toward the ground on the far side of the valley, her heart in her throat. Lord Laverstock stood on the edge of the tree-studded slope. The expression on his face could not be seen clearly at this distance, but she somehow felt reassured knowing he was there.

Her hand on the steering bar trembled slightly as she tilted the elevator, holding the rudder stable. The ground seemed to rise to meet her and she tried to recall what it was George had told her to do when she landed. His ideas hadn't worked too well last time, so now she merely held the glider steady, raising the nose to prevent the sort of damage that had occurred on the first flight.

There was a bump, followed by a bounce, and she was on the ground. Safe. Lord Laverstock rushed to her side, pulling her from the craft, holding her very close in comfortingly strong arms. Samantha clung to him a moment, ignoring her jockey cap, which again flew away to the grass below.

"It was wonderful!" exclaimed Emma, tightly hanging on to Alfred's hand, with great joy—and relief—beaming from her face. Looking at the glowing Emma, Samantha couldn't tell if her happiness was for Samantha's achievement or simply for being with Alfred.

Alfred gave a lopsided grin and added, "Well done, Samantha, old girl."

George strode up to inspect the construction of wood, wire, and canvas, checking to see if damage had been done in the landing. He turned to where Lord Laverstock now quietly stood, close to Samantha in a very protective attitude.

"You see, this will land safely with the new design," George said enthusiastically. "Once we can arrange for it, I believe it really can be lifted up beneath a balloon. They tried something like it with a parachute in 1797. I think this could not only be steered but flown for quite some distance, which could not be done with a mere parachute. Cayley figured it ought to sail perhaps five to six times the distance horizontally that the balloon is above the earth. You see how the maneuverability of the glider is superior to the less controllable balloon. The pilot can exercise a surprising amount of direction. I think I shall use silk for the sail next time," he said reflectively.

Charles gave George a severe look. "But not, I think, with your sister at the helm."

That George was startled by this statement was most clear. He might have questioned Laverstock's defense of Sam, but for the appearance of Percival. The dandy walked slowly toward them, taking great care not to damage his pantaloons on any of the bushes along the path. Aunt Lavinia joined him, her expression curious. They all watched as the grooms hurried up the hill. Once at the glider, the grooms, along with George and Alfred, picked up the craft to return it to the barn.

Percival observed all this with a remote expression on his face. "I trust you suffered no ill effects?" he inquired of Samantha in a bored, but extremely polite voice.

Beside her, Lord Laverstock stiffened. Samantha lightly touched his arm in a warning gesture. "I fared quite well, thank you." She was disappointed. All the others had been so happy

she had flown and was now safe. Percival had flashed her a
pettish look before his usual mask of indifference dropped over
his features.

Aunt Lavinia drifted forward to inspect her wayward niece.
"I believe that now your part is done and over with, you can
proceed to the house to change." She sniffed with distaste at
the picture Samantha presented in her tight breeches. White silk
stockings displayed shapely calves and ankles. The worn linen
shirt revealed the delicate lace trim of the shift underneath. It
seemed Samantha had omitted her stays this morning, and it
showed. Most improper.

A glance at Lord Laverstock told Lavinia that his lordship
was probably well aware of Samantha's lack of decent under-
garments. Might as well kiss the notion of a marchioness in
the family good-bye. He was fastidious in all he wore and did.
Lord Laverstock had been a jolly good sport about this flying
business, but there was a point beyond which—well, Lavinia
knew. Samantha could be left behind. The tea leaves had never
failed before, but then, Samantha defied all odds with her
behavior.

"Dear, you and Lord Laverstock ought to present yourselves
in the village. Now the sun has dried up the ground sufficiently,
they will raise the maypole and decorate it properly. You both
should be there to observe. Perhaps the others will wish to join
you? You will wish to change, Samantha." She moved closer
as though to hide Samantha from the others. "Remember,
tomorrow is to be a busy day."

Lavinia took Samantha by the arm, leaving Lord Laverstock
and Twistleton glaring at each other before they fell in behind
the ladies.

"I believe your pretty white muslin, the new one your papa
sent up to you not too long ago, will do quite nicely for this
afternoon." Lavinia chattered on, little caring that her niece
paid her scant attention.

The four were joined by Emma and Alfred near the house.
Emma looked radiant, though she darted frequent puzzled
glances at Alfred.

Samantha deduced that Alfred had not sought to explain his
feelings or position to Emma. Men! They really were most

tiresome, Samantha concluded once again. Witness Lord
Laverstock. That he had been worried about her safety was quite
evident. Yet, now it was as though nothing had occurred.
Odious, horrid man. If only she did not care one whit about
his opinion. The trouble was—she did.

In Samantha's room, Hetty waited with a soft white muslin
dress that displayed the skill of the finest dressmaker to be found
in London. It had an elegance of style not expected in such
simplicity. Samantha could not help but be pleased with the
result. Her papa certainly revealed a nicety of taste. Proper, too.

Breeches and shirt were tossed aside; for once Samantha
hoped she might not have to don them again. Then she stretched
out her arms to welcome the dainty new dress she hadn't fully
appreciated before now. The skirt had a flounce, an advantage
for her with her tendency to forget narrow skirts and their
restrictions. She tied her neat little bonnet on, pleased with the
small white plume that curled about the brim. Smoothing wrist-
length white gloves over her fingers, she left her room with
high hopes.

Downstairs, she found Lord Laverstock waiting for her. It
hadn't been necessary for him to change, yet he looked as though
he had stepped from a painting on the wall, so impeccable did
he appear. The walk from the landing site had left him in good
order. And helping Samantha from the glider had disturbed his
attire not one whit. Percival would have to look to his laurels.

"Charming." Charles bowed to the young lady he was to
escort. One would never know she was the little hoyden of an
hour past. It was difficult to put aside the memory of her appeal
in those snug breeches and that soft shirt that had clung to her
full young breasts with disturbing effect. Try as he might, he
found that vision superimposing itself over the now well-covered
form.

He was not happy about the proposed trip to the village. It
seemed a lot of nonsense to him. However, he concealed his
impatience admirably, ushering Lady Samantha out to the landau
with nice courtesy.

It was obvious to Emma that Samantha felt ill at ease next
to the elegant Lord Laverstock. Exquisitely polite, Lord
Laverstock could be rather intimidating to a girl such as her

impetuous cousin. Emma smoothed out her soft silk gloves, then shyly glanced at Alfred seated so cozily next to her. Something had altered between them, yet she wasn't quite certain what it was. All she knew was that she was extremely happy. If only Samantha might be as joyful when the May Day celebration was over and gone.

Touching the treble ruff of pointed lace around her neck with a nervous finger, Samantha decided that her dress was most decorous. Lord Laverstock—indeed, the fustiest person—could not find any fault with it in the least. Long, rather full sleeves ended at the wrist in dainty lace which fell over her gloved hands. From beneath the broad flounce of the skirt peeked the toes of her slate-colored slippers. Anyone looking less a hoyden, she couldn't imagine. Yet she could see the expression on Emma's face and sense a stiffness in Lord Laverstock. Or was it merely that he wished he was elsewhere? George always fought occasions such as this. Perhaps Lord Laverstock was merely bored. Samantha devoutly hoped that was the case.

It was Percival who commented on Samantha's appearance from where he sat on the other side of Emma. "You look most lovely this afternoon, Lady Samantha."

Her eyebrows rose a bit at his use of her rank. That was unlike Percy, who usually was most informal with her. Perhaps he was inspired by her ladylike image. She nodded at him graciously, repressing a grin with difficulty. "Thank you, Percival." How could she be suspicious of a gentleman who noticed what she wore and complimented her on how nice she looked?

The group entered the village green to the sight of the artistically painted maypole in the process of being erected. Samantha was impressed at the height. She had been here every year she could remember for this celebration, but this year everything looked bigger, brighter, and fancier. More daunting, too.

"The maypole is an ancient fertility emblem, you know," teased Alfred, darting a look at the proper Lady Emma by his side. "At first it was a tree, decorated with flowers and garlands of greens. The young people would leap and dance about it in a most pagan manner."

"Alfred," scolded Emma, "that is enough. We are here to observe the three elected Pole Men raise the freshly painted and furbished maypole. I want no nonsense, if you please." She then totally spoiled her reprimand by laughing at him.

Turning to Lord Laverstock, Samantha said in a soft voice, "The maypole must be taken down every three years to be painted and fixed up. Three men are elected to oversee this and then see to it the pole gets erected once again. That is why we are here, to watch it go up." She felt her cheeks grow warm at his look. Whatever had thawed his attitude, she could only be thankful for it.

A group of children danced about the carriage, demanding that their queen and king join them in watching the tall pole go up. Samantha gave Lord Laverstock a helpless look, then carefully gathered her pretty skirt in one hand to descend. A Mayne family groom stood proudly by the side of the carriage to assist her. Samantha was sure she caught a faint wink before she had to extend her hand to the child who offered her a bouquet of wildflowers.

A pretty rose color bloomed in the little girl's cheeks when Samantha gently thanked her. Then Samantha clasped a soft, pudgy hand, smiling down with pleasure at the soap-scented girl who beamed a shy smile in return. Behind her Lord Laverstock, looking more regal than any king in the history of the village, stepped down from the landau to join the group. They all strolled across the green to where the husky men were assembled by the pole. Samantha was glad Aunt Lavinia had reminded her to be here today.

Using a system of ropes, pulleys, and ladders, the men carefully maneuvered the tall, gaily painted larch pole into place. Amid the cheers of the assembled children, an intrepid volunteer climbed the near-sixty feet to release the positioning ropes. Then he slid to the ground after a saucy wave of his cap. Samantha crossed to congratulate him on his feat of daring.

"Now what must we do?" The familiar husky voice sent a tremor through Samantha.

"I expect we might adjourn to the Blue Lion for a glass of refreshment. There will not be any celebrations until tomorrow morning. I rather hate to go home just yet." She cast a wistful look about the green. The ribands and flowers would be attached at dawn the next morning. And she, rompish little Samantha Mayne, would reign as queen for the day. And Lord Laverstock would be her king. She smiled, her eyes lighting with pleasure at the thought.

Charles offered her his arm, then walked toward the inn. Lady Samantha appeared to know everyone in sight, for she nodded—most correctly—and smiled—most engagingly—at one person after another.

At the Blue Lion, they were greeted with a deference Samantha found charming. Of course, having Lord Laverstock present ensured a nicety of attention. But her own self in the form of this year's queen was a plus. Off to one side the visiting morris dancers had gathered following their practice session. They were laughing and slapping backs, and sipping their ales as well. On a table lay their purple scarves and wooden poles. Tomorrow they would be dressed to the nines with their bells strapped on their legs and hats decorated with paper flowers.

Lord Laverstock gave them an alarmed look before glancing to Samantha in question. She could almost hear his words, wondering if it was proper for her to be in here.

The landlord bustled forth to insist the "royal" party take over the private parlor. They assumed possession of this immediately, leaving the morris dancers the happy occupants of the common room. Their host assured them that ale, cakes, and lemonade would be brought in a trice.

" 'Tis a busy time for him. Tomorrow will be more so. Aunt usually brings a hamper of things to eat and drink to avoid crowds. We all enjoy Cook's picnic." Samantha flashed a smile at Laverstock.

The door opened, bringing not the serving maid but George. It was a very troubled George, too.

"What's happened?" Lord Laverstock crossed to greet George, drawing him aside from the others.

Sighing deeply, George shook his head in disgust. "The lock to the barn door has been forced and broken. New, it was, too. I did not notice it at first until we tried to get the glider back inside. Once inside I saw some papers were messed up, others on the floor." He gave Charles a worried look. "There are two missing. I know you told me to put them in a safe place. I forgot to put these away with the others," he said with a sheepish expression.

"Which ones?" Charles frowned at this serious turn of events. Somehow he ought to have anticipated this, but he hadn't, although he had suspected George might be absent-minded about the plans.

George glanced to where Samantha sat with Emma and Alfred. Percival had said he intended to wander about the village in hopes of finding some amusement. "The drawings for the new elevator design plus several sketches I made for a new type of sail I hope to use when I send up a glider with a balloon. You realize there ought to be a modification of the present design." George sighed and gazed off into space. "At least the remainder of the plans are safe. I wonder if Sir George has had any problems? Since he lives nearer the coast, he might."

"Perhaps, since you have met the man, you ought to seek him out, discover if there have been any unusual occurrences around his place." Charles also glanced to where the others sat. "You note that Twistleton is absent. I wonder if there is any significance to that?"

"Percy?" said George, his surprise at this query clear. "I doubt it. You can well imagine that he would have little taste for this tame gathering."

"I still think we had best keep our eye on him tomorrow." Then Charles recalled his duties as May King soon to begin and shook his head. "I will not be of much help until after that. You'd best post men by the barn, and try to duplicate your designs if you can in the meantime. It might do well to leave some false plans about," he mused. "If someone attempts to gain the rest of the drawings, you could lead him astray with some just a wee bit inaccurate." Charles was convinced Twistleton had played a part in the disappearance of the plans. He suspected the Frenchman was involved as well. The trick was to catch them at something incriminating. "We have no idea as to when or if they actually intend to do anything."

Slowly nodding his head in agreement, George added, "Aye. If Percy has violated our hospitality we shall find out soon enough. I have this odd feeling that things are coming to a head.

Something Aunt Lavinia said this morning to me after she read
my tea leaves.'' He shrugged somewhat defensively at Laverstock's incredulous look. ''Well, she has been right in the past
about a good many things.''

''And what did she say?''

''To beware of a green man.''

Laverstock laughed at that nonsense. ''Green man? Now I
wonder who that can be? Someone like your family ghost,
perhaps?''

George merely dropped his gaze and strode from the room.
He had been too close to Aunt Lavinia all these years to ignore
her readings. It would bear some thinking, but the clue was
there.

13

Dawn had not yet appeared when Samantha crept from her room. She met a silent Emma at the top of the stairs and together they quietly made their way down, and out through the side door.

"Are you sure we ought to be doing this?" whispered Emma, though they had indeed gone some distance from the house and there really was no need for secrecy.

" 'Tis an old custom. Aunt Lavinia is convinced I ought to be partaking of it this year, being May Queen and all." Samantha didn't mention that she had decided to try the ancient belief of her own accord, regardless of her aunt's urging.

"Precisely what is it we are to do again?" Emma was still not quite awake and felt chilly, not to mention faintly annoyed, at this uncivil hour of the day.

"We are to wash our faces with dew," replied Samantha, feeling rather silly now, although it had seemed romantic last evening when first suggested by her aunt.

"Whatever good is that supposed to do?" Emma walked along the path to the garden, wondering if all the soaring of the day before hadn't done something to Samantha's brain.

" 'Twill improve our complexions, although yours is lovely and in no danger. I could do with a bit of help on these freckles of mine though," Samantha glanced at Emma self-consciously before she continued. "Also, 'tis said that if you wish hard enough while washing your face, you will perhaps get a husband in the coming year."

Emma longed to dismiss the scheme as nonsense. But she also yearned for a husband of her choice, namely Alfred. It would be nice to think it could come about within the year ahead.

"Well, let us get to it then," she replied with a calm demeanor, as though not in the least eager for the results.

"First, it must be beneath an oak tree and there must be ivy growing. Ivy is thought to be the more powerful help." As oak grew in fair abundance, that proved an easy matter to find. The ivy was not as simple, but soon they spotted a neat patch beneath a splendid old oak.

Finding the ivy heavily laden with dew, Samantha knelt and began earnestly to pat it on her face, grimacing as the cold drops hit her skin. At her side, Emma followed suit.

"I think there is a bug on my ivy," Emma said with distaste. "I shan't wish it on my face."

"Do hurry, Emma. I am very cold." Samantha shivered, rubbing her hands up and down her upper arms and stamping her slippered feet.

Sniffing with disdain, Emma replied, "Well, you would rush about and not dress properly. One's wrapper could hardly be deemed appropriate for outdoor wear, you know."

"Oh, pooh," said the irrepressible Sam. "Who in the world would see us at this hour? I am certain everyone is sound asleep. In this gray light, we might be mistaken for ghosts. Rather colorful ghosts," she amended, glancing down at her red-gold silk robe embroidered with black and gold dragons and fanciful flowers.

Rising from her knees, Emma glanced about her in the faint light of predawn. "Pity I do not believe in fairies or the like. I have no doubt they would be out about now."

"Or the ghosts, Em. If you are going to help Alfred, you'd best get accustomed to such." Samantha tugged at Emma's hand to urge her return to the house. She intended to seek out a cup of something hot before returning to her room.

They had gained the warmth of the kitchen and Samantha had begun to heat up some milk when the door creaked open. Startled, Samantha glanced about with alarm. Seeing it was only Alfred, she relaxed and added a bit more milk to the pot. "Another early riser? I trust you will join us in a cup of hot chocolate?"

"I should like to know what it was I saw out my window.

What are you up to now, Sam?'' Alfred directed a kindly look at the discreetly attired Emma, her neat gown buttoned to her neck, before shaking his head at Samantha. She wore some sort of a Chinese-style wraparound robe that undoubtedly was not supposed to have been seen outside of her bedroom. Judging from its condition, it may have been something she had found in the attics.

"It is all a part of the day, you know. 'Tis the custom for unmarried maidens to wash their faces in dew before dawn the first morning of May.'' She busied herself locating the chocolate and then stirred the pot with vigor. The aroma of steaming chocolate wafted over the gloomy kitchen, imparting a sense of warmth in spite of the cold flagstone floor.

"I seem to recall that nonsense. Surely you do not believe such silly stuff, do you?'' He looked at Emma as he spoke the words and she blushed a rosy pink.

"Well,'' offered Emma in return, "I expect these things do not harm one . . . and anyway, Samantha said we must rise early today as she wished to go out to try the dew.''

Samantha thoughtfully refrained from saying she had noted that Emma had been most eager to participate once at the oak tree and patch of ivy. Instead, she poured out three cups of chocolate and led the others close to where the great stove gave out heat. "We'd best not linger. The kitchen maid will be here any time now to start the baking. I do hope she has set some of her special bread to rise,'' Samantha crossed to peek beneath a cloth in a corner of the kitchen to check the rising dough. At the second creak of the door, she turned about, expecting the kitchen maid, only to find Lord Laverstock staring down at her. "Oh, drat,'' she muttered.

Laverstock appeared neatly dressed for the day but for an elegant dressing gown atop his shirt and the long hose that could be glimpsed above his shoes. Samantha was extremely conscious of her lack of proper dress. She gulped the remainder of her chocolate, nearly scalding her tongue in the process, then inched toward the hall door. Lord Laverstock didn't budge. She gave him a wary smile, then began to edge around him. "Good morning, sir. I shall see you later, when 'tis time to leave.''

Pushing against the door, she fairly ran from the room and up the stairs.

She had looked like an entire bed of flaming lilies in that outrageous get-up. Across the bright silk, snarling black dragons edged with gold lashed tails amid fanciful blooms of every color. Above that curious robe, her beautiful hair tumbled in charming disarray. She must be mortified, Charles reflected. Her eyes had been wide with distress. How utterly exotic she appeared, and quite breathtakingly lovely. Pity she ran from him. It was a novel experience for him, to have a woman flee from his presence.

Charles turned to face the others as the kitchen maid slipped into the room to stir the oven fire that the scullery maid had lit earlier, and then put the bread to bake. Gentry folk did strange things, so she took little notice of the three in the kitchen other than a few curious glances. It wasn't worth her while to be overly inquisitive.

Placing their now empty cups on the scrubbed deal table, Emma and Alfred walked to the door. Charles couldn't refrain from a grin at their guilty expressions. Over his shoulder he tossed a polite request for a pot of coffee, then preceded the others into the hallway. In the library they found a maid finishing up her work at the fireplace. Yesterday's ashes filled a bucket, while neatly stacked wood on a freshly blacked grate waited to be lit. She hastily folded up the length of drugget that had protected the carpet, struck tinder to light the fire, then scurried from the room.

Charles rubbed his neck as he walked closer to the slight warmth, welcome even on a spring morning. "Does this kind of thing go on often here? Pity to think I have been wasting time in bed when I could be so entertained."

"Aunt Lavinia suggested Samantha might wish to try one of the traditions of this day," began Emma.

"Corkbrained notion, if you ask me," muttered Alfred.

Leaning against the mantel, Charles surveyed the most correct young lady he'd had the pleasure to meet for some time. She now looked very flustered, as though she wished she were miles away. "This tradition . . . what is it?"

Emma bloomed a deep rose. "Nothing at all that you might find of interest."

Curiosity leaped higher at her reluctance. "I believe I should find it so."

With the expression of one about to be hanged, Emma replied in her soft, high voice, " 'Tis said that if a young maiden washes her face in the predawn dew of May Day she will be wed in the coming year." She sank onto a chair as though her legs refused to hold her any longer.

Alfred's gaze sharpened, though he said nothing for the nonce.

Coffee was brought in and Laverstock poured himself a generous cup, then took one of the small rolls from the tray. He seated himself on one of the fireside chairs, crossing his long legs while pinning Emma with his direct gaze. "And Lady Samantha went out before dawn to do this thing?"

Feeling remarkably like she had when as a child at school she was called to the headmistress's room to answer for something her younger cousin had done, Emma nodded.

"Hmm." He sipped his coffee and said nothing more.

Emma took the opportunity to murmur vague excuses and escaped from the room.

Alfred followed her to the door. Before she left, he asked softly, "And did you do it as well?"

Glancing up through thick brown lashes, her brown eyes shyly meeting his, Emma boldly whispered, "I did," then fled.

An hour or so later Samantha primly sat bolt upright in the landau, quite as though she had not been skittering about in her Chinese robe earlier that morning. She peered about eagerly from the carriage as it rolled into the village. Emma, Alfred, and Aunt Lavinia sat opposite her. George was to follow shortly.

An imposingly regal, and incredibly good-looking Lord Laverstock sat at her side. His white garb was stunning; when she had first glimpsed him, she had caught her breath in wonder. Long, well-shaped legs disappeared beneath a white velvet jerkin with a padded doublet above. The outfit became him well, like a heroic figure from an old tapestry, she reflected.

Of Percival, there was no sign. Alfred had raised a brow at

Laverstock, and murmured something about people who stayed in bed regardless of the day.

At the green they discovered the villagers gathering in spite of the early hour. The sun slanted across the neatly scythed grass to highlight the gaily dressed girls holding garlands of greens and wreaths of flowers in their hands. Samantha and Charles exited the carriage and strolled over to join them. Ribands floated from the top of the maypole, dancing with a life of their own. A man climbed up a ladder to attach the last of the garlands and flowers to the pole to the cheers of the same children who had greeted Samantha and Charles the day before.

Behind them in the distance rose the squat Norman tower of the village church, tall elms in their spring dress setting off the gray stone. Along the stone-paved walks that bordered the cottage-lined roads, people thronged toward the green, intent on their holiday and the festivities promised.

The village of Sawham boasted a mayor, who, with the village constable, now approached Samantha and Laverstock in a slow, stately walk. Following behind them were a dozen of the prettier girls wearing flowers in their hair and dressed in simple muslins, all carrying ribands and garlands. Two exquisite crowns composed of the finest flowers selected from the sheltered garden belonging to Squire Dowdeswell were carefully held before the first two girls.

Samantha moved forward, conscious of the rustling of her silver tissue gown that sparkled in the sunlight with every movement. At her side the disturbing presence of the white-clad Lord Laverstock seemed almost intimidating. He had been kind not to mention their earlier meeting in the kitchen. Her cheeks had burned with embarrassment all the way up the stairs after that confrontation, though he had said but very little to her at the time.

"An honor, my Lord Laverstock, Lady Samantha," wheezed the decidedly overweight mayor, Mr. Jennings. At his side the taciturn constable, Mr. Mackrell, nudged the corpulent mayor, hoping to avoid one of the lengthy speeches the man loved to spout. A few words were said, then the mayor urged the girls holding the crowns forward.

The flowery crowns were respectfully placed on the heads

of the queen and king. The tall, beetle-browed constable had to do that job, the mayor being far too short. Then the village children danced forward to lead the new royalty on a procession around the green to where they would sit and command the May games.

From off to one side came a pyramidal creation about seven feet in height covered in holly and ivy leaves, weaving and bobbing in a manner to cause the children to squeal with delighted terror. It was the Jack-in-the-Green, come to join the celebration. It was impossible to guess as to his identity, for only a carefully placed slit allowed him to see out of the leaf-covered wicker structure.

He bowed slightly when Samantha neared, then cavorted on along the edge of the crowd, bringing laughter to the older ladies as he drew too close, shrieks from children as he threatened them with his large shape.

Around him danced the fiddler, making funny faces as his bow arched across the violin. Capering beside him was a merry andrew dressed in typical jester fashion. He blew a reed whistle which clashed with the fiddle quite awfully.

Amid all this foolery, Samantha and Charles walked with great stateliness to where they were to sit for the festivities. She cast a pleased glance at Laverstock, then at last pronounced in her clear, sweet voice, "Let the games begin."

First came the morris dancers. They were guests of the mayor, brought from the town of Abingdon because the mayor's wife was related to one of the men, and she thought it prodigious fine to have such a treat.

They impressed Samantha far more today than yesterday at the Blue Lion. Now, dressed in their white shirts and pants, bells strapped to their legs, and purple handkerchiefs waving in the air, they were awesome in the precision of their steps. Their splendid hats sat firmly atop their heads in spite of their jumping up and down with such vigor. Nearby, a similarly dressed fellow played a concertina. One merry tune after another poured forth as the men performed the complicated steps.

They paused to substitute wooden sticks for their fancy silk handkerchiefs, and resumed positions. The sticks made loud clacks when struck in what appeared a most dangerous manner while the men performed another of their repertoire. Back and forth, in and out they wove, their faces serious with their intent to dance well.

Samantha leaned over a little to whisper an aside to Lord Laverstock. "We have knife-dancers here in Yorkshire, but they only perform in January. Our mayor's wife thought it would be lovely to import a May Day ritual dance for us just once. I must say, 'tis most impressive." She flashed him a spontaneous smile, one of her sudden, breathtaking variety, before turning back to watch the dancers.

After the morris dancers finished it was time for the archery contest. Lord Laverstock officiated at this, somehow inspiring each man to outdo all previous efforts.

There were ten men from the village and surrounding area competing this year. Each man was highly skilled in the ancient sport. Four arrows were to be shot at the butt, a center hit gaining five points, a score of three for a hit outside the center. The first man made three out of four hits to the center and the assembled throng buzzed with shrewd comments on the chances of the remaining contestants.

Aunt Lavinia hovered behind Samantha's chair, waving her new white handkerchief about in the air while keeping up a running commentary with Samantha about the festivities, who were there and dressed in what—as though Samantha couldn't see for herself. Samantha dutifully watched the archers, trying to appease Aunt at the same time.

"I still do not see that lazy Percival. No wonder his mother despairs of him. I shall be quite glad once his quarter day arrives; he has developed a rather insinuating address. I expect he feels a need to retrieve his disgrace with a rich wife. I do not wish you to encourage him, Samantha." Aunt Lavinia gave a pointed look at Lord Laverstock which, fortunately, was lost on Samantha.

"But Aunt Lavinia, I could hardly do such a thing."

"Don't 'but Aunt Lavinia' me, my dear. I saw the manner in which he stuck to your side the other evening. Discourage him, my love."

The command was given kindly, in such a way that Samantha could hardly dislike it. Besides, she had no intention of ever encouraging Percival Twistleton to do anything, much less offer for her. Ignoring the closeness of the Jack-in-the-Green, who might be able to overhear her words, she impetuously replied, "It would be a boiling day in January before I would consent to the likes of him, dear Aunt."

The eighth contestant shot all four arrows to the center, much to everyone's delight, for there was clapping and whistling at his success. Shortly, he was pronounced the winner.

Her conversation with Aunt Lavinia ended abruptly, to Samantha's relief.

Lord Laverstock returned to sit on the high-backed wooden chair from the Blue Lion that served as his throne. It was time to make the awards. He handed a silver arrow to the winner, then gave medals to the second- and third-place men. Laverstock performed the task with gracious aplomb.

From where he now watched, Charles found the subdued madcap amusing. She was trying so very hard to be dignified and regal, and had he not seen another side of her he could well think her such today. He hid a smile behind a suddenly raised hand when he thought of how she had scampered across the path this morning, her Chinese red-gold robe fluttering about her in a delightful way, glimpses of her modest white muslin nightdress revealed now and again.

Not wishing to cause her discomposure, he had leisurely dressed, then gone downstairs to see what was afoot. How rosily her cheeks had bloomed when she had turned her head to discover him in the doorway.

He was distracted from further thoughts by the appearance of a group of young women carrying gay ribands and garlands of greenery and flowers. Laverstock watched with interest as they formed a circle. While the fiddler joined in with the concertina player, the women picked up the colorful streamers and danced complicated patterns about the maypole, in and out, making a pretty scene.

"I believe this is called the Spider's Web," offered Samantha in an attempt to be helpful. She had inquired about the charming dancing from one of the girls in order to learn more about the dance form. It was one thing to merely observe and quite another to understand the intricate figures performed. In some villages the morris dancers did the patterns. Here in Sawham the young ladies had taken firm control. Since they made a very lovely picture in their soft muslins and flowers, with their bright ribands fluttering in the breeze, it was doubtful anyone objected.

Charles tilted his head as he observed the women twine, then untwine, the ribands; kneel; then rise and whirl about. It was a graceful dance, one that looked to have ancient origins.

His eye was suddenly caught by the figure of the Jack-in-the-Green bobbing its way behind the throng. Charles could glimpse that peak of holly and ivy leaves as it moved along and wondered why the man hadn't remained with the rest of the royal party. Then his gaze sharpened as he saw the Jack pause by the Frenchman through a brief separation of the crowd. What could the Jack possibly have to do with the foreigner? Most intriguing. He wished he were free to follow them. Perhaps there would be some action tonight.

When Charles had stopped at the Blue Lion after the Scarborough trip to subtly inquire about the Frenchman's activities, he had discovered little of use. It seemed the man really did pay visits to local drawing rooms to teach the latest in steps from London, and the rest of his days seemed to be spent in dull regularity. Still, Charles couldn't refrain from his suspicions. He knew well that appearances might be deceiving.

His attention was claimed by Samantha as the dancers began another dance she informed him was called Gypsies' Tent. He set aside the peculiar incident while watching the young women, then the entrancing Samantha.

Aunt Lavinia saw to it that Samantha and Charles got fed. Trust the older lady to understand that this celebration business made a person hungry and thirsty. A cold collation was set up behind their chairs and a plate of food slipped to each to nibble while they watched the events taking place. Among the crowd Samantha could see others following suit, packets of food appearing by some kind of magic.

At last there was a conclusion to the various entertainments for the day and the time that Samantha had dreaded arrived. She carefully wiped her mouth on a napkin, then smiled bravely at Emma, who appeared to sympathize greatly. Alfred sent a

cheeky grin, one Samantha remembered well from childhood
days. Beast. He was altogether too knowing.

The fiddler motioned the royal couple to their feet. Lord
Laverstock held out his hand to her in a courtly gesture, retaining
hers and adding to Samantha's sense of unease. She had no idea
how he would behave. However, there had been signs of that
deplorable stuffiness of his receding, and he had so far taken
the foolishness of the day in good cheer.

"I believe the children are ready for us to go with them on
the round of the village, sir." Samantha smiled warily while
the crowd dispersed to their homes. Of course they would be
waiting to see if the king and queen passed along their street.
Although desirous that a nice sum be collected for charity alms,
Samantha hoped that either no one would be to home or no one
would donate. "Coward," she muttered to herself.

"Did you say something, my dear?" Charles's voice was soft,
barely reaching her ears as they walked forward to meet the
four young boys who were to escort them.

Samantha gave him a startled look, then laughed, "I confess
I have a few apprehensions. Have you none?"

"Not about this." The glance he bestowed on her caused her
heart to flutter with a touch of uncertainty. His look had carried
a certain warmth she had not caught before. Then her mind
jumped back to his words. If he was not apprehensive about
this remaining walk, what did concern him?

Charles looked over to where the Jack-in-the-Green now
capered along the edge of the green with the merry andrew at
his side. The Frenchman was nowhere within sight, but somehow that failed to reassure Charles. A highly developed instinct
warned him that something was not quite what it ought to be.
He drew Lady Samantha closer to his side, enduring her
questioning glance with fortitude.

The four boys, their faces solemn with the importance of the
escort duty now given to them, came forward, each bearing a
miniature maypole. Samantha was certain their faces hadn't been
so well scrubbed in months, for they beamed with that new-
washed appeal, red-cheeked and soap-scented.

The Jack-in-the-Green went first, followed by the merry

andrew loudly playing his reed whistle, and then the fiddler, who seemed to have an inexhaustible supply of tunes. A band of children and adults trailed behind Samantha and Charles.

Samantha was grateful for the support of Lord Laverstock's strong arm beneath her hand. Somehow this was not quite the way she had envisioned the day. True, she had been treated like a lady of rank by all and sundry, and Lord Laverstock had acted with great gallantry toward her, but was there a twinkle of amusement lurking in those gray eyes? She glanced up at him to note a lock of dark-brown hair had fallen down over his forehead, giving him great appeal. Could she admit, even to herself, how much she cared for him? Well, she did, a great deal.

He wouldn't be around much longer, she suspected. With no suggestion of a spy at work, he would shortly return to London and her father to report that all was quiet along the coast in Yorkshire. Yet hadn't George reported something? Those odious men had kept everything possible from her, no doubt wishing to spare her worries. Could they not understand she might worry all the more because of their stupid notions?

The four boys stopped before a neat cottage, primroses and columbine blooming in dainty beds along the path. A woman opened the door, greeting the noisy group with a smile, then stepping forward to drop a few coins in the receptacle.

The boys placed their maypoles so they crossed directly overhead while Charles first gave Samantha a mocking look before raising her hand to his mouth to place a lingering kiss upon it.

Samantha was shocked at her response. Having seldom attended affairs where this was the practice, she was not accustomed to it. She decided she quite liked it. Next time she went to the Assembly Rooms in Scarborough, she would see to it that she reaped this manner of attention. Although it was doubtful she would react to another as she had to Lord Laverstock. Who else would possess such a fine pair of gray eyes and cast such speaking glances? How she wished she knew what was in his thoughts.

The crowd was not best pleased by such a tame kiss on the hand, and a few derisive hoots were heard—safely in the background.

At the next cottage, more coins were offered and this time Charles drew her close in his arms to place a light kiss on her cheek.

"That's more like it, guv'nor!" shouted one stout man on the fringe of the group.

Samantha tried for a semblance of serenity, but it proved utterly impossible. She was definitely discomposed by the riot of her feelings while she was held close to him. The velvet of his jerkin had brushed against the soft skin of her shoulders. She had felt the unfamiliar touch of his mouth on her cheek . . . and known the insane desire to turn her head so she might again experience a true kiss. She ought to blush at the mere thought, but it was far too appealing.

As they wandered down the lane, a few houses were found to be empty, much to her disappointment. The same men were teasing and joshing about the kiss on the cheek. Even the little boys who held the miniature maypoles looked expectant. At the corner of the lane where it met a tree-shaded alley they came to a house where the lady waited for them at her door, a wide grin on her face. She dropped in her coins, then placed hands on hips while she waited.

Charles pulled Samantha close once again. Dare he do as he wished? By heaven, the lass was enticing. She glowed with that inner fire he had noted before. How well and truly she had ensnared him with her beauty and charm. Once back in London he would approach her father to see how his suit might fare with him. He could not leave here without making an effort to keep her his forever.

"Samantha," he whispered, "may I?"

Not sure of what he intended, she nodded, hope rising in her heart.

The four poles again crossed over their heads. Charles drew her closer to him to place a light kiss on her sweet lips. Oh, how he longed to have her away from this noisy crowd, away where he could indulge his passion for her without restraint.

Her hands flew up to rest on his velvet-covered chest. Startled eyes flew open as his lips left hers. "Charles . . ."

A commotion was begun by the merry andrew, who acted with great nonsense. The fiddler struck up a familiar tune. Charles was distracted from the question in Samantha's eyes by several of the children who tugged at his jerkin, wanting a bit of attention from this elegant lord.

From one side of the lane, the Jack-in-the-Green called to Samantha. She went to his side promptly to see if he needed assistance or some such thing. The wicker framework must be vastly uncomfortable. "May I help you?" she queried politely, though impatient to return to Laverstock. The noise of the throng increased with a round of loud laughter at a sally from the king.

"Er, yes." There was a slight pause. "Please help me to get a drink. I am near faint with thirst."

Not asking why he didn't seek aid from one of the men, the tender-hearted girl quickly walked to the pump in the alley and proceeded to get him a cup of water. She turned to stare with astonishment as the Jack tipped off the cumbersome cage.

"Percival!" she whispered in amazement. It couldn't be. But it was!

The cup was dashed from her hand as Percival scooped her into his arms and then thrust her into a carriage that stood waiting in the shadows. He jumped in beside her, grabbing the reins. The horses took off in a wild rush out of the village on the Scarborough road. Samantha fell back against the cushions, her head in a whirl.

Behind them the people clustered about his lordship, totally absorbed in him, ignoring the uninteresting actions of the more familiar Lady Samantha and the Jack-in-the-Green.

"What *are* you doing, Percy?" cried Samantha above the noise of the carriage as it rattled over the road.

"I have need of you, dear Sam."

14

"Where is she?" With a feeling of unease, Charles disengaged himself from the children when he sensed an emptiness at his side—Samantha's absence. "Where is Lady Samantha?" he asked the people near where he stood. He searched the throng of people with growing concern. She had been next to him all along their stroll down the lane from the green. Now she was suddenly missing. "Has anyone seen her?" Surely that gentle kiss hadn't frightened her away.

The four young boys standing nearby looked abashed. They had been waving their miniature maypoles about in the air and paid no heed to the queen at all.

A confused buzz began, as one villager turned to another. "Gone?" one after another murmured. Surely that couldn't be. "She was just here. Perhaps she merely stepped aside for a moment?"

A shy young girl stepped forward. "She went with the Jack, milord. Down there." The child pointed a trembling finger toward the alley, a dim place much covered over with the branches from low-hanging trees and darkened by the shade from a stone building. She retreated as she saw the flash of bewilderment, then worry, cross his lordship's face.

In the alleyway could be seen the wicker cage that had been the Jack's costume for the day. It looked as though it had been hastily abandoned, tumbled against the stone wall in a quick exit. Puddles of dirty water provided an attraction for a lone duck.

Heedless of his gorgeous white attire, Charles ran down the muddy alley to where a village pump stood. Then he saw the cup on the ground, and evidence that water had been splashed from it. There were wheel tracks, partly obscured by a few foot

181

prints that might have been made at any time in the past day. Not a real clue. What had happened here? What had the Jack-in-the-Green to do with this? "Did no one see her? Who was the Jack this year? Where is he now?" Charles took a frantic look at the blank faces about him, wondering if there was someone hiding information regarding Samantha.

"We mayn't know 'at, milord." A plump, narrow-eyed woman, curiosity oozing from every pore, was the only one to speak. The other villagers stood in silence, dumbfounded at this turn of events. Lady Samantha was well liked. No one would wish her any harm.

"I must find out who was the Jack today. Who can tell me? Someone must know the answer. The mayor?" He gave the hapless cage a kick, his anger and feeling of utter helplessness spilling over into physical reaction.

The crowd of people was melting away as though by magic. Charles couldn't ever recall feeling so baffled. In all his years of investigation this was the first time that the subject was close to him, important to him. He must get a rein on his anger, he was frightening everyone away.

A husky young lad came running down the alley, concern showing clearly on his face. "Is somethin' wrong?"

"Lady Samantha has vanished. Do you know anything that might help locate her?" Charles rubbed his neck in frustration. It was as though Samantha had disappeared from the face of the earth without a trace. And she had just called him Charles, such a promising sign. He had hoped to build on that. He had rapidly come to see that the impetuous, madcap girl had wound herself around his heart. He tore his thoughts from her with difficulty. "The Jack has gone as well."

The lad's face paled. "An't please you, milor', he paid me a guinea for hisself to take th' cage for a bit. Said he wanted ter play a joke on his friends, he did. I had no notion he meant to do somethin' bad." The young fellow bent over to examine the wicker cage, still well covered with holly and ivy leaves. He picked up the awkward seven-foot piece with ease. "That feller had a time with this, so lean was he."

Charles described the Frenchman to the young lad, who merely shook his head. It was no use. Obviously the Frenchman was not the one who had spirited Samantha away. But then who had? Clearly, there was no more information to be gained from this lad. The description drawn by him was like no man Charles could recall, not even Percival, who topped Laverstock's list of suspicious characters.

Anxiously, he raced down the lane to the green. There he saw Lady Emma and Lady Lavinia sitting in the landau discussing the day. Alfred stood close to Emma, chatting with ease. George was not far away, talking in great earnestness with a stranger. Beyond, several people were setting up for tea and cakes.

"Where is Samantha? Did you get a lot of alms for the church?" asked Emma with a mischievous gleam in her eyes. Then she noted his breathless and less-than-perfect condition. Her countenance grew alarmed. "What is it?"

The stirring kiss briefly flashed in his mind, then was pushed aside by the pressing urgency. "Samantha's gone! She walked down an alley with the Jack and now both are missing. Have you seen her?" he demanded.

Alfred shook his head and strode over to talk to George. In moments the two men returned, George frowning in concern.

"I doubt she would do anything today without telling at least Emma, here. Not like her to just run off." George looked to where Emma sat.

"Not a word," replied Emma to his unspoken question. She had paled, placing a comforting hand upon Aunt Lavinia's, though to be honest, it was Emma who sought consolation. Her sensibilities threatened to be overcome.

"I have fear of foul play. We'd best make a search of the village. Perhaps we can find out something of help. I wish to know who played the Jack today." Charles strode down the street to the Blue Lion Inn to ask a few questions, while Alfred and George began to query the workers who had helped set up for the day. The poser that lurked in the back of their minds was that of the missing Jack. Why? And, more curiously, who?

Discouraged and perplexed, George and Alfred met the ladies at the carriage in a half hour. Emma had checked with the Moores and Holcrofts.

"I spoke to the Dowdeswells and they have not heard or seen a thing," reported Aunt Lavinia.

Emma noted the white fan that now dangled from Aunt's wrist, but ignored its implications. "What do we do now?"

The men looked at each other in silence, then turned to stare as Laverstock hurried to join them. "I discovered that a horse and carriage was hired this morning, but the lad who handled the arrangements cannot recall what the gentleman looked like. I fear whoever it was that arranged for the carriage is also the missing Jack." Charles explained to the ladies about the switch that had taken place between the original Jack and a slim young man who resembled no one any of them could recognize from the description given.

"They have no idea as to the destination? When is the carriage to be returned?" Emma clasped her hands tightly before her. She loved her cousin Samantha dearly. It was unthinkable that something terrible might have happened to her.

"I wish I knew. If only someone had managed to note which direction they went. Undoubtedly the carriage will be left at a point where the Blue Lion has arrangements, but that could be one of many different locations." Charles wished he had kept her hand on his arm, kept her close to him. The thoughts that raced through his head at the moment were grim, far beyond being merely unpleasant. If anything happened to a hair of that red-gold head there would be the devil to pay!

The mayor and constable joined Charles, expressing polite concern for the distressing event, but little in the way of firm assistance. The two officials walked off toward the Blue Lion, murmuring something about the strange Frenchman having gone away as well. So much activity for the normally sleepy village must be discussed over a pint of the best ale to be had.

"Tea! We had best return to Mayne Court and have tea. That will help us think, I believe," declared Aunt Lavinia, waving the dainty white fan about in the air for added emphasis.

Charles looked about the deserted green with frustration. He wanted his horse . . . and to find his Samantha.

Since no one else offered any better ideas, they entered the carriage and gloomily clipped along the road to the house, each with unanswered questions darting about in his or her head.

"Forgot to tell you in all the fuss. Talked with Sir George Cayley. He lives not too far away, you know. That was the fellow I was chatting with when you came dashing up. He says he has had no trouble at all at his place. Nice gentleman," said George reflectively. "Wants to discuss my new design for the elevator sometime. Haven't wished to intrude on him before," he added with the typical consideration of an aristocratic gentleman.

Charles studied George while considering the earlier bit of information. "I have the most peculiar feeling that it is all of a piece. I suspect there is a connection between the missing papers at the barn and our missing Samantha, not to mention the Jack."

No one commented on his referring to Samantha in such a familiar way, if indeed anyone gave it a thought. Lord Laverstock had gone through that mysterious process that turns one into a member of the family, so to speak. He was an accepted part of the inner group—the leader, in fact. It was as instinctive as breathing to look to him to solve the family dilemma.

They straggled in from the carriage and headed for the drawing room. Lady Lavinia instructed Peters regarding tea, then paused to ask, "Is Mr. Twistleton about?"

"Mr. Twistleton is not here, my lady." Peters stood very correctly, perceiving that something was afoot, his butlerish senses telling him that a difficulty had arisen. That was not an unheard-of circumstance in this particular household, yet it paid him to be alert.

"Did he say when he might return?" Really, guests could be so tiresome.

"He has departed, my lady. His valet as well. One of the maids reported to me this morning that his room was empty, portmanteaus gone." Peters delivered the news with great satisfaction.

"How strange," declared Emma, feeling oddly weak. She sat down abruptly, determined not to be missish about the turn of events. Her nerves would just have to wait to be overset.

"Well, I cannot say I am sorry," said Aunt Lavinia. "Although I care not for his family—a clutch of loose screws if I ever saw any—I daresay they have reasons for being annoyed with the boy.''

"Indeed," agreed Alfred, keeping an eye on Emma. She was holding up better than he might have expected under the circumstances. Actually, he was most proud of her.

Charles wandered away, stricken that he had not foreseen the possibility of this. He had not anticipated that Percival would strike *during* the festival, and certainly not that he would use Samantha. Charles was most angry with himself. This ought *not* to have occurred.

It was Emma who poured tea, a job usually accomplished by Samantha. Emma was quite fine until it was time to pour out the final cup of Chinese green tea, adding two spoons of sugar before handing it to Alfred.

"Somehow it does not seem right that Samantha is not sitting with us, making us laugh with her amusing talk. I hope the dear girl is all right," said Aunt Lavinia, using her new white handkerchief to dab at her eyes.

It was too much for Emma. There was a clatter of dishes as she plunked the tea cup and saucer on the tray. The brave girl burst into tears and fled from the room, followed closely by Alfred.

The two hurried down the stairs and out the rear door to the garden. There Alfred stopped Emma, placing his arm gently about her. Relieved there was one stronger and wiser to turn to in a crisis, Emma allowed herself to lean against him, dropping her head against his shoulder as though she had done it a hundred times. She cried the tears she had been trying to withhold for so long, her shoulders trembling with delicacy. She accepted the handkerchief he offered, wiped her eyes, and sniffed.

Raising her face to his, she pleaded, "Oh, Alfred, she cannot be dead, can she? My fears are great for her." Emma knew wondrous comfort in Alfred's closeness. How lovely it might be to know such consolation always.

"Your tender heart does you credit, my dear. But you know your cousin. If some man has abducted her, he will live to regret it." Alfred spoke with more optimism than he inwardly felt. It was difficult to talk of Samantha when his arms were full of his darling Emma. He had been wanting just such a proximity as this for a long time. And now to be in such a situation.

Emma gave a watery smile. "She is rather fearless, is she not? I am not at all inclined that way." She nestled closer to her comforter and protector.

"Thank heaven, my sweet. I would not have you any other way." He tilted her chin up to search her eyes for some clue to her feelings. It was encouraging to see the warmth in those lovely brown eyes. Her soft rose-tinted mouth was a most precious bud.

"But I thought you did not want me . . . in any way," said Emma, speaking in an unusually daring manner, for her. Deciding that she might as well plunge forward to know what her heart desired above all, she continued. "Samantha"—her voice broke on the name—"told me how you felt about my rank and fortune. It is all a piece of nonsense, you know, dear Alfred. As if rank is all that important to me . . . or to us."

"Am I your 'dear'? How I have longed to be just that. I suppose I have been foolish to hesitate. I felt you deserved better than a mere scribbler." Alfred led Emma to a marble bench, where they sat down to gaze into each other's eyes, the calamity of the missing cousin momentarily forgotten.

"Oh, how could you even think such a thing!" Emma, in a rare burst of nerve, leaned forward to bestow a hesitant kiss on Alfred's cheek. To him it felt like the soft stroke of a rose petal. "You are the most intelligent, the bravest, the very kindest of men!" she declared fervently. "There could be no one better, as far as I can see." That her eyes had been fixed only on Alfred for some time made little difference to her. He was the man she was determined to wed. Hadn't she washed her face in dew this morning?

From here on, the conversation degenerated into the usual lover's nonsense of "When did you first know?" and "You truly do care?" Somehow a declaration of love was offered, along with a proposal of marriage. This last was promptly accepted by a starry-eyed Emma.

"My parents will be pleased, I believe. Aunt Lavinia shall write to them immediately. I know she will approve." Recalling the proprieties, Emma reluctantly rose, Alfred assisting her as though she were a piece of fragile Wedgwood. "We'd best return to the drawing room." Emma trilled a delicately musical laugh. "I fear our tea will be quite cold by now."

They strolled back to the others, hand in hand, to discover George and Laverstock in animated discussion.

"What has happened?" said both pairs simultaneously.

"Alfred has offered for Emma, and she has sensibly accepted him," said Aunt Lavinia. "I read it in her tea leaves this morning." Aunt fanned herself while the others, particularly Lord Laverstock, looked at her in astonishment.

"Did you read anything else, dear Aunt?" Emma left her beloved to sit by her aunt on the sofa.

"I wonder if you recall the night I read Percival's tea leaves? I saw a gallows in his cup! That meant he had bad luck coming, danger as well. I thought perhaps his creditors were pressing him, for it also showed he had suffered losses. Might not all those elements combine? What I mean to say . . ." She waved the fan in her hand in a vague gesture, while looking at Lord Laverstock. Indeed, it seemed they all turned to him for the solution.

"Yes, I believe that Percival is the one who has absconded with Samantha!" declared Charles in a hard, tight voice. While anticipating trouble to come, Charles hadn't calculated any threat to Samantha.

"How can we be certain?" queried a bemused Emma. She had not quite recovered from her longed-for proposal. How like Samantha to create a distraction, without even meaning to do so.

"I believe you must have the right of it, Laverstock," declared George. "Twistleton needed money, and rather badly, if I am correct. How easier to come by it than steal the plans? But he has not got them all," added a worried George. He mentally reviewed the newly repaired lock on the door, the hiding place for his plans.

"But why take Samantha?" worried Aunt Lavinia aloud. "If he has formed an unfortunate tendre for her, he cannot elope, he has no funds. He knows my brother would never consent to such a union, regardless." She gazed at Lord Laverstock, noting with satisfaction the grim tightening of his lips at her words.

"Alfred says Samantha will make him rue the hour he kidnaped her." Emma patted her aunt's hand to reassure her, if possible, that all would be well.

"Even if he is able to get the plans, and he can manage to build the glider, he will need a pilot. Who better to use than Samantha, who has the experience?" Charles shared a concerned look with George. He knew full well what the dangers might be. Twistleton must return for the full set of plans, then embark for France. With him would go Samantha to serve as pilot for the craft. If the plans were fake, might not Samantha be injured? It was a risk, but one that he was compelled to take. He could but pray Samantha might be saved.

"Absolute crinkum-crankum, if you ask me. Can the lad actually have that much derring-do in his blood?" Since no one had the answer, and all were deep in thought, Aunt Lavinia fanned herself while she considered the situation.

Samantha . . . in her lovely silver tissue gown, the crown of flowers sitting so regally on her head, had appeared like a princess, a vision of incomparable beauty. Charles recalled how she had begun the day in such delight, scampering out to wash her face in the dew. Had she hopes for the coming year? Was there some young man, unknown to Charles, that she yearned to marry? The thought was not a happy one. He turned to Alfred.

"My belief is that once Twistleton discovers the plans are lacking some of the pages, he will return in the night to steal the remainder of them. George will replace the present set of plans with ones that *look* right but are false. We can only hope that Samantha will be all right. I propose to try to find her. There must be a clue we have missed."

"You could be right about that," admitted Alfred, deciding the best thing for him to do was get out of the house and away from Emma. While still near her, he had the strongest urge to take her in his arms, and he would be no help at all under those conditions.

"Well," offered Aunt Lavinia, rising from the sofa where she had been deep in thought, "we had best all prepare for possibilities and eventualities. I am encouraged, however." At these words of hope, the others gave her questioning looks. "There is a broken sword on the near side of my cup. That means defeat, you know. And on the far side, there are wings. That tells me a message is coming from overseas. Whether it brings good news or bad depends on whom the sword is intended for. I believe there is a shoe to one side and that always means a change for the better. So you see," she looked at Lord Laverstock, "we must do what we can."

Lavinia smiled to herself. She felt assured Sam would be safe. She was nicely spoken for, unless the tea leaves were horribly wrong. But George needed tending to, and the Wyndhams had a remarkably pretty daughter due home from school ere long. Lavinia discounted the gossip about some scandal. Never from a Wyndham.

Not seeing at all what Lady Lavinia might mean by her words, Charles merely nodded his agreement, deciding it was the best course to take.

"Emma, we'd best prepare for what lies ahead." Aunt Lavinia took Emma by the arm to steer her toward the stairs.

"But what is that?" replied a confused Emma. There were times when it was very difficult to follow what her aunt meant.

"Why, danger, of course. Do you not recall I foresaw danger in Samantha's cup the other night? Now, if I can just figure out where she might be." The strange little lady, her wispy white hair a trifle wilder than usual, fanned herself vigorously while Emma made a mental note to keep a watch on the said article.

The three men watched the ladies leave and climb the stairs to where the bedrooms were.

"I propose we change out of our festive clothes for something more practical," said Charles, giving his now-rumpled white velvet and silk a disgusted look. "Say . . . our black garments? Then we shall be prepared for any event that presents itself."

The others agreed and followed the ladies up the stairs, and on to individual rooms. In an amazingly short time, considering how Lord Laverstock's valet tut-tutted over the condition of the white outfit and deplored the change to clothing of a ruffian, the men met on the stair landing.

"Well, how do we produce a convincing set of plans?"

demanded Alfred, suddenly alert now that his beloved Emma was out of sight.

"Best go down to the barn," replied George. "I have paper there and a goodly supply of quills. I believe I can draw a set of plans that will produce a glider not capable of soaring. It is in the design of the canvas wing, you see." He began to explain the finer points of wing design to a curious Charles, while Alfred took a lingering look up the staircase where Emma had disappeared before joining the men on their walk from the house.

Upstairs, Emma walked to the window of Samantha's room to gaze out. In a few minutes she could see Alfred heading toward the barn with the others. Turning to her aunt, she said with great curiosity, "You knew, dear ma'am. Did the tea leaves tell you?"

Aunt Lavinia had the grace to blush, an amazing feat for a lady of her acknowledged years. "Well, not actually. All I needed was a pair of eyes in my head and the good sense to use them. You two have been prickly as hedgehogs whenever together. That was a promising sign. I may be a maiden lady, but I know love a-blooming when I see it."

"I have often wondered why you never married. A woman with such charms as you must have received countless offers." Emma strolled restlessly about the room, while Lady Lavinia paused in her task of rounding up things she thought Samantha might require.

"I did. But my brother had need of me to care for his children when his wife died. I have sometimes wondered if I did him a disservice. Perhaps had I not accepted the joyful task he gave me, he might have remarried and the children had a real mother." Lavinia held a warm cloak in her arms, cradling it close to her as her face crumpled with concern.

Emma hurried to place a gentle arm about her beloved aunt. "No woman could have been a better mother to those two. And you know Samantha loves you with all her heart."

Lavinia's face cleared and she beamed up at her niece. "Not her entire heart, my dear. There is a gentleman who claims more and more of that every day."

"Will she be happy? Can Lord Laverstock possibly see our precious Samantha as we do?" Emma moved about the room, smoothing the bed, tracing a line across the dressing table.

"Never the same, but I believe better, perhaps. There was a ring in his cup, you know." Aunt Lavinia's eyes crinkled up with amusement and anticipated pleasure. There had been a ring like his in Samantha's cup, too.

With that bit of wisdom, the two ladies went about their work with lighter hearts.

"Place that lanthorn a bit closer, will you?" George waved a hand to where he needed more light. He had pulled out several sheets of paper precisely identical to those he had used for the originals. The hours were passing and soon it would be getting dark outside. He must finish these plans before night fell in case Percival returned.

It was almost a relief, in a manner of speaking, to know it was Percival who had taken Sam. While George guessed Percy might have an interest in Sam, he also knew that if his sister disliked the dandy, she was safe from assault. Unless he tied her up with rope or something of that sort. George firmed his lips and began the clever drawings of a glider that appeared remarkably similar to the originals.

Once each drawing was completed, Charles took it and began a queer process. At Alfred's questioning look, Charles gestured to the originals. "These look too new. He might suspect something. I decided to give them a wrinkled and worn appearance."

When George finished, the originals were carefully rolled up and placed in a metal cylinder that Charles took.

"Where can we put the replacements so they won't be obvious yet he will be able to find them?" George searched the commodious barn for a likely spot.

"Where did he find the two he removed while we were gone?" Charles nodded thoughtfully as George pointed out the location previously used. "I suggest you put them up here." He took the original set and tucked them under his arm. "I propose we store these under my bed for the moment. Since there is usually someone about, it would be difficult for him to locate them. Besides, George has always left his plans in the barn. Twistleton won't even consider they might be elsewhere."

The three walked to the door, surveyed the scene, doused the lanthorn, then closed the large wooden door. George carefully locked it behind them. They seemed incongruous wearing their black garments in the soft early-evening shadows. Around them the white blooms of Aunt Lavinia's garden gleamed picturesquely, showing how romantic her notion might be to those inclined to stroll in the evening breezes. Two guards stood where later they would be concealed by shadows.

"We have a wait until it becomes dark out. Perhaps there will be some dinner up at the house." George glanced at Charles, who looked about to protest. "I gather you do not feel much like eating, but consider this . . . you will need your strength for this night's work."

Charles nodded. Alfred bent to pluck several white primroses to bring up to Emma while Charles watched, wondering when and if he would be able to do a like thing for his Samantha. Oh, that his dear little love was safe! He felt as though his heart was frozen.

When they entered the house, they were met by Aunt Lavinia and the announcement that dinner was to be served promptly as they all had need of sustenance.

The food was excellent, yet none did it justice, for all assembled at the table thought of Samantha. Where was she now? Was she chilled, hungry? Was she safe?

Charles wondered if she had been violated by that rat, Twistleton. If he had touched her in any manner, Charles would see his carcass thrown to the fish off Scarborough coast.

15

"Whatever are you up to, Percy? I have no desire to go anywhere with you." Samantha had been repeating this thought in various forms for the past thirty minutes. "Take me back to the village, if you please," she demanded in what she hoped was a polite manner. It was nearly impossible to attempt dignity while the curricle was racketing along the road to Scarborough. She had tried in vain to convince Percy that she wished to remain in Sawham; he had been deaf to her entreaties.

Samantha was distinctly annoyed with her brother's friend. He had not said one word since tearing out of the village as though a pack of demons were determined to make him their dinner. She glanced sideways at him. He was not his customary dandyish self at the moment. His usually carefully rumpled hair now flew every which way, and his clothes were wrinkled—no doubt from wearing that wicker cage affair. There was a rather wild look about him that had begun to frighten her a little.

It was a lovely afternoon, if one were inclined to go for a drive. The sun was shining and spring flowers popped up here and there to cheer the view. There were a few gray clouds in the distance, but not the sort to bring a rain, she hoped. Any young miss should have been pleased to have so determined an escort.

Samantha was not. "Percival Twistleton! This has ceased to be amusing. You have had your bit of fun. I insist you turn this carriage about and return me to the celebration. It may have escaped your notice—though I fail to see how—that I am the queen of the festivities. My presence is required there, I believe."

Her crown, now reposing sadly on the floor of the curricle,

was a total loss, yet added a colorful and rather bizarre touch to the scene. She would have picked it up to attempt a restoration of its appearance, but that was impossible, given the careening nature of their drive.

For the first time, Percival spoke to her. "Ah, yes, so you can receive the kisses of his noble self, Charles Winford, the Marquess of Laverstock. Are they better than others, Sam?" The mockery in his voice confused Samantha.

"What utter nonsense, Percy. Surely you cannot believe Lord Laverstock might have an interest in a girl like me? Those kisses were for charity. Quite innocent, they were, too." Samantha clutched at the side of the carriage as they went over a particularly nasty bump. The drive into the country was becoming most alarming. The painful stab she felt at admitting the disinterest of Lord Laverstock was firmly set aside.

"Have a care, do, Percy! You will have us in the ditch and then where would we be?" She clung to the seat with one hand and the side panel of the vehicle with the other. Oh, that no one should know of this terrible trip. She had no desire to marry a loose screw, and Percy was showing evidence of being a prime one. Yet society demanded a young woman's honor be protected. Her aunt could well insist that Percy marry Samantha if this precipitous drive came to the attention of others. Was that what he wished?

"If you are doing this ridiculous thing to force me to marry you, you may as well turn about or dump me right here! I have no intention of getting wed to you. Not now or ever!" Samantha emphasized her point by a neat punch to his arm. She was strong—she had needed agility for all the various schemes her brother contrived. She had climbed trees, ridden like the wind, and even learned to swim when George had shown an interest in working on some peculiar design for a boat that could submerge.

Percival winced at the jab to his left arm. "Leave be, Sam. Rest assured, I have no desire to marry you. The man who draws that task has my sympathies." He now kept his eyes on the road ahead. As far as he could tell, no one from the village or Mayne Court followed them. Frequent glances behind them the first few miles out of Sawham had assured him of that.

"Well," huffed Samantha indignantly, "I am not all that far past redemption. I have merely led a varied life," she declared virtuously.

"Varied! That's a good one. 'Tis a wonder there is an unbroken bone left in your body, the way George has led you on over the years." Percival clamped his mouth shut. He had no intention of revealing to Sam what his present plans involved. If she got him to talking, she might be able to weasel information out of him. He recalled from past experience her tenacious ability in that regard.

"George means well. However, I am determined to end my participation in his many schemes. He will simply have to train a new slave to do the work." She emphasized her intent with a sharp nod. It was a pity her brother couldn't have seen her.

"I should like to know what you mean to do with me," she continued. "If you don't plan to marry me, what do you intend? I have no fortune, unless my father might spare a few pounds for my release. Is that what you seek? A paltry few pounds? You may as well know that my father is as likely to demand marriage once he knows you have hared off across the country with me in a carriage. After all, Percy, 'tis a bad thing to do, to kidnap a young woman against her will." Her spirited words didn't please the listener.

"Do be quiet, Sam. You are giving me an aching head with your incessant jabbering. And you didn't come against your will. Precisely." Percival gave Sam an uneasy glance, then stared ahead, trying to retain control of the horses while urging them to full speed. If he could manage to make it to Scarborough with these nags before they were winded, he would be well on his way to success with his scheme.

"I thought I was giving a drink to a thirsty Jack-in-the-Green. How was I to know there was a villain lurking beneath that wicker cage?" she demanded in a rising temper.

"You are too trusting. Comes from George's giving you free rein all these years. I warned him time and again. Don't think he considered you a grown-up miss until he saw you in that get-up you're wearing."

Samantha studied her pretty silver tissue gown, now sadly

umpled what with being tossed into the curricle, and the chaotic
nd dusty drive along the Scarborough road. "Do you need
oney very badly? We might think of a way for you to get some
a an honest way. Alfred became a writer."

"Writer! Bah. I have no wish for the ink-stained fingers of
scribbler of foolish novels," he gibed.

"There are a goodly number of people who think him to be
prodigious fine writer. Why do you need the money?" She
turned to the subject at hand with the tenacity of a hungry
errier.

"Leave me be, Sam." His patience was wearing thin, and
had never been very great to begin with.

"I think that is the least you can do. Tell me why you need
ue money and how you intend to get it if you have no plan
) marry me for whatever dowry Papa will bestow?"

Sighing like a man pushed beyond endurance, Percival
xclaimed, "I have a mountain of debts. To be in the swim of
ue *ton*, one must have proper clothes and a fine place to live."

"And gaming?" inquired Samantha shrewdly. "I expect you
o a bit—or more than a bit—of that as well. I declare, you
uen are far more silly than the ladies. Fancy clothes, a fine
lace to live, and the approbation of a covey of fine birds with
uore hair than wit seems your highest goal."

"And you women seek a marriage with a peer—the higher,
he better," he said, sneering at her.

"Never say such a thing. Emma cares naught that Alfred has
ot a title and is of lower rank than she. 'Tis the man himself
uat matters to us," she assured Percy in firm tones. She knew
hat she wouldn't care whether Charles was a plain mister or
lord, if she could share life with him.

"Hah! If I believed that, I should have to confess to faith in
airies as well." Percival subsided into silence. She was doing
t again, drawing him into speech when he had vowed to remain
ilent.

"I still wish to know why we are on our way to Scarborough.
really want to go home, Percy. By now, they must surely be
earching for me. I have no desire to upset Aunt Lavinia," she
aid earnestly.

"What a taradiddle," he was goaded into snapping back at her. "If she did not faint dead away at the sight of you soaring across the valley, this will scarce make a dent."

"That is not true, and you know it. Mayhap she read something in the tea leaves and is prepared for such an event as this." Samantha mused that her aunt had been reading those tea leaves a good deal lately, and that the results of her reading had not been shared as was her wont.

"Be silent," thundered Percival. If he had the nerve he would stop the curricle and bind her mouth closed. But they were getting near their destination now and with meeting a cart or carriage on the road, he couldn't take any chances. In fact, he had best prepare for the cart coming their way at this very moment.

Samantha saw the approach of a farmer's cart as a chance to be saved. She sat up straight, then leaned forward so as to shout to the man. However, instead of calling out, she clamped her mouth shut like a startled clam. There was something against her ribs that felt suspiciously like a gun. She glanced downward. She had been right; it was a gun. There, poked against her side, was a double-barreled pocket pistol. And it very much appeared that the trigger was at full cock.

"Be a good girl and sit very nice as we pass the man, Samantha. And smile. You are out for a jolly little drive with a gentleman friend." Perspiration beaded Percy's forehead. He had never stuck a gun up against a body before. Driven by need and greed, he had no alternative. He was too close to his objective to permit her to spoil his plans now.

Samantha sat frozen in place. Was that gun one of those hair-trigger things that went off at the least jiggle? She had heard George talk of such. She hoped the road remained very smooth until they passed the cart. She smiled—a wide smile—then breathed a sigh of relief as they whizzed past the slow-moving cart and the immediate danger was over.

"Do take the gun from my side, Percy. It makes me exceedingly nervous. I shall endeavor to comply with your wishes without your resorting to it again." She remained quite still, breathing carefully. It was clear Percy had lost is senses and must be humored. To take a gun on her!

"No more talk." He removed the pistol from her side, yet kept it close to hand. "Be assured I am a good shot. I've not spent hours at Manton's shooting gallery for nothing." He watched Samantha warily settle back against the seat, then gave a grim smile of his own. This was more like it.

Scarborough had never looked more welcome to Samantha. He dared not shoot her while within the city and in full view of the populace. She darted a glance to the tight-lipped man at her side, while furiously wondering what she might do to save herself. It reminded her of a few of the novels she had read, the kind where the heroine was shut up in a slimy old dungeon, left to die, and the hero charged through impossible barriers to save her. Samantha knew better than to expect help in real life. But she did wonder what the others back home were doing now. She might be able to escape if she could only persuade Percy to stop the curricle. Not knowing if he had the gun at the ready, she was reluctant to create a scene while in the carriage. Then she saw an opportunity.

"I am hungry. Could we not purchase a bit of bread and cheese? Look over there." She—rather cleverly, she thought—pointed to the remains of a Saturday market, a couple of stalls with odds and ends left to sell. Because of the festive day, more bread than usual had been baked and heaps of cheese had been brought to market, some of which remained.

Percy gave a grim little chuckle. "Think you to jump from the carriage and run off? Not on your life, my dear girl. My plan requires your assistance. I foresaw the need for a bit of sustenance, so I tucked in some bread, cheese, and wine . . . lemonade for you, if you prefer."

"You know I never drink wine, Percy." She had underestimated Percival, it seemed. He was not at all what he appeared to be. Rather than being the empty-headed dandy, he had a very devious mind hard at work.

They went speeding through the north end of Scarborough with dispatch—avoiding the central area and possible trouble completely. Few people were to be seen; it seemed all were attending festivities in the heart of the town. He directed the horses and carriage out along the street toward the crest of the promontory where the ruins of Scarborough Castle rose in barbaric splendor.

Returning to angry silence, she watched with great curiosity as they wove in and out along the twisted streets until they came to a steep open stretch of road. She must try to remember every twist of this road. Ahead of them, with only the top of the keep visible, towered the ruins.

The sun was slipping toward the horizon and a freshening breeze brought goose bumps to her skin. Sam shivered, wishing she had a shawl to draw about her shoulders. She glanced at Percy, wondering what would happen next. She wasn't precisely afraid of him, in spite of the gun. She couldn't accept that he would actually do her harm. Yet he was desperate. She could see it in his face, hear it in his voice.

What would he do with her? Her eyes strayed off toward the sea far below. What was it George had told her? That the cliff rose nearly three hundred feet from the water's edge? A sudden foreboding seized her, causing her to tremble.

The carriage rattled through the broad arch of the gate of the barbican, or gatehouse, of the castle, slowing in pace due to the steepness of the climb. Samantha stared down at the sheer drop of the cliffs on one side and the rugged moat on the other, and shuddered. The double bridge that crossed the chasm still seemed in reasonable repair, but even the horses appeared uneasy. The castle had been built as a fortress. It was certainly forbidding, even now. She turned a troubled face to Percival as he brought the curricle to a halt around the back of the keep.

"Now what?" She would not permit him to see that she was becoming frightened. The best way to face a bully was head on, and show no fear. As far as she was concerned, any man who would take a defenseless girl as hostage . . . or whatever . . . to achieve his aims was a bully. Chin up, she told herself.

"Come." He motioned her from the carriage, but offered no assistance as she scrambled down. He stood with the gun in one hand, watching her with very careful attention.

Percival gestured toward the keep of the ruined castle. Samantha hastened to walk over to stand by one of the piles f stones scattered about. The castle had been under siege many imes over the years. Now only one wall remained at full height, he others partially down, while the west wall was nearly gone. A staircase led upward to nothing, only a gaping space was beyond the doorway. She sank down upon one of the larger stones while watching Percy tie the horses to a post, then rummage in the back of the vehicle. From a curious-looking box strapped to where a groom might normally have sat, he brought forth a packet of food. He crossed to where she sat, handing it to her.

She possessed no appetite in the least. Who could think of eating at a time like this? She glared up at him, then opened the packet to find rolls and neatly sliced cheese. Apparently he didn't trust her with a knife.

"Fix me something while I open the wine," he ordered. Percy uncorked the wine, then opened a bottle containing lemonade and set it down not far from where she sat. He returned to the curricle and the odd-looking box once again, pulling out a roll of papers that looked familiar. She stifled an exclamation of recognition.

The plans! George's plans for the glider! She would know them anywhere. She jumped to her feet, clasping the rolls and cheese to her lest she do something foolish. "What are you doing with my brother's plans? Is this the manner in which you repay our hospitality? A fine person you are, Percival Twistleton."

The flash of anger that crossed his face stilled her tongue. An angry Percy was beyond her ken.

He again gestured with the gun. It almost seemed to Samantha that he rather enjoyed waving it about in the air. She obeyed the unspoken order, sitting once again amid tumbled rocks and weeds. She looked about in desperation.

The remains of an impressive stone curtain could be seen off to one side, a high stone wall hanging between what was left of two towers. There was a crenellated parapet atop the tower and keep. As she sat, a rock broke lose from the parapet and tumbled down, disappearing into a large hole just outside the entrance to the keep.

"I really do not care for this place," she announced in a small, yet brave, voice.

"How fortunate you do not have to like it. It is merely a temporary waiting place until we are to depart. We will not be observed here, and when it is time to go, we can make our way down to the sea by way of the postern Alfred mentioned. So clever to have a means of hasty exit."

Samantha could not equate this present Percy with the person she had known over the years. He looked to be more outlaw than dandy. What had happened to him? He placed the gun in a pocket, after restoring the safety lock. Amazing how an object merely a trifling six inches in length could strike terror into the heart.

Percy began to eat his roll in a hurried, undandified way while Samantha merely sat watching. She could not eat. Although the lemonade might wash the dust from her throat, she made no move to fetch it. Loathe to admit it, she was afraid of him. She did not know what he might do next. An unpredictable Percy was most disconcerting.

He had picked up the plans once again to peruse them, she supposed. Though what Percy could possibly know about the design of a glider was more than she could guess.

A muffled oath drew her attention to his face, which was contorted with anger. "There is something odd here." He crossed to stand before Samantha. Thrusting the plans before her, he demanded, "Are these complete? Seems to me I saw more than this on George's work table."

It was difficult to know how to proceed. She fingered the top sheet of paper. Ought she admit the plans were only partially there? Or should she pretend those two sheets of paper consisted of the total number? "How should I know?"

"Balderdash! Don't try to gammon me, Sam. You could not lie to save your neck, I believe. 'Tis plain as your nose that part of the plans are missing. How many sheets should there be?"

When she refused to say a word, he tossed the plans to the ground, giving her a furious look. He chewed at his bread while pacing about before the entrance to the keep.

In the fading light of the day, Samantha took note of her surroundings. It was a bleak, hostile scene, so remote and far from others. What had it been like long ago? she wondered.

Would that she had roamed here with her brother in years past. She could recall his talk about an inner and outer bailey and the great fun of exploring the prison pit. There was a well. She could remember George talking about its reputed depth.

The stairs to the basement were a broad spiral, she remembered him saying. She could see no sign of windows in the lower area. It looked cold and grim. She gave an involuntary shudder.

She tried to quell the fear rising within her. Was it too much to hope that Percy would merely leave her here, out in the open? After all, there was no one she might signal. Wouldn't it be a simple matter for him to block the bridge by which they crossed from the gatehouse? This had been a fortress, and as such, would kept people in as well as out if need arose.

"There is no way around it. I must ride back to the barn to get the rest of the plans. I'll leave you safely here, dear Samantha. Quite safe." His little chuckle quite chilled her blood.

She didn't trust that cocky grin for some reason. "Do you not fear my brother or Lord Laverstock?"

"I will take the greatest of care that they shall not know I am about. When I return the three of us shall escape to France." He appeared to relish her startled reaction.

"France?"

"Yes," he replied with satisfaction. "I shall be well paid for bringing these plans. Not only will they have the means to spy on Wellington's troop movements, but the English will be without the advantage."

"You fool," Samantha snapped back rashly. "If George can design the glider, he can redraw those plans."

"Not if his only sister is with me, the penalty for his effort being your death. Ah . . . I shall live well on a small estate near the border, everything I require to hand."

Keeping a tight rein on her alarm, she said, hating the slight quaver in her voice, "You said three. I gather the Frenchman who has been in the village will join us?"

"We shall meet him later tonight. He will have a boat for us." There was no mistaking the grim pleasure in Percy's voice. How he seemed to relish it all.

"And you trust him?" Samantha almost laughed, that frantic sort of laugh one has when trying not to cry.

"But of course. He gets the glory of bringing my offering to his country. He will be rewarded very well for his efforts." Percy's self-assurance seemed overmuch to Samantha.

She wondered what made Percy think that he wouldn't be dumped overboard on the crossing to France. They didn't need *him*. However . . . "What shall be done with me?"

"You . . . ? Why, you shall have the privilege of training those who shall use the glider once it is completed."

"I see." She saw far more clearly than Percy did, she suspected, and her apprehensions gave way to near panic. If the glider was not constructed properly she would plunge to her death—if she survived that long.

"I shall have to contact my man to inform him of the difficulty." Percival wandered about the darkening bailey while Samantha had the insane desire to call for the guards or whoever had attended the queen of this castle long ago.

She didn't feel very queenly at this moment, however. She was frightened, truly frightened. And chilly. The silver tissue gown was not intended for warmth. The strange, hard gaze from Percy was even more chilling than the breeze.

"I shall remain here," she offered cunningly, hoping he might believe her, "but I could wish for a shawl. You would not like me to catch an inflammation of the lungs. Think how poorly it would set with your new friends if you turn up without the very person needed to test your glider?"

Percy continued to stare at her, his face not revealing a hint of his thoughts. "Very well, I will fetch you something. Do not move from where you sit."

It wasn't difficult to obey. Her feet longed to flee, but some factor prevented her from trying. She scolded herself for being chicken-hearted. But she did wish to remain alive, and she didn't trust that mad gleam in Percy's eyes when he waved that little pistol about in the air.

He returned carrying a soft, old shirt in his hands. "It is all I can spare, but I think it will help some." He handed her the garment, leaving her to cope with pulling it over her head. She thrust her hands through the sleeve openings, then tugged the

body down. It was large, but blessedly it offered a fair amount
of warmth.

Once clothed in the old shirt, Samantha faced her brother's
old friend with guarded hope. "I shall be quite all right while
you are gone." Her eyes flickered a glance to the staircase,
which rose upward to nothing.

A rather nasty gleam crept into Percy's eyes as he watched
her proud figure sitting on the slab of stone like it was some
sort of throne. Even with the wretched shirt on, she had a
queenly air about her, which was odd, considering what a
hoyden she had always been in the past. Being Queen of the
May had affected her, it seemed.

He gave her an amused look, then handed her the bottle of
lemonade. "Better drink up. You might get thirsty while
waiting."

He gestured with his gun and Samantha obeyed. Percy made
her even more nervous when he waved it while it was pointed
at her. The lemonade was horrid stuff, far too sweet and rather
odd tasting. She put it aside as soon as she could without making
him annoyed.

Percy debated as he watched her. He had to make certain she
didn't escape. It wasn't unlikely that she might try a daring
attempt at her freedom. To have her alert the constable or
someone else if she got free was not in his plans. He gestured
toward the towering keep.

"I believe I know of a better place to ensure your silence.
Come on with you, now. Move."

Samantha rose slowly from where she sat, terror slowly
growing in her breast. He meant to put her down below . . . in
the dark. She just knew it. "Do not do this thing, Percy." She
hadn't wanted to plead with him; that only made a bully happy.
But she feared going down to the dampness of the basement,
even if she could see that it was open to the sky. It would be
much darker there, cut off from the waning light.

Percy merely grinned, while pulling a candle stub from his
pocket. Samantha shrugged her slim shoulders and took the
proffered candle—so very small, it was—using the tinder box
he then handed her to light it. She shielded the flame with one
hand as she walked toward the stairs, her heart in her mouth,

to use a phrase she had read in one of her novels. It had seemed overly dramatic at the time. Now she knew full well the cold trembling that gripped her.

"You shall be quite safe, as I promised. Though once the candle burns down you might have a spot of trouble. But then, I know a hardy girl like yourself won't be troubled by that. Will you?"

Samantha thought he had become quite unhinged and so strove to humor him. "I suppose you will not be gone all that long, will you? I expect your Frenchman will be eager to get on his way before the excisemen catch sight of his boat. Although the caves where the smugglers usually land are south of here, I imagine a few might have found that postern you mentioned a handy means of hasty exit. I have no doubt there will be patrols about tonight, it being cloudy and no moon." She firmly quelled a shiver that threatened to become overwhelming.

They carefully made their way up the broad flight of steps to where a vestibule once covered the entranceway. Now there was a yawning chasm before her. She glanced back at Percy, a question in her eyes.

In the flickering light of the candle his smile was most unpleasant. "The prison pit. Note how steep the walls are, even today. No way out but by rope, I expect. Take care not to fall down there, Samantha. I do not carry a long rope with me."

Samantha shivered at the tone of his voice. So cold, so hard. At his urging she flattened herself against the remaining south wall and edged along a narrow ledge of sandstone until they reached the crumbled west wall of the keep. There she found herself facing the task of making her way, candle in hand, across a twenty-foot expanse of rubble that was all that remained of the shattered wall. She never quite knew how she managed to crawl that distance.

At last they reached the broad steps of the spiral staircase, the upper portion now gone, the lower descending into damp darkness. She risked a glance at Percy. He motioned her forward. With the gun. In his other hand was the lantern from the curricle.

"I expect you do not trust me," she said in what she hoped

was a neutral tone. "You could. If I gave my word, I would keep it." She might have saved her breath. He didn't even bother to answer.

Rubble was strewn on the steps, making it difficult to walk. She picked her way to the foot of the stairs, then halted. "Well?" Anger blazed from her eyes as she faced him. How could he do this evil thing?

The steps had made her dizzy, it seemed. She put her hand to her forehead, trying to steady her poor senses.

Stumbling almost drunkenly across the weed- and grass-choked basement by the dim light of her little candle, taking care to avoid stones scattered about, she found herself in one of the two arched recesses. Percival tucked the gun in his pocket, then produced a length of fine rope. He took the candle stub from her, placing it on a ledge. "I shall leave you with light, dear Sam. His chuckle was not pleasant.

Samantha gave the rope a wary look, then glanced up at Percy. The walls seemed to sway about her. She felt strangely disoriented and unresisting as he grabbed first one hand, then the other, tugging them behind her. She felt the rope tied firmly about her wrists as though it was happening to someone else. Then she slid down to the hard stone of the arch. It seemed her legs no longer wished to support her.

"I would have preferred the lanthorn, Percival. Bring it back with you." She blinked, wondering how long she could stay awake, and how long the candlelight would last.

"I'd best be gone." As Percy hurried up the stairs to scramble across the rubble to his carriage, he couldn't help but marvel at her bravery. What a pity he knew they would not suit. She wasn't like other women. He wanted a pliant, soft girl. Samantha was too strong-willed, too impetuous for his taste. Her one ladylike accomplishment was playing the lute, and that wasn't enough for him. What a shame she did not have her instrument here to keep her company. He laughed at the thought of Sam playing madrigals in the bottom of a castle. How fitting. Especially when that stub of a candle burned out, which it would before long.

Down below, Samantha heard that laugh and trembled. It

would be hours before Percy returned and the candle stub was nearly nonexistent now. Her head was nodding and she couldn't keep her eyes open. That rat Percy must have put something in the lemonade, for she knew she was going to sleep. A breeze whipped about the corner of the keep and blew the little candle out.

About her was total darkness.

Samantha lost her fight to stay awake and slumped down on the cold, comfortless stone.

16

The horses stamped restlessly while Percy removed the small trunk from the curricle. Quickly, he changed into black shirt and breeches. Once all his possessions were placed to one side by the keep, he got in the carriage, kicking the crown of flowers out when he espied it on the floor. He wanted nothing obtrusive to call attention in any way to him or the vehicle.

Percy drove the carriage through the barbican and down the steep, narrow road with reckless abandon. The ground dropped off sharply on both sides of the road, and on the outer side of the barbican the forbidding cliff guarded the castle well. Even after some six hundred years the place was a fortress. What a shame that the portcullis was no more; that vertical drop-gate would have been such a simple solution to his problem. Instead, he had been required to tie Samantha's hands and leave her to doze in a basement arch of the keep.

He could only hope that the amount of laudanum in the lemonade was sufficient to quiet her until he returned. Pity he'd had to use the drug now. He'd originally intended it for subduing her during the trip to France. He had no illusions about Samantha: she would fight every inch of the way otherwise. He feared the Frenchman would have no patience with her. She could well be knocked unconscious; Percy didn't want that to happen to her. In a way, he had some fondness for her.

Glancing at the dark sky, where heavy clouds threatened, he gave a worried shake to his head. Leaving Samantha unprotected in the basement had not been part of his initial intent, but he was quite certain that she would not have remained at the castle. With that stub of a candle, she would have made her way to that ledge, then down the steep staircase to the ground level.

The darkly forbidding clouds that reduced his light so drastically might have restrained her a little. Few young women liked to scramble about in the dark over piles of rubble, not even the intrepid Sam. But he also knew her well enough to know she would never give up, once determined to get away.

The curricle tore along the twisting road leading from the castle into the town. Here he found the Crown and Scepter, the inn the boy at the Blue Lion had named, and left the carriage there plus a message for the Frenchman.

Within a very short time he was on the road from Scarborough to Sawham on a surprisingly acceptable steed, wondering how he was to evade the three men at Mayne Court.

He had bragged to Samantha that he would have no trouble, but he knew better than that. He was no cock-sure boy to think he could merely walk up to the barn and help himself to the plans. No, it would take a bit of planning. He had no way of knowing whether they had connected him to Samantha's disappearance or not. Nor did he know if they had discovered that the plans were missing. Though if they had, they would have no notion of who had them. They might possibly be wary, but not prepared, surely, against a clever thief.

As the horse pounded over the miles, and the clouds threatened him from above, Percy devised a scheme.

It was a frightening place to awake in, Samantha decided, striving to retain her reason and a bit of calm. She listened, hearing strange sounds, the faint rush of the North Sea against the cliffs in the far distance.

There was a sea gull who had stayed up late. Or was it all that late? Clouds had been rolling in behind them all the way to Scarborough. They hadn't appeared to be rain clouds, but they darkened the sky so that the hour had seemed late. She had no idea what the time might be. She couldn't see anything about her. It had been four or thereabouts when they left Sawham. The ride to Scarborough had taken at least an hour, then the slower ride up to the castle. Percy had eaten the bread and cheese in a hurry. And now? Early evening? But such darkness.

How woozy she felt. She longed for a drink of water. There was a well somewhere in the castle. George had talked about how deep it was. Was it outside, in the inner bailey? Or was it located down here? If she managed to free herself and strayed from the arch, might she fall into its depths?

She had to get out of here, she decided sleepily. Off to one side of her she could detect the steady trickle of water. If she remembered rightly, the spiral staircase was just beyond the spot on the wall where slimy green moss cascaded down the cold gray stone. What a predicament to be in, her hands tied behind her and no light by which to see. She closed her eyelids—for just a moment. Her brain couldn't seem to think of a means of escape, no matter that she wished to flee.

Percy skirted the edge of Sawham. He felt it wise to avoid recognition by anyone. Even though he felt reasonably certain that no one—other than the young lad who worked at the inn, and was likely to be busy now—would know him, still he used caution. The horse he rode seemed to welcome the quiet walk through the woods that rimmed the village.

Once safely beyond Sawham, Percy again urged his horse to cover the ground at top speed, and it wasn't long before he entered the road that led to the Court. He dismounted, tying the reins to a low-hanging branch. From here he must creep along under cover of what brush there was, flitting from tree to tree, at all times remaining as hidden as possible. Though it was dark now, and he was dressed in unrelieved black, he didn't trust Laverstock. George and Alfred were not as formidable. But Laverstock? The man had come from London, and Percival doubted he had come to rusticate as claimed.

His senses alert, Percy found no evidence that anyone was about the grounds. There were lights above the stables. Up at the house he could see candlelight from the dining room and entry hall.

His stomach rumbled in protest. How he would have liked to sit down at the table to have a good meal. Lady Lavinia was a good hostess; the food was usually delicious. He pulled out a chunk of the cheese he had had the foresight to put in his pocket to take a bite. Later he would dine on Burgundian beef.

His foot accidentally broke a twig in half and he froze, waiting in suspense to hear a rush of steps in the dark. Nothing.

At the barn, he found the door well locked. He had expected that. Had it not been secured, he would have worried. With a little device his valet had picked up in London from a less than savory character, he undid the lock, then slipped inside. What a pity the man hadn't revealed it earlier. He stood very still for a few moments.

Had he heard a rustling of straw? He glanced upward, then decided to risk lighting a lanthorn, keeping the flame low. Nothing but the barn cat, he saw with relief. In spite of that little gun in his pocket, he had no desire to shoot anyone. The sooner he got the plans and was on his way, the happier he would be.

A trickle of sweat ran down his face as he studied the bench where George usually kept his plans. Gone. Well, that was to be expected, he supposed.

He moved about, searching below the bench first, then overhead. In a small space below the loft floor and next to a beam he espied a roll of papers. It was slightly crumpled, with marks of grease and glue along the edges. Percy smiled. He had found them. It had been so simple he wanted to laugh.

Quickly grabbing the papers from their place of hiding, he doused the lanthorn, then waited a moment until his eyes adjusted to the darkness. It remained silent. He liked that. Silence was most welcome right now. He made his way out the door with little difficulty.

Percy decided he had better take the time to slip the lock in place once again. Then he crept along through the brush, keeping the plans close to his body, until he reached the hired horse, now munching on grass. First tucking the plans into a cylinder he'd brought for the purpose, he vaulted into the saddle and prepared to rush back to Scarborough. Samantha could be awaking before too long, though he hoped not.

Suddenly, brilliant light from a previously concealed lanthorn blinded him, causing his steed to rear up in affront.

"I hope you did not have intentions of leaving without us,

wistleton, old boy. We would be utterly devastated to think
e had missed a bit of fun.'' Laverstock moved forward so that
ercy could see him, and grabbed his horse's reins to restrain
. The twisted smile on Laverstock's face was most unpleasant.

"Where's m'sister, Percy? What have you done with her?''
eorge took a step forward, the expression revealed in the light
om the lanthorn he carried as menacing as Laverstock's.

Trying to appear more courageous than he felt at this moment,
ercy swallowed with care, then attempted nonchalance.
Samantha? How should I know where your madcap sister is?''

"Because you were the Jack and she went off with you in
carriage.'' Alfred appeared on the opposite side of the restive
orse, placing a firm hand on the reins.

Deciding that silence was his best refuge, Percy shrugged his
houlders and said nothing.

"At a loss for words? Perhaps I can help you find some.''
harles grabbed a handful of Twistleton's clothing and dragged
im from his mount. Taller, more powerful, and fearsomely
ngry, Charles shook his quarry like a terrier shaking a
articularly nasty rat. As a matter of fact, he roughed up Percy
vith a considerable amount of relish. The hours of waiting,
vondering about his dear Samantha, had built up a tension that
ad snapped when he viewed the contemptible Twistleton astride
is nag. The gentlemen at Jackson's Rooms would have
ppreciated the neat display of fisticuffs. Charles knew he had
ever been more provoked to action.

"I'll lead you,'' gasped Percy at last, little fancying further
nanhandling. He wiped a trickle of blood from the corner of
is mouth with the back of his hand, then backed away from
Charles, staggering slightly.

Charles followed him closely. "I believe we shall check you
irst. Sorry, old fellow.'' Laverstock ran his hands over him,
letected a slight bulge in one of Twistleton's pockets, and
hortly brandished the deadly little gun in the air, after
scertaining that it was not cocked. He then pushed Percy toward
is horse, letting the battered man scramble up as best he might.

Percy cast a baleful look at the three men who held him in
estraint. His brain worked feverishly at a plan to escape at

Scarborough, so he could make his way to the sea where the boat would await. He held his tongue for the present.

Charles turned to wave to someone behind him. One of the grooms who had stood guard led forth one of the horses that had been kept at a distance to ensure quiet. Tucking the pistol in one of his coat pockets, Charles vaulted upon his horse, then motioned for horses to be brought to his friends.

Alfred moved in close to Percy on the one side, with George closing in before the miscreant.

"Lovely, Twistleton. We now have the advantage. I always like this kind of odds, do you not, gentlemen?" Charles gave Percy a look that gave the younger man pause, before grinning at his fellow accomplices.

It might be well to remember the strength of Laverstock's arms and use extreme caution, thought Percy.

Alfred and George laughed—grim, terse, chilling laughter— then mounted their horses as well. The lanthorn was held aloft by one of the grooms who led them all at a discreet distance on horseback. A load of other lanthorns, guns, and any other items the men had thought might come in handy was also loaded on a pack horse by sturdy grooms, along with the bundle gathered by Aunt Lavinia for Samantha.

The cavalcade set out for Sawham, voices stilled, Percy at the center, his horse now controlled by a rope held by Laverstock. Once in the center of the darkened village, Charles stopped the little procession.

A few lights burned in the Blue Lion. All other houses were dark.

"Did you take the Scarborough road?"

Percy reluctantly gave a nod of his head. He was determined to shake them once they reached the city. They could hardly ride through the streets as they were now. Realizing the gloom concealed his silent affirmation, Percy muttered his reply. "Aye."

Charles gave a jerk at the rope, startling the horse Percy rode. The men turned toward the Scarborough road and were off. Although the clouds were heavy, the rain had not yet begun. With luck, none might fall. One of the grooms continued ahead with the lanthorn to show the way, and the party rode forward, though not at the pace they might have maintained during daylight.

Charles was worried. Even though Twistleton had turned up as hoped, there was the matter of Samantha. Where was she? Dare he trust she might be inside an inn, safely asleep on a comfortable bed? Looking at the sullen Percy, whose expression might just barely be made out, Charles doubted his optimistic desire to be reality. He tightened his grip on the rope, as he considered the possibilities for his dear Samantha.

The miles were covered in relative silence. The men sensed little could be extracted from Twistleton, and did not feel much like talking among themselves.

Samantha woke again when she shivered violently from the sharpening breeze. It had whipped about the corner of the keep, cutting her to her very bones. Percy's shirt was little help in this sea-damp, mist-laden wind.

She struggled to sit up, huddling her body in a small little ball. It wasn't simple, with her wrists tied behind her. Percy had tied them well. She could not work them loose. But she refused to sit here and catch her death of cold. Now that her mind was clearing some from the drug-induced fog, she considered her problem as best she might.

Perhaps one of the many rocks that had nearly tripped her up earlier could aid her freedom. She felt about with her feet, thanking divine providence Percy had not thought to tie her ankles. Ah, a very sharp piece of rubble, one with a good, clean edge. She worked her way about until the goodly sized stone was behind her and began to saw away at her bonds.

Time was in her favor, as she saw it. Percy would take hours to travel to Mayne Court and hunt for the missing plans, then return here. Would that someone thought to watch for him, and follow him back to Scarborough. But she'd best not look to others for her deliverance. Hadn't her aunt always said that the good Lord helps those who help themselves? A disturbing thought occurred to her—she didn't know how long she had been asleep. It served to make her rub harder.

Then the thin rope that bound her wrists broke, and she was able to move her arms. They were stiff, and ached a good deal. But she could work her way to freedom! She remained on her knees, the better to make her way.

An encounter with a rock in her path caused her to wince with pain. She sat back to rub a wounded knee, thinking it would be so much better had she her jean half-boots, or better yet, her riding boots, on her feet instead of these dainty slippers. Then she might try to walk, rather than crawling like some babe.

More cautious now, Samantha continued to move forward, she hoped in the right direction. Oh, if she but had that stub of a candle lit again. It seemed to her that behind her towered the highest wall of the keep, for it appeared blacker there. Before her must be the spiral staircase leading up to the pile of rubble that was all that remained of the west wall.

Was that the first step her hand had reached? She felt about, exploring, reluctant to rise or place her weight on the stone unless she could be sure she had attained the staircase. If she recalled correctly, the stairs would be in about the middle of the wall, constructed as a part of it. She then heard the slight trickle of water as it dropped down the wall, which she knew was close to the staircase.

Satisfied she had indeed found the steps, she rose and cautiously began to make her way upward, feeling for the wall as she went. The steps were broad, but in a sad state of repair, with bits of rock in her path. Well, she philosophized, you could hardly expect the work of six hundred years past to last forever.

It was fortunate these remains of the spiral staircase were intact. Hadn't Alfred, that fountainhead of odd bits of information, said that some castles had used nothing more than ladders? She shuddered at the mere thought of coping with a ladder while wearing long skirts and in darkness.

She must look a dreadful sight, with dirt and weed stains on her gown, her hair a tangle of snarls. Hardly like a queen. She gave a watery chuckle at that vision, herself in the silver tissue, covered with Percy's old shirt, her gown a filthy mess. Hardly presentable to travel to France. She would have to make her way to a stable, now. There was not an inn in the country that would allow her entrance, looking as she did.

She reached the top of the stairs and scrambled as best she could, feeling her way along the remains of the west wall until she reached the corner. Below the ledge she had traversed earlier was the prison pit. Only a narrow space remained for her to cross, but what danger if she should misstep! She clung to the wall on her left then dropped to her knees to crawl, sending prayers that she would be able to make it safely past this awesome hole from which there was no escaping. Inch by inch she groped her way toward freedom. Her nails dug into the sandstone, seeking a purchase. Percy's promise of the trip to France echoed in her ears. She was not going with him! It was better to die here than betray her country.

Suddenly she could see a faint light. It seemed to come from around the far corner. As she raised her head to squint, then rose, searching for a clue as to what might be its source, she stubbed her toe on a stone and stumbled forward.

The horses clattered over the cobblestones as the party from Mayne Court entered the city of Scarborough. At this hour of the night there were few about to see the curious group. Percy still rode in sullen silence close to Laverstock, but he had been studying the rope tied to his saddle and now managed to work it loose. As soon as they reached a confusing crossing of streets, he made his move.

"What the . . . !" Charles stopped, then wheeled in the direction Percy had taken, followed by Alfred and George, the grooms trailing behind, not wishing to be lost.

Cleverly, Percy led them through the maze of back streets that wove in and out below the twisting road to the castle. He ducked his horse into an alley, drawing well into the inky shadows and holding his breath until the men rode past him; he expelled a long sigh of relief as the hoofbeats faded into the distance.

Then he doubled back, turning up the castle road with haste, thinking he heard the clatter of hoofs once again.

George stopped his horse, then Alfred did likewise. Turning back, Charles gave a resigned sigh. Percy had eluded them as neat as could be. "He gave us the slip," admitted Charles. "Where do you suppose he has gone?"

"To the sea," said George, thinking Percy must desire to flee the country.

"I am not so sure about that," mused Alfred aloud. "Do you recall the day we came up here to find a costume for Laverstock? Percy overheard us talking about the castle then. It's possible he might have gone there."

"And taken Samantha with him?" Charles noted the chill, damp air and the brisk wind. If Samantha wore no more than that silvery tissue gown, she would feel frozen by now.

Alfred nodded. "If you think we'd best check the wharves—"

"The postern!" exclaimed George. "Remember we talked about a hasty exit to the sea by way of that gate? Egads, if he can find that, he can slip away and we shall never see him again. It's devilish hard to find by day. By night . . ." George shook his head, trying desperately to recall precisely where that elusive gate was located.

"I say we try the castle. If he has taken Samantha up there, she will not make it easy for him to attempt to remove her to France." Alfred looked first to George, then Laverstock.

"France," echoed Charles, recalling the mayor's mention that the Frenchman had left that May morning it had all begun. Yesterday. A glance at his timepiece while near the lanthorn had revealed the hour—past midnight.

Alfred agreed, while George looked angry. That meant Percy was most definitely a traitor. The three turned to look up at the crest of the headland where the castle remained hidden in darkness.

"Let's go," commanded Charles, leading the way with his horse. They pounded over the ground, Alfred shouting directions, yet not seeking to go ahead. He knew how he would feel if his darling Emma were being held by some traitor. More than merely angry—murderous.

At the barbican, Charles stopped his horse, motioning to the others to halt.

"We'd best go on foot from here," he said softly. "Better put out the lanthorns as well. We want to steal up there as quietly as possible. Not a sound out of any of us. I have seen no trace of lights, but if Percy believes he has shaken us off, he may feel confident enough to set up a lanthorn of his own.'' Charles looked to the others, then dismounted. He admonished the groom to wait for them, then, grabbing the bundle for Samantha, strode up the steep hill without waiting for the men he knew would follow.

The lanthorns were hastily extinguished. The horses were tied to a post, then each man took some of the gear with him.

The light was flickering. Cautiously peeking around the corner Samantha saw two figures seated by a fire—Percival and the Frenchman. She withdrew to sit rubbing a sore toe while she debated what she must do. Thank the Lord she had made it past the prison pit and down the stairs before she had stubbed her toe and fallen so heavily. Shivering as the breeze bit through her gown and Percy's shirt, she knew she must go on. She could not even contemplate the notion of the trip to France and all it meant.

Could she manage to flee from here before they came to fetch her for the journey? Taking a deep breath, she looked away from the beckoning light toward where the gate house must be, wondering how in the world she could find her way through this darkness. For there was no moon to bless her path, no stars to help light the way, and she hadn't that stub of a candle—which wouldn't help anyway, because they might see it, and her.

Refusing to sit merely awaiting the fate Percival had decreed for her, Samantha hesitantly backed away from the faint light and resolutely set her face in the direction of the gate house. Then she began the trip that was to haunt her sleep for weeks to come.

She could distinguish a certain amount, certainly between the rocks that loomed up from the hard, pebbled ground and nothingness. The trick as she saw it was to avoid the nothingness if possible, and cling to the solidity of what little she could discern.

The rocky terrain was cruel to her hands and cut her silver gauze gown to tatters before long. But she crawled across the open area to the south of the ruins and around to where the ground began to slope steeply toward the bridge. Tears stung her eyes as she cut her hand on a sharp edge. She held the wound against her cheek, then froze.

Did she hear a noise? Other than the restless sea pounding at the base of the cliff far below? She sat quietly, waiting for a moment. There followed no crunch of gravel, no whispering of clothes, so she continued her torturous way across the rubble-strewn bailey, then began to make her descent.

She had crossed the hard-packed ground of the bridge and was beginning to breathe easier when she truly did hear a sound. There were footsteps approaching. But were they friends or foe? Percival had mentioned the Frenchman, and it had seemed as though the two worked alone. But did she know that for a fact? Retreating against the cold stone wall, and thankful there was a vine of sorts to pull across her, she waited while they neared. They spoke not one word; she had no idea as to who they might be. Charles? She shook her head slightly in rueful amusement. Now, would that not be lovely and convenient? It was possible. They might have followed Percy to this lonely spot. But could she be certain—beyond any doubt? No. She refused to take the chance. These men might be on Percy's side. The gloom permitted the barest hint of the figures, but hardly enough to risk her freedom for. She waited until the sound of the footsteps faded away up the hill, then resumed making her cautious way down . . . toward the city and freedom.

The road was steep and narrow, and there were disconcerting gaps in the wall. She well knew what would happen if she failed to use care. She would fall to certain death below.

Sam crept into the gate house and felt her way along the wall. There were horses not far away. Although they were quiet, she could hear the jingle of reins, the creak of a leather saddle; she could smell the pungency of horse. Were they alone?

Inching along, she came to the gateway and stopped. Her ears strained to hear if there was someone there. Sounds were magnified in this dismal darkness. She heard steps. It was better to hide for the moment. Freedom was too close to take more risks.

It was a silent group that hurried along through the barbican

nd up across the double drawbridge. As they neared the keep,
flickering light could be seen.

Charles held up his hand in caution, whispering a suggested
lan to the others, who nodded their agreement. The five men
arted. Three went around the keep by the far side, to surprise
Percy from behind. The other two, Charles and George, crept
orward to the corner of the keep, edging along the sandstone-
ronted wall with great wariness.

Smoke drifted past. A fire. Percy must be more adept than
Charles had given him credit for. At the corner of the keep he
dged forward, moving carefully so that he could see before
eing seen.

Percy was with the Frenchman. A small fire crackled
longside a pile of stones. The wood must be the remains of
ome of the timber used here at one point or another over the
ears. The two men sat with their backs to Charles and George,
rinking wine while discussing something, possibly the bogus
lans Percy now held in one hand. Samantha was nowhere to
e seen.

Charles motioned to George to follow his lead. From the other
orner of the keep, Alfred and the two grooms were creeping
oward the pair by the fire. As he moved, Charles thought of
Samantha. If not here, where could she be? Then he saw the
attered crown of flowers, and knew she had been there at one
ime. He firmed his resolve to find the truth and his precious girl.

With the stealth of determined and careful men, the five
dvanced slowly until Charles raised his hand in signal. They
ose with varying degrees of sound and rushed the two by the
ire. It might have been comical—indeed, in later years it would
e recalled in that manner—such was the surprise on the faces
f the Frenchman and the traitor, Twistleton.

In a matter of minutes the fight was over. A resigned Percival
glared at Charles. The Frenchman, identified by a paper in his
acket as André Montreaux, stood in sullen defiance.

Charles took a deep breath, adjusted his coat, then placed a
eavy hand on Percy's shoulder. "Where is she?"

"Samantha? I don't know. As God is my witness I have not
seen her. She was tied up and now she has gone." He darted

a look at Montreaux, who merely shrugged. The woman ha
been a necessary evil as far as he was concerned. He had neve
approved of that part of the plan in the least.

After studying Twistleton's face a few moments, Charle
backed away, his face a mirror of his disappointment . . . ar
worry. "Where was she tied up?"

When he heard what Percy had done he wanted to wipe th
ground with the dandy's once-pretty face. Instead, Charle
discussed what was to be done with the captured two, the
explained what he intended to do. George and Alfred nodde
in sympathy as Charles took one of the lanthorns and stroc
off toward the south side of the keep.

Behind him the others tied up Twistleton and Montreaux
preparing to bring a little "gift" to the constable in Scarborough
In short order, they marched down the hill to the gatehous
where the horses waited.

As he ran up the steps, Charles wondered what he might fin
Evidence, he hoped. A body, he hoped not. He paused at th
top of the prison pit, swinging the lanthorn around, staring dow
into the hole with relief as he saw it was empty. Had she falle
there . . .

He inched his way over the ledge and around the side to th
west with more speed than grace, scrambling over the rubb
to the stairs, then tearing down the steps to the basement. B
the first arch he found a small length of rope, frayed as thoug
worn by a rough cutting. She had been here and was gone

Determined to find her, he leapt up the stairs as fast as h
could manage, then slid and stumbled down the west side o
the keep, managing to hold the lanthorn free and clear.

As he began his search, he could hear the other voices fadin
in the distance. Where was she? Hiding? He called to he
"Samantha?"

There was no answer. Proceeding across the doubl
drawbridge, he peered over one side, shuddering with fear a
he observed the steep incline leading to the sea far below. C
the other side, the moat was a treacherous drop, overgrown wi
thorny shrubs.

He continued on until he reached the barbican, a sort of pan rabbing him as he again called her name. "Samantha!"

There was a flurry of movement, then a figure dressed in
attered white ran across the gatehouse area to throw herself
against Charles, her arms wrapping around him in a deathlike
grip. "Oh, Charles," Samantha sobbed. "Why did it take you
so long?"

She had decided while imprisoned in the basement of the keep
that she wished she were not quite so intrepid. From now on
she would gladly leave the soaring to others, the queenship to
pretty young things from the village, while she would sit quietly
at home by her hearth. If only she might have her love. Perhaps
she had given him a disgust of her that could not be overcome.
Her answer to this question came in a most satisfying
manner.

Charles tilted her chin up to study her face. Poor girl, bruised
and battered, those amber eyes looking so very afraid. Her fiery-
golden hair hung in wispy tendrils from the elegant style of this
morning. Her dress was in tatters beneath what appeared to be
an old shirt. And she appeared infinitely precious to him.

He set the lanthorn on a ledge, as he needed both hands.
Wrapping his arms about her, he lowered his head to take—
and give—a kiss that sent Samantha into transports of delight.
It warmed her; she would never be cold again, she blissfully
decided. Not as long as she might have Charles with her.

"I will undoubtedly rue this day," he said, his voice rough
with emotion. "You are a mad, impetuous girl, given to im-
pulsive, spur-of-the-moment actions, and I'll probably wish to
thrash you every other day of our lives—but on the other hand,"
he said in a deeper, huskier tone that thrilled Samantha to her
heart, "if I don't, I will regret it the rest of my life. For I am
wildly in love with you and can only hope that you will have
me. Besides," he added with a wicked gleam in his eyes, "I
hear you need a strong man to keep an eye on you. Alfred said
you need a keeper. You will marry me, a May wedding," he
pronounced, not giving her a chance to argue the case.

Sam meekly agreed, but for one point. "Aunt Lavinia says
May weddings are unlucky. We shall wait until June." Her eyes
glowed with a delightful sparkle that ought to have warned

Charles if he but knew it. Life with Samantha would never b
tranquil.

"If needs be, until then, my little love."

Anything he might have added to his admirable proposal wa
lost, as Sam impetuously reached up to bring his face to he
once again. Enough of these words. She wanted action.

She got it. For the rest of her days.